Fighting SHADOWS

ON THE ROPES BOOK 2

ALY MARTINEZ

Fighting Shadows
Copyright © 2015 Aly Martinez

Fighting Shadows is a work of fiction. All names, characters, places, and occurrences are the product of the author's imagination. Any resemblance to any persons, living or dead, events, or locations is purely coincidental.

Cover photo by FuriousFotog (www.onefuriousfotog.com)
Cover Model: Brendon Charles
Cover Design by Jay Aheer of Simply Defined Art
(www.simplydefinedart.com)
Edited by Mickey Reed at I'm a Book Shark
(www.imabookshark.com)
Formatting by Stacey Blake at Champagne Formats
www.champagneformats.com)

Other Books by Aly Martinez

The Wrecked and Ruined Series
Changing Course
Stolen Course
Among the Echoes
Broken Course

On the Ropes
Fighting Silence
Fighting Shadows
Fighting Solitude

The Fall Up
The Spiral Down

The Retrieval Duet
Retrieval
Transfer

Guardian Protection Series
Singe

Savor Me

Prologue

Ash

"WHERE THE FUCK HAVE YOU been?" a man's voice growled as soon as I entered the conference room.

My eyes flashed to his for only a single second before I recognized them. The door had barely clicked behind me, but I already wanted nothing more than to bolt. My heart raced, and my mouth dried.

I have to get out of here.

"Um . . ." I stalled, giving myself time to formulate a plan.

"Sit. Down," he ordered, pushing out the chair next to him, but there was no way I was getting that close.

"I'm good," I said, taking a step backwards toward the door.

"Don't even think about it," he snapped. "I swear to God, if you so much as open that door . . ." His words might have trailed off, but the threat had been clearly stated.

I swallowed hard and slowly walked to the chair farthest away from him, perching on the very edge—waiting for the right moment to escape.

He looked down at the name badge around my neck and quirked an eyebrow.

"Victoria?"

"You can call me Tori if it's easier." I tried to fake a smile, but it

1

only seemed to infuriate him.

He took several calming breaths, which did nothing to dampen the blaze brewing in his angry eyes. "I've been looking for you, *Ash.*" He snarled my name.

"Oh, yeah? Well, mystery solved. Here I am." I pushed back to my feet, but I was halted when his fist pounded against the table. My whole body flinched from the surprise.

When the room fell silent, I slowly looked back up to find him staring at me with a murderous glare. Even while he was sitting down, I could tell he was huge, and as he held my gaze, the tense muscles in his neck and shoulders strained against the cotton of his grey henley. He blinked at me for several seconds before finding his voice again.

"You live in a homeless shelter," he stated definitively, as if the words told a story all of their own.

And maybe they did.

"I *work* at a homeless shelter," I quickly corrected.

Only he corrected me just as fast. "In exchange for a permanent place to live . . . in. A. Homeless. Shelter." He enunciated every single syllable.

I looked away, because it was the truth.

A truth I hated.

But the God's honest truth nonetheless.

Tears welled in my eyes, and I battled to keep them at bay.

My life was hard, but his being there made it infinitely harder. If I could just escape that room, I could disappear again. It wasn't ideal, but neither was his showing up.

"I want you to leave," I lied with all the false courage I could muster.

"I can't do that. You stole something of *mine.*"

"Look, I don't have your book anymore."

A knowing smirk lifted one side of his mouth. "Liar," he whispered, reaching into the chair beside him, revealing the tattered book, and unceremoniously dropping it on the table.

My eyes widened, and without a conscious thought, I dove across the table after it.

That was *mine.* Not even he could have it.

Just as quickly as the book had appeared, he snatched it away and grabbed my wrist.

I slid off the table and tried to pull my arm from his grasp. It was a worthless attempt though, because even if he had suddenly released me, his blue eyes held me frozen in place.

"Three fucking years," he seethed.

"I had to," I squeaked out as the tears streamed down my cheeks.

"Three. Fucking. Years, Ash. You took something that belonged to me." He let go of my arm and pushed to his feet.

My mouth fell open and a loud gasp escaped as he took two *impossible* steps forward.

Pinning me against the wall with his hard body, he lifted a hand to my throat and glided it up until his thumb stroked over my bottom lip. Using my chin, he turned my head and dragged his nose up my neck, stopping at my ear.

After sucking in a deep breath, he released it on a gravelly demand. "And I want *her* back."

My breath hitched.

I'd waited three years to hear those words.

If only I could trust them.

"Flint, please."

CHAPTER

Flint

I REMEMBERED IT ALL.

I *heard* the gun.

I *felt* the bullet.

I saw *her* fall.

In less than a second, my life as I knew it was over.

But, unquestionably, I would do it all over again.

For her.

"Flint!" Eliza cried from underneath me.

It wasn't the way I had dreamed of at least a million times over the years. Her voice hadn't broken in ecstasy. She hadn't called my name as I'd been claiming her as my own, nor was it followed by confessions of love and declarations of forever. Instead, there was a sharp ringing in my ears and a tsunami of tears welling in her deep-blue eyes.

My heart was already pounding, but the earth-shattering pain on her face spiked my pulse even higher. I knew I had been hit, but that wasn't what scared me.

"Are you hurt?" I rushed out.

"I'm fine," she choked around a sob. As much as I hated to see her cry, the weight of my world disappeared with only two words.

"Are you sure?" I studied her, but she was focused on something else completely.

Peering over my shoulder, she lifted her hand off my back. Blood dripped from her fingertips to the floor.

"Oh God!" she exploded, scrambling from under me.

"I'm okay," I tried to reassure her, but as I attempted to push up off the floor, I knew my words were in vain. I was nowhere near fine. "I'm . . ." I started, but the thought was stolen from my tongue. Pain overtook me, causing me to collapse face first to the ground where Eliza had just been lying.

I desperately tried to keep myself from passing out, but it was a battle I was quickly losing.

"Flint. Stay with me. Just hang on, please," she said calmly, kneeling beside me. But as soon as she sat up, her true emotions were revealed. "Help him!" she cried. "Please, God, someone help him!"

My mind was drifting, rendering me unable to focus, but even amongst the chaos of Eliza pleading for help and security rushing into the room, I somehow homed in on the announcer's voice on the television blaring in the background.

"I really expected more from Till Page in the ring tonight," he said.

It was then that I was reminded of a pain far worse than any bullet could inflict.

Till.

Her husband.

The father of her unborn child.

My brother.

He deserved her, but damn it, so did I.

My eyes never left hers as her screams drifted into silence.

I awoke to a searing pain in my back, and panic immediately flooded my thoughts.

"Eliza!" I screamed as loudly as I could, but it came out as nothing more than a gurgle.

"I'm right here." She appeared at my side. "Oh God, Flint. Don't do that again. You have to stay awake." She began smoothing my hair down.

"Eliza," I repeated when further coherent thoughts failed me. I was terrified—I knew that much. But my mind fought to catch up and answer the why. "Are . . . are you hurt?"

"No. I'm fine," she assured me, leaning down and kissing my temple—a gesture I would have killed to be able to return.

Instead, I blindly reached out to the side, searching for her hand. "Stay with me."

Firmly grasping my palm, she vowed, "I won't leave you, Flint. I swear."

If only she'd meant those words in the way I would have liked. However, right then, as I lay facedown, bleeding on the carpet of an upscale Vegas hotel floor with a bullet in my back, I would take it.

It wasn't enough.

But it would have to be.

She isn't mine.

She never was.

As she whispered soothing words into my ear, I went willingly into the darkness.

I slowly roused back to consciousness. I couldn't quite figure out where I was or why my throat felt like I had swallowed a truckload full of burning embers. Even through my grogginess, I could feel an ache in my back. It wasn't until I spoke that I realized how fucked I truly was.

"Ewliz." *What the hell?* "Elyz."

"Oh thank God!" Eliza cried, suddenly appearing at my side.

Breathing a sigh of relief, I tried to pry my eyes open, needing nothing more than a glimpse of her dark blues. They held no superpowers, but I still believed they could heal me with a single glance. Hell, just knowing she was there with me worked miracles.

I tried to fight, but I couldn't seem to convince my eyelids that light wasn't the source of all evil.

"Shh. It's okay. Just relax," she whispered, reading my struggle. "Are you hurting? Do you need more pain medicine?"

"Nup. Juz you," I said drunkenly.

"What's wrong with him? Why can't he talk?" Quarry whimpered from somewhere nearby.

I'd never forget how he sounded in that moment. His voice shook like that of the frightened child he never got to be. He might have only been thirteen, but he hadn't been a boy in a long time. Just like Till and me, he'd been forced to grow up too soon. Hearing the inflection of fear in his voice cleared my groggy mind.

"Em good, Q," I slurred on a laugh, even though nothing was remotely humorous about the situation.

I was lying facedown on a hospital bed, drugged out of my fucking mind, and pining over my brother's pregnant wife. The same woman who was the closest thing to a real mother I'd ever known. The levels of fucked-up could not even be described.

On second thought, maybe laughing really was the right response.

My brother, Till, was quite possibly the best man I had ever met. He was only six years older than I was, but as far as I was concerned, he had always been a father to me. Lord knows that the man's DNA I carried was not. My mother was a work of art, but my father was in a category all of his own. Clay Page was the reason I was lying in that bed and recovering from a bullet in the back, the reason Till had almost lost his wife and unborn daughter, and the reason Quarry had almost been kidnapped.

All I had left in life were my brothers, and in turn, *I had Eliza.*

If I could have been half the man Till was, I would've been better than ninety-nine percent of the male population walking the planet. God, I wanted to be as selfless as he was. But I wasn't even close. Instead, over the years, I'd become increasingly jealous of his life and the way Eliza loved him. Sure, they had their fair share of problems, but they always weathered the storm together, never wavering in their devotion to each other. Only a year earlier, my older brother had suddenly lost his hearing—something that would have easily sent a lesser woman running for the hills. But not Eliza. She gave him unconditional love, and it stung so fucking much to watch her give it to *him*.

The older I became, the more I found myself consumed by guilt and anger. Guilt because no two people had ever deserved each other more. And anger because, despite knowing that, I wanted to shove my brother out of the picture completely. I wanted to own Eliza Reynolds Page in every possible way, but especially in the way where she never left me and loved me forever.

I wanted the comfort and security only *she* could offer me.

"Eliza?" I called as I went back to battle against my eyelids and was finally victorious. I was greeted by the sight of Till holding her tight, his arms folded around her swollen stomach.

"Hey, bud," he cooed, visible relief washing over his face.

But I didn't have eyes for him. Eliza stood in his arms with tears flowing in a steady stream down her cheeks.

My lips twitched in the most unlikely of smiles.

She always cries.

"You 'kay?" I mumbled.

"I am. Thanks to you." She took a step forward, joining our hands.

I laughed, using our linked knuckles to rub her belly. "How's ma baby?"

"What'd he say?" Till asked.

Eliza removed her hands from mine long enough to translate for him through sign language.

I attempted to roll over so I could have the use of my hands to communicate with him, but I was stilled by the sudden shouts.

"No!" they yelled as I tried to push up on the bed.

"You can't move . . . I, um, I mean you shouldn't move." Eliza squatted down in front of me.

I lifted a hand to wipe her tears away. Her eyes were red and puffy, but as she brushed my short hair off my forehead, she'd never looked more beautiful. Her fingertips trailed over my skin, soothing my aches from the outside in.

"Let's get you some more pain medicine." She grabbed a red button off the corner of my bed and pressed it repeatedly.

I wasn't in any real pain, but within seconds, my entire body relaxed even further.

She remained squatting in front of me, and her tears began to dry while she whispered soothing words I couldn't quite make out among the myriad of beeping monitors. It didn't matter what she was saying though.

She was *there*.

With me.

For *me*.

My vision was blurry, but time stood still as I stared into her eyes and slurred the words I had absolutely no business saying.

I had been harboring them for years. But no matter how I tried, no amount of time made them right.

"I love you, Eliza. Soooooo. Fuuucking. Mush."

Even drugged out of my mind, I knew that my admission was going to do more harm than good, but that didn't slow the words—or the pain.

Maybe, if I just told her how I felt, I could let it go. Move on to a day when I wasn't teased by the unattainable. It was a grand idea, but fruition was a different story.

She replied, "I love you too," but I knew she didn't understand.

In that second though, I *needed* her to understand. It wasn't a choice.

For her.

Or me.

"No. I loooove you." I exaggerated the word but not the truth.

"Shh," she whispered, resting her hand on my cheek. "I love you too, Flint. We all do. Just go to sleep."

We all do.

They wouldn't after I was done. I was sober enough to realize that.

"No. Lizen to me. I . . . love *you*. Like Till loves you. Like . . . I-want-to-have-sex-with-you love you. Really. Gud. Sex." I laughed.

"Oh fuck," Quarry groaned.

"And marry you, and . . ." I stopped to lick my dry lips before spewing the ultimate slap to my brother's deaf ears. "That should be my baby, not his."

"Oh fuck," Quarry repeated.

"Uhh . . . um . . ." Eliza stuttered, looking up at Till, who was standing only a few feet away.

"What? What'd he say?" Till asked, stepping forward.

"I said I'm in love with your wife!" I yelled for some unexplainable reason.

Well, maybe only unexplainable to them; I understood my frustrations completely.

Till needed the chance to hate me. He had given me everything in life and provided for me even when he'd had to sacrifice himself. I owed him the truth about the way I felt about his wife. Regardless that it proved what a dirt bag I truly was.

I lifted my one free hand in the air and began to sign out the letters, but Quarry stepped between Eliza and me and forced my hand against the bed.

"Yep. That's enough. Go to sleep, asshole."

"He needs ta know. Tell him fur me."

Quarry lifted his hands and signed to Till without words. *He said he loves us all, and then he got all weepy and called Eliza mommy. I'm just trying to keep him from embarrassing himself. That's all.*

"Dat's bullshit," I replied when he finished.

"We love you too, Flint. Get some rest," Till said, folding his arms across his chest, not buying into Quarry's explanation.

"No! I said, 'I love *her.*' Eliza." I began to point in her direction, but Quarry once again slapped my hand down.

Turning his back on Till, he leaned into my face. "Shut your goddamn mouth. I'm trying to help you here."

"I love her," I repeated for the umpteenth time.

Eliza wedged her way back to my side. "No, you don't. You're just drugged up right now, Flint."

"Bullshit," I declared adamantly.

Drugs didn't cause the way I felt any more than they could fix it. I'd have been a junkie long ago if there were something that could've quelled the burning in my chest every time I saw her with Till.

"This isn't somethin' new, Eliza. I think about you when—" I'd started to spill all of my embarrassing secrets when Quarry's hand slammed over my mouth.

"I said, 'Shut the fuck up,'" he seethed.

"Stop cussing," I mumbled from behind his hand.

He looked to Eliza. "Can you press that button again? Maybe see if he'll pass out."

"What the hell is going on?" Till snapped from behind us, losing his cool with being in the dark.

Nothing. He's acting like a bitch. Just doing my job as his little brother to protect his manhood . . . or something like that, Quarry signed then flashed Till a tight grin.

"No, I—" I started, and his hand once again landed over my mouth.

Quarry gave Eliza an impatient glare.

"He has a few more minutes before the pain pump will give him any more meds," she answered, frazzled by my confession.

And just that small reaction to my admission hurt more than whatever the hell was happening on my back.

"Well, I'll just keep my hand right here until it's time," Quarry hissed at Eliza.

"Um, I'm gonna step out and get some water," she announced uncomfortably.

"Eliza, wait," I tried to shout, but Quarry wasn't lying about not removing his hand. "Get off me." I weakly swatted it away.

Glancing back at Till, he lifted a finger in the air to signal one second. Then he turned back to me. "Shut up. Shut up. Shut. Up. You're in love with her, fine. Now, shut up."

"Not until he knows," I replied.

"Go to sleep, Flint. If you still want to make this mistake when you wake up, I'll sign it out to him myself." He urged me with a hard stare.

I *was* tired. Sleep didn't exactly sound like torture. I'd been sitting on my feelings for Eliza since I was twelve. What was one more night?

"I would take her from him," I declared as my lids began to droop.

Quarry busted out laughing. "Then, when you wake up, I'll sign out your warning. Oh, look! Time's up." He grabbed the red button and gave it a push.

I moaned as the glorious burn of the medication hit my vein.

"Thank God," he breathed as I drifted off to sleep.

When I awoke some hours later, my determination to tell Till had fortunately disappeared.

Unfortunately, so had my desire for Eliza to know.

But the truth was out.

As the embarrassment set in, I tried to convince myself that maybe it was for the best that she knew how I felt.

It wasn't.

It was a hell of a lot worse.

CHAPTER
Two

Flint

THE DAY I FOUND OUT that I might never walk again was unlike anything I had ever experienced in my life. And that's saying a lot for someone who had seen more heartbreak in eighteen years than most people experience in a lifetime.

Hell, I was a fucking pro at heartbreak. I lived with the knowledge that my mother had abandoned me. And the fun fact that my father had spent years in prison after he'd almost gotten my brother killed. I'd witnessed firsthand the night Till had suddenly gone deaf. And I'd had a front-row seat the day Quarry had found out he shared the same silent fate. Most recently, I had spent hours reeling as I'd watched my family fall apart while we had frantically tried to find the man who had taken Eliza at gunpoint.

Heartbreak was nothing compared to the road I had ahead of me.

I was paralyzed after having taken a bullet in the back to protect her. At least, that was the way other people saw it. Till especially hailed me as a hero. It was a lie though. I had taken that bullet to protect *myself.* I wouldn't have been able to survive a single moment without her. My actions that day had been so selfish that I couldn't even be devastated.

I made the choice.

"We have high hopes that you'll walk again, but until your body starts healing, we just don't have any clear idea of when that will be."

"Have you had other people with similar injuries walk again?" Till asked when Eliza finished signing the information for him.

"Of course!" the doctor answered enthusiastically.

But I felt like I had been punched in the gut. "You've also had some not though, right? I asked, bitterly.

"Well, yes. Every patient has a different recovery."

"So, it's basically a coin toss, huh?"

He didn't respond as he exchanged a knowing glance with Till.

"Right. Well, you should know, Doc. The coin fucking hates the Page brothers." I laughed without humor. Pointing at Till, I announced, "Deaf." Then I waved my arm at Quarry. "Going deaf." Then I stabbed my finger at myself. "Paralyzed." I shook my head, looking down at my worthless legs, cursing them for failing me.

"It's not permanent, Flint. We're gonna fight this. We'll get you back on your feet. I swear to God we will," Till vowed, barely able to contain his emotions.

I wanted to scream and yell that he couldn't possibly make that promise. But it would have only added to my mounting guilt.

I know, I signed back to him with a forced smile. "Really. It's okay," I whispered as Eliza, who was securely wrapped in Till's arms, broke down.

My attention was drawn away by a knock at the door.

"You up for some company?" Slate asked as he walked in, his wife, Erica, in tow.

Slate Andrews was the former heavyweight boxing champion of the world. But to me and my brothers, he and Erica were the parents we'd never had. Slate owned a boxing gym for underprivileged kids, and considering that the three of us had never fit into a category more, we'd spent most of our time at On The Ropes. He was tight with a lot of the kids at the gym, but it was obvious to everyone that he had formed a special bond with us—or, more accurately, with Till. Like so often in our lives, Quarry and I were just part of the package.

A few years earlier, Slate had given Till the opportunity of a lifetime by bankrolling his efforts to become a professional boxer. A fated chance that had ultimately led us to a moment where I lay paralyzed in a bed and my brother sat across from me as the current heavyweight champion of the entire fucking world, holding the woman I loved.

It didn't exactly seem fair, but not much in my life was.

"Yeah. Come on in," I replied, looking around the room at the solemn faces.

My eyes landed on Quarry, who was in the corner, peering out the window. If it weren't for the softest shake of his shoulders, I wouldn't have thought much of it.

"Hey, Q," I called.

He didn't turn to face me as he answered, "Yeah."

"You crying over there?" Yep. I went right for it. He was my little brother. Even in a moment that, by all means, should have been emotional, it was still my job to give him absolute hell.

"Fuck you," he barked at the window.

My lip twitched at his response. *"Hey, you can't be a man and a baby. Either cuss or cry,"* I teased, making sure to sign as I spoke so Till could join in the fun.

Slate groaned beside me, and Till shook his head before kissing Eliza's temple.

"Leave him alone," Erica urged.

I couldn't do that at all though. I needed that interaction to keep my mind from spiraling out of control.

In an exaggerated baby voice, I mocked, "Q, you want me to ask the nurse if she has a lollipop?"

"I hate you," he mumbled, pushing to his feet and storming toward the door.

"I'm just kidding, Quarry. Christ, don't be so sensitive," I yelled after him.

When he reached the doorway, he looked up and flipped me off. Tears painted his face, and it would have been a lie if I didn't admit that it fucking killed me to see him like that, but at least the attention was on him.

"Seriously, Flint? He's worried about you. Cut the kid some slack, " Erica huffed as she went after him.

Cut him some slack.

Cut him some slack?

What exactly that meant, I would never understand. We were the

Page brothers. Slack was not something we would ever receive—and truth be told, we couldn't afford to. You know what slack did to a person? It made you soft. Slack left you unprepared and gave you a false sense of safety, all the while slowly working its way around your neck, leaving you a tangled mess and fighting for your next breath. *Fuck that.* I was doing Quarry a favor by keeping him on his toes. The world didn't hand out slack.

Where had my *slack* been when I'd been scrubbing the filth off the floors of our shithole apartment just so Social Services wouldn't place Quarry and me in foster care? No one had cut me *slack* when I used to stay awake all hours of the night waiting for my father to come home because I'd known he'd have drugs in his pocket—drugs I could trade to the old lady next door in exchange for a fucking meal to keep us fed. Had *slack* helped me as I'd searched through the bins at the local church drive for jeans that fit Quarry who, for some reason, wouldn't stop growing?

No.

I'd had to fight for everything. The same everything that had absolutely never been enough. For God's sake, hearing and walking weren't even guaranteed for us.

Fuck the slack. Give me the tension.

Erica was right though. I should have apologized to Quarry, but where would that have left him? He needed to learn that it's not okay to cry. No one cared about his tears any more than they did the billions I'd shed in my eighteen years. Emotions didn't pay the bills, or I would have been Donald fucking Trump. You had to get up, brush yourself off, and figure it the fuck out. You found a solution, even if it fucking sucked, and then you moved on. Wallowing got you nowhere, and pity was for the weak.

So, as I lay there in front of my family, I made a decision.

One choice.

Infinite possibilities.

One gigantic lie.

"I'm gonna be okay," I told the room. However, the announcement was entirely aimed at myself. "Even if this isn't temporary. I'll be fine."

If only I could have found a way to keep from losing myself in the arduous process of pretending to be *fine* and *okay*.

CHAPTER
Three

Ash

"HELP ME! PLEASE!" I SCREAMED, almost plowing the well-dressed man over. The concrete was cold against my bare feet, and the torn sweater did little to protect me from the freezing wind swirling around the city.

"Whoa!" he exclaimed, grabbing my shoulders to still me.

"Please. You have to help me. My dad . . . He . . ." I faded off as tears sprung to my eyes. "I need to call my mom. She has no idea where I am." I grasped his wrist and pulled his arm around my shoulder, burying my face in his jacket.

"Wait." He took a giant step away, unraveling me from his involuntary embrace. "What the hell is going on?" His forehead wrinkled as his eyes scanned my face, searching for answers I would never be able to give.

"Oh my God!" I whispered, peeking over his shoulder. "He's coming. Quick, hide me!"

Using the lapels of his suit coat, I dragged him against me. His arms hung at his side, but his confusion was obvious. Mine was not. I had but one focus.

"Please, mister, just help me. I can't go through that again," I sobbed.

His tense body momentarily slacked. "Okay, okay. Calm down." After glancing up and down the busy downtown sidewalk, he guided me into the small alley between two buildings. "Better?" he asked.

Not yet.

I lifted my head off his chest and peeked up through my lashes to give him the weakest of nods. "I'm sorry." I shoved my hands into the pockets on my sweater.

"What's your name?"

"Danielle," I responded then started chewing nervously on my bottom lip.

"Okay, Danielle. How old are you?"

"Seventeen," I answered. I would have gone younger, but I was five foot nine with a thirty-two double-D bra. No one bought the truth anymore.

"Shit." He swallowed hard.

I pressed to my tiptoes to look over his shoulder, and he followed my gaze.

"Who are you looking for?"

I cleared my throat. "I'm not looking *for* anyone. Can I, um . . . Can I just use your phone to call my mom?"

"Yeah. Sure." He began to pat down the pockets on his slacks. "Shit, I must have left it in my car."

"Oh God." I started to cry all over again.

"No. It's okay. I'm just parked right out front. We can go grab it." He smiled, forcing me to look away.

"I can't go back out there. He'll see me. You don't understand what he'll do if he finds me. I just want to go home." My teeth began to chatter as I wrapped the ratty sweater tighter around my body.

He dragged his suit coat off and draped it around my shoulders. "You have to be freezing."

"Thank you," I said softly, the smallest of smiles growing on my lips.

"Listen, I'll go grab my phone. You hang out here for a few minutes."

I nodded and leaned against the brick wall of the building.

"I'll be right back." He held my gaze as he backed away. My Good Samaritan cautiously looked up and down the sidewalk before exiting our hidden alley.

"I bet you will," I mumbled, inching myself to the corner to watch him go.

When he got a few feet away, I made my move.

Once I'd shed his jacket, I dug through my sweater pockets and pulled out the car keys I had easily lifted from his pocket. After a quick swipe with my sweater to remove, or at least smear, any possible prints, I dropped them to the ground beside his jacket.

He seemed like a nice man. It was the very least I could do.

Feeling guilty as hell, but without so much as a backward glance, I sprinted in the opposite direction down the alley. I zigzagged through a few of the side streets finally stopping to pull out his phone and dial the number to my father's latest disposable phone.

One ring later, he barked, "Where are you?"

"Corner of Price and Fourteenth." I pressed end.

I waited several minutes until my father's sedan came rolling to a stop in front of me.

"What the hell took so long? There is a very good chance that I'm going to lose a few toes to frostbite," I snapped, climbing inside and sliding on the pair of Oscar the Grouch slippers that were waiting on me. "Remind me again why I had to be barefoot?"

"Studies have shown that men are more likely to help women who are barefoot. Here." He offered a large, plastic cup of water.

Knowing the drill, I dropped my newly acquired iPhone inside. Within seconds, the screen blinked to black.

I cried a little each time we had to inhumanely put such a beautiful beast to sleep. I could have given that phone a wonderful home in my back pocket. He would have been so happy sending out my tweets. I could almost imagine his delight while helping me create cat memes. Unfortunately for me and the shiny little guy, cell phones were traceable. So, regardless of how many of them I managed to pickpocket, they all suffered the same fate.

"Ash, don't look at me like that! We'll get you a new phone soon," he lied.

I heard that promise along with numerous others on a daily basis. All. Lies. I was never getting a new phone, not after he had given mine to his beautiful new wife. *The whore.*

"Here. You want this one?" He spun the cheap, disposable flip phone in his fingers.

I rolled my eyes. "As amazing as that offer may be, I'll pass," I retorted sarcastically, causing him to chuckle.

"All right. What else did you bring me?" he asked, rubbing his hands together.

I dug into the pockets of my sweater. "Watch."

He lifted it to inspect it. "Oh, come on, Ash. This is fake!"

"Wow. I'm so sorry, Pops. Maybe you should hustle yourself from now on. Are there any studies that show how men react to a comb-over? We should give it a try." I smirked.

"Don't you dare catch that attitude with me. That is, unless you *want* to move up to Minneapolis." He quirked an eyebrow.

"What? No!" I shouted. "You said we could stay in Tennessee."

"Then quit your bitching. This place isn't cheap. If you want to stay here, you need to bring me back something better than a fake Rolex. And don't even act like you didn't know the difference when you targeted him."

I gritted my teeth.

Oh, I knew the difference, all right—which was precisely why I had taken that one instead of leaving it. I wasn't a bad person. Sure, I was a thief, but I only took what I needed in order to appease my father. I hated every single second of robbing people, especially the nice ones who seemed like they genuinely cared about me. It was freezing outside, and he'd offered me his coat. Unlike my father, who had taken my shoes and shoved me out of the car two blocks away.

I didn't want to rob people; however, I was willing to do whatever it took so I didn't have to move again.

Fifteen years. Twenty-two houses. Well, *house* might have been a little-too-liberal use of the word. Sure, we had lived in houses. Nice ones. *Big* ones. But we'd also lived in trailers, apartments, and, on more than one occasion, our car. Conning people didn't exactly provide a steady income.

Reaching into my pocket, I retrieved the rest of the man's belongings. "Here."

"That's my girl!" He snatched the wallet and business card carrier from my hands. "Where's his car keys?"

"I don't know." I shrugged, awkwardly looking out the window. "Maybe he carpools."

"God damn it, Ash!" he boomed.

"He was nice! I took his wallet. He wouldn't have been able to pay for a cab!"

"Oh, yeah? Poor guy. Maybe you can write a letter apologizing to him?"

It wasn't a completely bad idea, but I was relatively sure he was going somewhere else with that statement.

"While you're in *jail!*" he finished. "Your prints were on those keys. The first time you get caught, they will have you for every asshole you've ever turned."

"Nuh uh! I wiped 'em."

"Well, for your sake, I hope you were thorough! Stop leaving the fucking keys!" He banged the heel of his palm against the steering wheel.

"It's rude. We don't do anything with them anyway. They just go in the trash."

"I'm gonna need you to listen to me very carefully." He pulled off to the side of the road just as we got out of the city. "Your job is to take everything you can get from their pockets. That's it. If your fingers touch something, it comes home with us. You got it?"

I rolled my eyes.

And he narrowed his. "You know what? Maybe Minneapolis would be a good change for you."

That got my attention. "No!"

"You're getting sloppy, Ash." He sucked on his teeth with a slurping sound that made me want to vomit. "A change might be exactly what you need." He pulled back onto the road, cool as a fucking cucumber.

I, however, was livid. "Fine! I'll take the keys!"

"Nah. You've gotten *too* comfortable down here in the South. Everyone's an easy target. You need the challenge of a bigger city."

"Dad! No. You *swore* that we could stay here for a full year. It's only been three months!"

"I can't take that risk with you leaving your prints all over the goddamn city. Besides, I've got a lead in Minnesota. It could set us up for a while."

"School starts next week! You promised me I could enroll after Christmas."

"Well, you know what? Sometimes, shit doesn't work out the way we've planned." He reached over and opened the glove compartment, pulling a toothpick out and shoving it in his mouth. I had an overwhelming urge to stab it in his eye. "Especially when you bring back five hundred bucks and a fucking case of business cards."

What he didn't know was that the nice guy I'd just worked over also had his social security card in his wallet along with that five hundred bucks—or that I'd snuck it out while he'd checked the watch. I'd probably saved that poor schmuck three years of his life trying to get his identity back after my father got done with it. But . . . he was nice.

"Asshole," I mumbled under my breath. Although it wasn't nearly quiet enough.

"Just forget it, Ash. I've changed my mind. I don't think school is going to be a good fit for you. Besides, what the hell do you know about algebra?"

"Nothing!" I yelled. "I know nothing about algebra, English, or history as far as you're concerned. It's a goddamn miracle I can even read and write."

"Oh, don't give me that shit. You always have your nose stuck in some book. Plus, I got you that computer so you could take classes online. Stop being so dramatic." He went back to staring out the window.

"You did not *get* me a computer. I *stole* a computer! From a ninety-year-old man whose grandkids bought it for him so they could video chat with him every day because they missed him so much."

"What the fucking hell are you talking about?" He laughed. "He was sixty-five and loaded. His grandkids hated him."

"You don't know that! It could have happened my way." I crossed my arms over my chest, full-on pouting.

"Yes, I do. How the hell do you think you got a key to his house? His crooked son paid me to get that computer. There was quite a bit of information stored on that bad boy before you decorated it with puppy stickers."

Whatever. I liked my version better.

I changed the subject back. "I'm not moving."

"Debbie's packing your shit as we speak."

"No," I gasped.

"We don't have the money to stay. If you had actually brought me something of use, I could have squeaked us by a few more weeks, but business cards aren't going to pay the rent."

Tennessee seriously sucked. I had no friends and I slept on the couch in a one-bedroom apartment that had an ant problem. Yet I would've given absolutely anything to stay there. It was the first place my father had actually considered letting me attend school. I hated his wife, but thankfully, the feeling was mutual. She was so desperate to get rid of me that she'd actually convinced my father that school would be good for me. I wasn't exactly bi-curious or anything, but when he'd finally said yes, I'd wanted to throw her down and hump her.

I'd been begging my father for as long as I could remember to let me go to school. But he'd always answered with a resounding no. He had given me a ton of bullshit excuses over the years, but I knew the truth. It all boiled down to the paper trail. Ray Mabie used a hundred different identities. Very rarely were they actually his own. However, if Ash Victoria Mabie enrolled in a public school, he would have to provide some sort of documentation. God, I would've killed to go to an actual school, with actual kids my age. I'd heard that teenage girls were bitches, but I was willing to take the chance. They couldn't be all that bad. I was pretty freaking awesome. Surely there were others like me.

I sucked in a deep breath and reached into my pocket, palming the social security card that I knew would buy me more than just a few weeks. I began to pull it out, but I stilled as I remembered the soft smile of the man who'd offered me—a stranger in need—his coat. He hadn't had to do that. He could have walked the other way, like so many others had that day.

Damn it. Why'd he have to be so nice?

"I hate you," I mumbled as I rolled the window down and tossed the social security card to the side of the highway.

"What the hell was that?" my father asked.

"Gum wrapper. You want some?" I flipped the pack I had hidden in my hand.

He eyed me warily. "Gum, huh?"

"Yep," I responded before blowing a bubble and popping it loudly.

"Don't litter," he scolded.

I couldn't help but laugh. The man had sent me out on the streets alone with zero protection, but a gum wrapper on the side of a road bothered him. To hell with his daughter, but let's not tamper with the fragile environment.

Fuck my life.

CHAPTER
Four

Flint

Eight months later . . .

"I HAVE TO GET OUT of here," I declared as if I were being held prisoner in the pits of hell. And in my mind, I really was.

I prided myself on being logical and levelheaded. I was a planner who thought out every detail, sometimes to the point of obsession. But right then, as the words flew from my mouth, it was a completely rash decision made in haste when I caught my brother innocently kissing *his* wife while holding *his* child. He had every right to do it, and I had every right to leave so I didn't have to witness it anymore.

Till and Eliza had gone to great lengths to make me comfortable in their new house. And by anyone's standards, they had done an amazing job. It was a far cry from the shithole we had grown up in. By all means, I should have been ecstatic. But I was suffocating in that one-point-four-million-dollar mansion. Sure, I had a bedroom that had been built especially for me—complete with an adjoining gym that was a physical therapist's wet dream and a bathroom that was fully handicap accessible. I had the freedom most people in my situation dreamed about.

I, however, felt like a caged animal.

"Okay," Till said, surprised. "Where do you want to go?" He crossed his arms over his chest and studied me carefully.

Any place where you aren't fucking the woman I'm in love with.

"College," I answered instead. "I'm feeling better, and I'm already a full semester behind. I'm ready to start."

Eliza smiled tightly, shifting six-month-old baby Blakely to her other hip. "You can live here and go to college. It's only a fifteen-minute commute."

Fuck. That.

"They have wheelchair-accessible dorms," I told her without making eye contact.

Yeah. And a yearlong wait list.

"I'm not sure that's the best idea, Flint. I'm all for you starting school, but we just hired that new physical therapist." Till lifted his eyebrows and tossed me a teasing, one-sided smirk. "I thought you liked Miranda?"

Oh, he knew I liked her, all right. He'd caught me fucking her a few weeks earlier. But what he didn't know was that she was a hardcore gold digger who had taken one look around that house and all but dropped to her knees the second I'd rolled into the room. She didn't want *me* though. She wanted the money she assumed lined my pockets. Those weekly *physical* therapy sessions were usually only beneficial to my cock. Till had essentially hired me a hooker with a college degree.

However, I was such a miserable bastard that, knowing my brother, he wouldn't have given a single damn that his money was being spent getting me off. Although I bet he would have cared if he knew that, not two minutes after he'd walked into the room and found Miranda riding my cock, I'd been forced to call her Eliza in order to come. Some things never changed.

Whoever said that time heals all wounds was an ignorant asshole. In my experience, time made everything worse. While I had been making great strides in my recovery, I was still stuck with useless legs and a suffocating obsession for my brother's wife. Visiting Eliza in the hospital the day Blakely was born had almost killed me. So, after that, I'd checked out from the whole family thing. The day Till had received his cochlear implant, which allowed him to hear again for the first time in over two years, I'd refused to go. I'd told my brother that I was in pain, and he'd quickly dropped the subject. Eliza knew I'd lied, and I knew that it'd broken her heart. Till deserved to have his hearing back, but I hadn't been able to sit there and watch him have it all.

Every day that had passed, I'd become more and more bitter toward him.

It wasn't fair.

It wasn't right.

Yet I wanted to make him pay for every single strand of happiness he'd worked his ass off to get.

Somehow, in my warped mind, I'd learned to hate the only person who'd ever given a damn about me. And it wasn't all about Eliza, either. Honestly, I wasn't sure what it was about. I just knew that Till Page had a life I would have killed for, but because of one fucking bullet, it was a life I would never even be allowed to fight for.

Living with them made it that much worse, too. It was exhausting. Every time I exited the sanctuary of my room, I was forced to paint on a fake-ass smile and pretend that I didn't want to punch Till in his throat each time I so much as ran into him while making a fucking sandwich in the kitchen.

His kitchen.

I needed my own goddamned kitchen. And, while I was at it, my own woman.

My cock worked; I at least had that on my side. But women didn't exactly get off on the idea of being with half a man. Fuck 'em though, because there was only one woman I really wanted, and with her, I had far bigger barriers than my wheelchair—a six-foot-two, two-hundred-and-fifty-pound barrier, to be exact.

For everyone's sake, I *needed* to move out, but as I stared at Till's concerned eyes from across the room, I knew he *needed* me to stay. Responsibility will do that to people. And that was exactly what I had become.

"Flint, just stay here a little while longer. You can do the college thing, but I think it's safest if you lived here with us," Till said.

"No!" I yelled. "You can't fucking stop me!" I propelled my wheelchair forward, stopping inches in front of him. Only months ago, I was a full two inches taller than he was, but right then, I stared up like the pleading child he apparently thought I still was. "I'm leaving. I'm not asking permission. I'm just letting you know."

He leveled me with an angry glare, which I fearlessly returned. I had lost so much weight since I'd stopped working out at On The Ropes that he was at least fifty pounds heavier than I was, but he was no match for me in the anger department. I had more of that than Till could ever dream of mustering.

"I'm nineteen. You. Can. Not. Stop. Me," I gritted out through my teeth.

"Flint, stop," Eliza pleaded from beside him.

I never dragged my eyes away from my brother, but I was positive there were tears streaming down her face. I couldn't care anymore though. That was Till's job. Not mine.

Not. Mine.

"You're right." Till began rolling his bottom lip between his index finger and his thumb. It was his nervous habit and also the sign that I'd won. "College will be good. When do you move in?" He wrapped his arm around Eliza's shoulders and kissed the top of her head.

Yep. There it is.

Looking away from their embrace, I replied, "Tonight."

"What?" Eliza gasped.

"I'm gonna stay with a friend for a couple of nights. Then I'll see if Slate can come over and help me move my stuff."

"Flint, what the hell is going on here? College, I get. What's the sudden rush to leave?" Till asked.

And before I could stop them, my eyes jumped to Eliza. Just as quickly, I flashed them away in an attempt to cover my accidental confession, but before I had the chance, her shoulders fell. She might not have been mine, but the way her chin quivered as she looked down at the ground absolutely belonged to me. And I *hated* myself for it.

"Nothing. I'm just sick of sitting at home all the time."

He tilted his head to the side, not completely convinced. "When do classes start?"

"Monday," I guessed. Fuck if I knew when classes started, but I was willing to tell him whatever bullshit it took to get me out of there ASAP.

"And you're sure about this?" he asked.

"Positive."

Sighing, he grabbed the back of his neck. "Okay, but if you change your mind, you can come back anytime. Let me get you a check. Pre-pay for the first full year of tuition and your room. Put the rest away for books. I'll set you up on a monthly stipend for food and shit." He released Eliza and started to walk from the room.

"Are you insane? I'm not taking your money!"

He stopped in his tracks and spun to face me. "Excuse me?"

"There is no way I'm taking your money."

"Yes, you fucking are!"

"That's your money. Not mine. Use it to take care of your wife and daughter. I can figure out college on my own."

"You're absolutely right. It is my money, and I busted my ass to earn it so I could take care of my family. *You* are my family," he bit out.

"Unfortunately, that's true," I mumbled.

It was childish and a lie, but they were the only words I could think of to hurt him. However, since he was standing across the room, Eliza was the only one who heard them.

"Flint!" she scolded, wiping her tears away and squaring her shoulders.

Fuck. I knew that look, and it didn't bode well for me at all.

"Till, take Blakely and go get that check. I'm gonna help Flint pack a few things." She smiled sweetly, and it quite honestly scared the piss out of me.

Till must have recognized *the look* too, because as he took the baby from her arms, he bit his lip to conceal a laugh.

Not even a second after he walked from the room, Eliza started in on me.

"Are you done?" She crossed her arms over her chest.

"Yep." Unwilling to listen to her lecture, I spun myself away. But before I could get turned all the way around, she lifted her foot and slammed down on the brake of my wheelchair, thrusting me forward from the sudden halt.

"You're not done."

"Oh, I'm not?" I laughed humorlessly, rolling my eyes. After re-leasing the brake, I began to leave again, but Eliza had other ideas.

Moving in front of my chair, she leveled me with a menacing glare. Bending over, she rested her hands on my thighs. "Kiss me."

"What?" I questioned, leaning away.

"You love me, right? You're leaving because of that, right? Then kiss me. Who knows? Maybe I'll like it." She shrugged and moved in even closer.

I had envisioned kissing Eliza no fewer than a million times. Never once had it been out of pity or desperation. Those two things were enough to ruin even my wildest dreams.

"Wow, Eliza. I didn't take you for a cheater."

"It's not cheating, because I would feel *nothing.*"

I laughed again, trying to hide the hole her words had carved in my soul. "Well, when you put it that way."

"Then tell me why you're leaving," she demanded, never moving away.

"I told you. College. Besides, I'm sick of you guys taking care of me. I need to do this on my own."

Oh, and because I want to rip the arms off my brother every time he touches you.

"Bullshit. You're leaving because of me."

"Wow. Aren't you full of yourself today? Not everything is about you."

"I'm well aware of that, but *this* is," she hissed. "I love you, Flint Page. And I know you love me, but not like this. If finally kissing me will make you see that this thing you have for me is nothing more than an infatuation, then I'll take the hit."

"The hit? Christ, now I'm in the mood," I said sarcastically, but my eyes dropped to her mouth.

Fuck it.

Suddenly, I grabbed the back of her neck, hauling her impossibly close. Her eyes went wide and her chin quivered, but she didn't back away.

I'd spent years pining over Eliza, but with her lips less than an inch from mine, I was hit by the overwhelming reality that it was never going to happen for me with her. I could steal a single kiss, but I'd *never* have more than that. I should have realized that about the time she'd married my brother, but it wasn't until right then—as fear and anxiety covered her gorgeous face—that the truth sank in.

My chest ached as I made the decision to *finally* let her go. She stared at me, pleading through her sparkling, blue eyes—a single tear spilling out then trailing down her cheek.

Fuck. That one fucking tear gutted me.

It was the end.

With that realization lingering between us, my angry façade melted away, leaving me stripped and vulnerable in its absence. I couldn't even stop the truth as it tumbled from my tongue.

"I don't know what to do. I'm so fucking bitter, Eliza. I don't even know why most of the time. I mean, of course, there's the obvious." I looked down at my legs. "But God, it's so much more than that. I'm starting to hate him because I love you. Yet, at the same time, he's my brother and I love him, but I hate you so fucking much for loving him too."

"You don't love me, Flint," she whispered.

"You can't say that! You don't know!" I boomed before falling quiet. "I just need to get away from here."

"Okay. Then I won't fight you. If you want to move out, fine. But I have this feeling that you're not planning to come back." She dropped to her knees in front of me. Then she squeezed my hand painfully tight. "I need you to swear to me that, even if your address changes, you're not actually going anywhere."

"I can't . . ." I trailed off.

"You don't have be around me if you don't want, but please don't do this to Till and Quarry." Her voice hitched.

Damn it, I'm such a prick.

"It's not just you, Eliza. I mean, that's part of it, but . . . fuck. I'm drowning. Everyone's so happy. Till's running the gym with Slate now. Quarry's destroying the amateur boxing circuit. And I'm . . . sitting in the stands, watching."

Releasing my hand, she inched even closer. Palming each side of my face, she said, "You're not sitting in the stands, Flint. You're just adjusting. You'll be back in the ring in no time."

"Don't," I whispered. "We both know I'll never be back inside that ring."

She shook her head in disagreement, but she didn't say the lie out loud. "God, you've had a hell of a year. You can't possibly expect—"

I interrupted what was sure to be a pep talk. "Let's just be real here."

She sighed then rested her elbows on my useless thighs. "Maybe you're right. As much as it's gonna kill me, your moving out and starting your own life might not be the worst thing to happen. You always were a nerd," she teased through tears. "College will be great."

God, she was amazing. And for that reason alone, I blurted, "You were right too. I am saying goodbye."

Her whole body tensed. I hated witnessing the verbal slap I had just issued, but if there was ever a woman who deserved the truth, it was her.

"I need a fresh start, and I can't do that here. I need to figure out my life now that this is my new reality," I told her. I could tell she assumed I was talking about being paralyzed, and I can't say that she was wrong. Although she wasn't right, either. So much of my life had been caught up in her. I wasn't quite sure how to move forward.

I was about to try though.

"I know you do." She sniffled, pushing herself off her knees. "Okay. No more crying. This is a good thing for you." She sucked in a deep breath and used the backs of her hands to wipe the tears away.

Then her shoulders squared.

Fuck.

"I'm gonna need you to take that check from your brother," she told me sternly.

"I can't do that. Till made his own way in life. I'm a grown-ass man now. I want to do the same."

"You might be a 'grown-ass man'"—she tossed me a pair of air quotes—"but you're still his little brother. Flint, he sat in silence for years to be able to earn enough money to write you that check."

"I'm sorry—"

"Shut up and listen to me."

I rolled my eyes, but she didn't seem to care.

"When Till initially went deaf, he gave me three excuses as to why he needed to continue boxing instead of getting the cochlear implant: to buy me a home." She waved her arms around the room. "To pay for the best specialist for Quarry." She crossed her arms over her chest. "And lastly, to be able to pay for your college. He always brags to anyone who will listen about how smart you are. He adores the fact that you actually enjoy school, and he wanted to be able to give you that. He doesn't want you to have to bust your ass the way he did."

"I can't take his money," I repeated.

"You have to. And if you want me to let this go and keep my mouth shut about the real reason you're leaving, then you will take that check and drive off in that van he bought for you months ago."

"I'm not taking the minivan. It's ridiculous."

"It really is." She laughed before getting serious again. "But you're gonna take it. And that check too. If you're planning to disappear for a while, at least give us both the peace of mind that you aren't struggling."

"I don't want—"

"Here you go," Till announced, walking back into the room. "I wasn't sure how much the dorms are. I tried to look it up, but I swear it just confused me more. Anyway, I think this should cover that and tuition. Let me know if you need more. I'll get a stipend set up for you next week." He extended the check in my direction.

I immediately backed away. "Listen—" I started, but Eliza cleared her throat, catching my attention.

"*Take it,*" she mouthed behind his back.

Till was absolutely not paying for my college, but I could take his check to keep the peace. Cashing it would be a different story.

I took it from his hands. "Thanks. I really appreciate it." I flashed my gaze back to Eliza, who continued our secret conversation.

"*And,*" she mouthed.

Shaking my head, I looked back at Till. "And can I have the keys to the van?" I mumbled.

His eyes lit, and a huge smile grew on his face. "She must have some serious dirt on you if you agreed to take the money *and* the van. Jesus, that woman is good." He let out a loud laugh, looking over his shoulder at Eliza, who innocently shrugged.

"That she is," I confirmed.

"Come on. I'll show you all the stuff I had added to it. The hand pedals are super easy to use. Let me grab the keys and I'll meet you out there." He squeezed my shoulder and walked toward the garage.

I started after him, but just before I made it to the door, Eliza stopped me.

"Hey, Flint."

I turned to face her.

"Come back, okay? Take some time and get your head straight. But please, just come back." She smiled tightly, tears once again flooding her eyes.

"I promise." I swallowed hard, praying that it was one I could keep.

Armed with a bag of clothes, a check folded in my pocket, and a handicap-equipped minivan, I pulled out of Till and Eliza's driveway. As I watched the mansion disappear in my rearview mirror, I had absolutely no plans of going back—despite whatever promise I had made Eliza. I couldn't even conjure a day where that place wouldn't send me into a tailspin.

My first stop was the college. I spent hours filling out paperwork: admissions, financial aid, and housing. Fortunately, they'd extended the acceptance I had received before the accident. Unfortunately, there was actually a *two-year* wait list on the handicapped dorms. The best news I received all day, though, was the fact that being broke had its advantages. The financial counselor set me up with enough loans and grants to cover tuition, with money left over to cover housing too. It would take several weeks to get the money, but that was okay. I still had the difficult task of finding a place to live first.

I left the college feeling marginally better. At least that was a step in the direction of getting my life back on track. After hoisting myself into the van, I drove around aimlessly. I considered calling Slate to see if I could crash at his house, but that would pretty much guarantee a conversation about why I didn't want to go home and probably an appearance from Till when Slate no doubt ratted me out.

Eventually, I found myself in an all-too-familiar rental office, begging for the keys to one specific *door.*

CHAPTER
Five

Ash

AFTER MOVING TO MINNEAPOLIS, WE only spent a few months in a two-bedroom trailer before moving to an extended-stay hotel on the outskirts of Chicago. Finally, we landed a sweet, run-down house in the slums of Indianapolis. Such was my life. However, of all the places I would ever live, Indianapolis became the golden standard against which everywhere else would be judged.

When I turned sixteen, my father started letting me drive. I had no idea why he'd made me wait; it's not like he took me to get my driver's license or anything. But I definitely didn't argue when he handed me the keys one night and asked me to go pick something up for dinner. And even though he didn't offer a single penny in cash to pay for said dinner, I still snatched the keys from his hands and ran out that door before he had a chance to change his mind.

He and the step-witch loved alone time. And I loved not being there during alone time. There were some things that even a set of earbuds blaring Taylor Swift couldn't cancel out. I took off at every opportunity I got.

With newfound freedom, I was able to branch out, and within a few weeks of being in the new city, I had actually made some friends.

True friends.

"Slumber party!" I yelled, dropping my bag onto the ground. "All right, which one of you is painting my nails?"

"Not me," Max declared, swiping the pillow from my arms.

"Okay. Donna, you're up," I announced, handing her a blanket and a bottle of polish.

"Honey, I ain't no damn manicurist," she snapped.

"Well, you two suck. Worst BFFs ever."

It was a total lie. They were the absolute best BFFs ever. Mainly because they were the only ones I'd ever had. Since the first night we'd literally run into each other on the street outside my favorite grocery store to shoplift from, they had always been there for me.

"You sign up for school today?" Max asked, opening the pizza box I had just deposited onto his lap.

"No. My dad's an asshole."

"They usually are," he replied, offering the box for me to take a slice.

"No, you two go ahead. I have to watch my figure."

"What figure?" Donna snarked before snagging a piece of pizza.

"I'll have you know I have excellent boobs. It's all the other stuff I have to worry about." I rubbed my stomach and glanced over at Max, who was shaking his head in defeat. He hated it when we talked about girl stuff, but as the sole penis in our club for misfits, he had to deal with it a lot.

Donna rolled her eyes. "Fine. I'll give you that, but some pizza on those hips wouldn't hurt anyone."

"Well, aren't you in a mood tonight? What has your panties in a bunch?" I asked, motioning for Max to hand me a piece of pizza. I really was starving.

"Same shit, different day," she answered, snapping her fingers until I passed her a napkin from my purse.

"No way. It has to be more than that."

Max filled in the blank. "Her sister stopped by today."

My eyes grew wide. "Oh my God. What the hell did that bitch want?"

"Don't know. Don't care. Just seeing her face was enough to ruin my entire fucking night."

Max shook his head again, taking another piece from the box and saying, "You should have talked to her."

"Oh hell no! I'm not talking to her. You think for a single second she feels bad about getting me kicked out of my own mother's house? Horseshit. I know her better than that. She's scheming for something."

"Like what?" I whispered.

Donna's family drama was exactly why I loved her so much. It was always something. I mean, I had a shit-ton of drama at home, but it was so much fun listening to someone else's problems for once.

"Who the hell knows!" she yelled. "That witch is up to no good. I'm positive."

"Good lord." Max rolled his eyes, not nearly as excited to hear about Donna's family issues as I was. "Ash, what's your pops's excuse for not letting you sign up for school this time?" he asked, changing the subject.

"No excuse. He just laid down the law." I sucked in a deep breath, pulling my ponytail over my forehead in a mock comb-over, and put on my best Ray Mabie voice. "'Ash, I said no. School will get you nowhere in life. Street smarts are what you really need.'"

"Well, he's not wrong," Donna said smugly, reaching for her water bottle.

"Oh, I forgot! I brought you guys a present!" I dug to the bottom of my overnight bag then revealed a bottle of vodka.

"Now we're talking!" Max clapped.

"Where the hell did you get that?" Donna asked, dropping her pizza back into the box before snatching the bottle from my hands.

I shrugged. "Stepmommy dearest."

"You don't think she'll notice?" he asked, taking it from Donna and twisting the cap off.

"Oh please. I'll divide one of her other bottles into two and tell her she drank it the night before. She's a dumbass."

"Cheers to the dumbass!" he lifted the bottle in the air before tossing it back for a long pull.

Donna slapped him on the chest. "Hey, Ash scored that shit. She should have had the first shot."

I curled my lip. "Ew. No, thank you. That stuff is nasty as hell. Give me some more pizza though."

"Fair trade." Max laughed, passing me the entire box and then tipping the vodka back for another gulp.

"All right, slow down." I snatched the bottle from his mouth mid sip. "I'm *not* washing the puke off your clothes again. Besides, I brought some more cards. I have serious intentions of winning back my money from last week."

He let out a loud laugh as I passed the bottle to Donna. "Oh lord, Ash. I spent my winnings about ten minutes after they landed in my pocket."

I huffed. "Fine. I'll loan you ten bucks, but I'm taking that back tonight. I still think you cheated somehow."

"Nope. You're the only magician around here, sweetheart." He gave me a knowing glare that made me burst out laughing.

I'd hustled the shit out of him the first night we'd hung out. I'd immediately returned his money, but he hadn't found it humorous in the least. Luckily for me, and thanks to Donna, I'd found out he had a soft spot for food and booze. It had taken me a full two weeks of "apologizing" to get back in his good graces.

"Laugh it up," he said seriously, but an unmistakable smirk grew on his face.

"Oh, I will," I shot back, almost falling over in hysterics.

Donna quickly joined me while Max sat watching us, unimpressed.

"Okay, okay." I sat up before bursting back into laughter. I wasn't even sure why I was laughing at all. But God, I loved that feeling.

Finally sobering up, I retrieved a deck of cards from my bag.

"Hey! Guess what?" I said as I began shuffling the cards.

"Hell no! Don't try to distract me. I'm watching you to make sure you don't stack that deck. You know what?" He reached forward, plucking it from my hands. "Let me shuffle."

I laughed but willingly let him take it from me. "No, I'm serious. So, apparently, Ray's wife has some kids. I overheard them talking about going to get the youngest tomorrow."

"Wait. How long have they been married? And you are just now finding out that she has kids?" Donna asked.

"A few years. And I mean, I knew she had kids, but I just assumed they were all older. She doesn't talk about them or anything. I know one of them is some big-time boxer, but the little one is only, like, fourteen." I shrugged, taking the two cards Max had dealt me. "I think his name is Corey or something. Anyway, I'm freaking stoked. It'll be fun having a little brother."

Donna quirked an eyebrow. "What if he's an asshole like his mom?"

"No way. He's gonna be awesome! I can feel it. I had a dream last night—"

"And here we go," Max moaned.

"Shut. Up. Don't be mad because I'm clairvoyant," I lied.

I wasn't even close to being able to see the future. I actually didn't have dreams at all. Every night, I would fall asleep, but never once did my traitorous synapses fire off during REM, leaving me unable to dream. I'd tried though. Hell, I couldn't even give myself a nightmare. I had always heard that dreams were inspired by a person's emotions or real-life experiences, so I decided to make up my own. I had a sneaking suspicion that what I created was a hell of a lot more fun than the dreams my brain would have made. Loneliness and robbery probably didn't combine to make glitter and unicorns.

"Trip Queens," I said, dropping my cards.

Max let out a loud curse.

"Just be glad that was a warm-up." I winked. "Anyway. This kid is going to be awesome. I can't wait to introduce him to you guys."

They both groaned, but it did nothing to suppress the giddiness I felt inside. Sure, he was a little younger than I was, but I was stoked about having some company around the house. A girl could never have too many friends, right?

CHAPTER
Six

Flint

FOR SIX MONTHS, I MANAGED to avoid my family. I'd wanted a fresh start, and that was exactly what I'd gotten. For the first two weeks, Till had blown my phone up with texts wondering where the hell I was. It had taken a month before Eliza had started messaging. I'd never engaged their conversations, but I had at least let them know that I was *fine* and *okay.* I understood why they were worried, but I was committed to my new life.

Alone.

I'd severed every possible connection they'd had to me. They didn't know where I lived, and I had even stopped going to the physical therapy sessions Till paid for each week. Instead, I'd started working with one of the PT students at the college. It was only once a week, and I knew I needed more if I ever wanted to walk again, but my head and heart were what needed the most healing.

Living in Eliza's old apartment had its perks. The memories were abundant, and they carried me through more than just a few lonely nights. However, it also had its downfalls. It wasn't wheelchair accessible, so it made even the simplest of tasks extremely difficult. I also had all of those memories haunting me but absolutely nothing tangible to ground me.

I missed her.

I missed Till.

I missed Quarry.

I missed Slate.

But most of all, I missed Flint Page.

I was wasting away. Hell, I'd thought I was half a man months earlier; I wasn't sure there was even a proper fraction to describe myself anymore. It wasn't just my physical appearance, either. My desire to fight was gone. Once my nemesis, wallowing became a way of life.

The only thing I was actually doing well in was school. Despite my advisor's recommendation, I was taking the maximum amount of hours allowable for a freshman. I fucking loved the distraction. School was probably the only aspect in life in which I didn't have to struggle. It had always come easy for me.

My life might have been a mess, but it was at least simple. I had a schedule that drove my day. Wake up, go to school, come home, do homework, study, go to sleep. Wash. Rinse. Repeat.

However, with a single knock on my front door, everything I had worked so hard to maintain crumbled in front of my eyes.

But like a second bullet to the back, it also changed my life.

"About fucking time," Slate said, pushing me out of the way as he strode inside.

"What do you want?" I replied with an attitude I never would have dreamed of using with Slate before that moment.

"Did you join a cult?" he asked, tilting his head to the side.

"What? No?"

"Then what the hell is that dead animal on your face?"

I rubbed the scruff on my chin. "Did you come here to critique my grooming habits?"

"No. But I would have brought you a razor if I had known you were having such a difficult time getting your hands on one."

I rolled my eyes. "How'd you find me?"

"Leo followed you from class about six months ago."

"Awesome," I mumbled.

"Till got worried after he knocked on the door of every dorm on the first floor of the entire fucking college. Don't worry. I didn't tell him where you're living. Your secret's safe. You really should have given him your address. That was a dick move."

"Why? So he could have busted in here like you? I'm doing my own thing right now. I needed some space."

He walked over to the couch and flopped down, stretching his long legs in front of him, crossing them at the ankle. "So let me get this straight. You decided to just disappear and take some *space*. To hell with your family. Flint's the only one who really matters, right? You're more important than the people who love you and miss you, right?" He popped a knowing eyebrow. "It must run in the family. Seems to me that's exactly what your mom and dad did to you."

My head snapped to the side, and rage boiled my blood. "That's not at all what I did! I am not my parents!"

"Could have fooled me." He shrugged. "Just for future reference, you can have space *and* family. Phone calls and the occasional visit wouldn't fucking kill you. But this little disappearing act you pulled *is* killing them."

I shook my head. He didn't get it. And short of spilling all of my dirty laundry at his feet, he never would.

"Awesome. Good pep talk. You done?"

"Nope, not even close." He smiled and pushed to his feet. "Your brother has been blowing up your phone this week for a reason."

"I've been busy."

"Well unbusy yourself. Your mom showed up at Till's with the cops on Monday and took Quarry."

"What!" I yelled, never wishing that I could fly to my feet more. "She can't do that!"

"She can and she did. The law got involved, and Till has no formal custody agreement. Even though she abandoned you boys, she is still biologically your mom. Quarry's only fourteen, so he defaults to her until a court date can be arranged."

"You have got to be shitting me," I breathed.

"We got a whole legal team involved and managed to get Till weekend visitation while we worked out a court date for next month. But that still means Q is gonna be living with your mom during the week until then."

"Son of a bitch." I raked a hand through my hair. "Is Till freaking the fuck out?"

"You can't even imagine. I actually just dropped him off at the gym. I spent the last twenty-four hours trying to bail him out of jail."

"Jail?" I exclaimed.

"Apparently, Till went to pick him up yesterday and your mom's husband refused to let Quarry leave with him."

"Her husband?" I clarified in shock.

"Yep. She married Ray Mabie, and that piece of shit was dumb enough to step between Till and Quarry. All hell broke loose."

Suddenly, I had a sickening feeling in my stomach. Nothing stood between "The Silencer" Till Page and his family.

"Did he kill him?" I asked.

"Nah, but Ray left in the back of an ambulance. Till was in the back of a police car."

"Fucking hell," I cursed in relief that the death penalty was at least off the table.

"Anyway, I need you to go pick up Q. Till isn't allowed within two hundred feet of Mabie's house, and it has to be an immediate family member to pick him up, which means Eliza and I are out."

Just the mention of her name twisted my gut. "I, uh, I mean . . . I can't."

"Excuse me?"

"I can't. I mean, I can. But—"

"Okay, let me rephrase this." He slapped the back of my head. "What the fuck is wrong with you? *Your brother* is sitting at your worthless-piece-of-shit mother's house. You remember what growing up with that woman was like, right? Don't give me any of this bullshit about can't. Get your fucking keys, get in your car, and, if you have to, break every goddamn traffic law on the way to pick him up."

"I'm not going back to Till's to drop him off. I'm just not!" I shouted.

Slate crossed his thick arms over his chest and narrowed his eyes at me. "You care to tell me why not?"

"Because I'm not going back there." I paused before throwing in, "Ever," so there was no confusion.

"Fine. Bring him to the gym. You know, it wouldn't kill you to come inside and put in a decent workout too. You look terrible."

"I'll *drop* him off." I had zero intention of going inside that gym, and no insult Slate could sling at me would change my mind.

"Flint—"

"Excuse me. I'm supposed to be racing to pick up Q right now. I'll drop him off at On The Ropes in a little while."

He sucked in a resigned breath and shook his head. "Fine. I'll text you the address. But for the record, don't for one second think that you have anyone fooled. You're not getting your shit together by holing yourself up in this apartment. *You're avoiding it.* But you know what? Problems don't need a map. They'll follow you everywhere. You can't hide forever, Flint."

"Noted," I smarted back.

He chuckled without humor, and the muscles of his jaw clenched as he gritted his teeth. "Man the fuck up, son." He shook his head then stalked out the door.

"Excellent advice, Slate! Bravo. Really," I yelled after him, but the door slammed without another word spoken. "Fuck," I whispered to the empty room.

CHAPTER
Seven

Flint

"FLINT!" MY MOTHER YELLED AS she opened the door. Clutching her imaginary pearls, she cried, "Oh my God, look at you."

"Debbie," I acknowledged without actually greeting her.

"You're in a wheelchair," she whined in the most nerve-grating way possible.

Folding my hands in my lap, I copped as much attitude as I could muster. I had so much indifference for the woman standing in front of me that even being an asshole, something I usually excelled at, was difficult. It was hard, but I still managed to snark, "Very astute observation."

"Don't treat me like that. It's not fair. I didn't know until last week that something happened to you. Till didn't even bother telling me."

"Really? He didn't call you or anything?" I questioned dryly.

"No! My son was paralyzed and he didn't even have the common decency to let me know."

"Wow. What an ass!" I said with a large dose of sarcasm that sailed right over her head.

"This is all his fault. I don't know where he gets off acting like he does. If it wasn't for him, none of this would have happened."

"You know, I never expected to say this when I came here today, but I absolutely agree with you. Me being in this chair is one hundred percent Till's fault."

Her eyes lit with shock that shifted to pride at my agreement. Mine lit when I realized I would be able to force them to dim again. Suddenly, being an asshole wasn't so difficult anymore.

"Actually, there are a lot of things that are Till's fault."

Her smile expanded. God, it felt so fucking good to see that on her face—it was going to feel amazing removing it. I became damn near giddy.

She checked over her shoulder before leaning in close and whispering, "Flint, he's an animal. Did you hear what he did to Ray? I thought he was going to kill him."

"I know! That's another one of Till's fuck-ups in life," I said seriously. I mirrored her move and leaned forward in order to whisper, "He *should* have killed him."

Her head snapped back in surprise and just as quickly as her smile fell, mine grew.

"Excuse me?" she asked.

"I'm actually really impressed with Till's self-control. You had the balls to show up at his house unannounced, with uniformed officers, to take a child he has been raising for years. I figured you'd be picking out a casket right about now." I laughed loudly.

"He belongs with his mother!"

"Are you shitting me? Quarry's gotten in his fair share of trouble, but he's never done anything that would warrant the cruel and unusual punishment of being forced to live with you again."

She gasped. "How dare you speak to your mother that way!"

"Oh, I dare, all right. How dare you think you're someone's mother! Were you thinking of Quarry when you decided to uproot him during this petty excuse of a custody battle?"

"I missed him."

"You *missed* him? Did you miss him when you abandoned us?" I roared. "What a load of bullshit," I sneered. "You are such a piece of work. You were absolutely right. It is Till's fault that I'm sitting in this chair right now, because if it wasn't for him, I wouldn't be alive at all. Who the fuck do you think cleaned up your mess when you walked away? Who exactly do you think fed us and put a roof over our heads for the last three years while you were off doing God knows what? We were kids! So yeah, it's all Till's fault. And thank fucking God for that."

"I should have known you three assholes would gang up on me. You have no idea what you are talking about or why I left. I didn't have a choice."

"We all have choices. Even worthless wastes of oxygen like yourself." I turned to wheel away. "Do me a favor and tell Q I'm waiting out front."

"No need," Quarry said, jogging out the door.

"No. I've changed my mind. You aren't going anywhere!" she yelled, but I heard Quarry's footsteps continue behind me. "Quarry Page! Get your ass back in here!"

"No can do! It's Till's weekend!" he shouted over his shoulder before grabbing the handles of the wheelchair to push me faster.

"Stop!" I snapped.

"Then go faster, before she calls the cops."

"Ray!" my mother screamed.

I glanced back while Quarry continued pushing me to the car. Ray Mabie came lumbering out of the house, and a simultaneous gasp and laugh flew from my mouth. His face was nearly unrecognizable, and I'm not just saying that I didn't recognize him as Ray—I didn't even recognize him as human.

"Holy fuck!" I cursed.

Quarry followed my gaze only to bark out a laugh. "Dude, you should have seen it. Till lost his shit!"

"It looks like Mabie's face found it."

"That guy is such a cocksucker. Mom doesn't give two shits about having me back. This is all about Till."

"No, they're up to something. This is all about Till's *money,*" I corrected, sliding into the driver's seat of the van. "Christ, when did you get so big?" I asked as Quarry shoved my chair into the back.

"When did you shrink? You look like dehydrated shit."

"I see that your stellar personality has remained intact."

"I see that you're still a cranky asshole. Must be from sitting on it all day," he sniped.

My lip twitched, but I quickly tucked it away. "Something like that," I mumbled, starting the van and becoming familiar with the hand pedals again.

"You look like a child molester driving this thing." He laughed, looking around the van. "When we get to a stoplight, I'm going to start crying and pounding on the window for help."

"You do that. I'm sure dear old Mom would be happy to come pick you up off the side of the road."

"Oh, please. No, she wouldn't. One of her reality shows might be on. I'd have a better chance hitchhiking while wearing an 'I'm a serial killer' T-shirt than getting her off her ass to do anything."

"I see she hasn't changed, either."

"Hey! Slow down for a second." Quarry jumped to his feet, scrambling into the backseat.

"What the hell are you doing?" I bit out as he slid the back door open.

Not two seconds later, a girl dove into the van.

"Fuck," I cursed, slamming on my breaks.

"Don't stop!" Quarry shouted.

"Go!" he and our new guest yelled in unison.

Quarry slammed the door. "Go! Before they see us!"

"Who?" I questioned, confused about what the hell had just happened and who this chick was. I still appeased them both by peeling off, complete with squealing the tires on the minivan. It was a sad new level of manliness.

"You drive a party bus!" the girl exclaimed, standing up off the floorboard and dusting imaginary dirt off her pants.

She was young, but I could tell she was a good bit older than Quarry—at least eighteen, maybe even nineteen. Judging by the way she crouched over to keep her head from hitting the roof, she was pretty tall. Her long, strawberry-blond hair cascaded down over her shoulders, stopping just before the curve of her large breasts. The same large breasts I allowed myself several seconds to check out before snapping out of it.

"Who the fuck are you?" I growled as I pulled into the gas station on the corner.

"Flint, this is Ash. Ash, this stud of a man is . . . Okay, okay. Enough about me." Quarry laughed. "Ash, this here is the king of the rolling throne, better known as my brother, Flint."

"Hey, nice to meet you. Can we stop and get something to eat?" She flashed me a bright smile.

"Sure!" I sarcastically returned her enthusiasm before dropping it completely. "Get out."

"Nah, I'm good," she replied, not even remotely fazed. "There's a really good burger place up the street." After flopping down on the bench seat, she crossed her long legs at the ankle and lifted her ne-on-green Converses to rest on the arm of my folded wheelchair.

I watched in disbelief as she intertwined her fingers and rested them behind her head. She might have been completely relaxed, but as her breasts strained against her tight T-shirt, I became the opposite.

"Shit," I whispered to myself. God, I needed to get laid.

"Come on, man. Don't be an ass. She's cool. I swear," Quarry interjected.

"Thanks, Q! I think you're pretty cool too." She smiled, and it was genuine—a fact that infuriated me. As far as I was concerned, those didn't exist anymore—at least, not in my life.

"I don't give a shit about 'cool.' Why the hell are you jumping in my car?"

"Your car?" she asked, looking back at me, crinkling her nose.

"Yes, my car. I could have run over you back there."

"Oh! You mean the party bus! Sorry. You confused me with the whole 'car' thing." She dug into her pocket and pulled out a pack of gum.

I was hard up. Since I'd walked away from Miranda the gold dig-ger, I'd been in quite the dry spell. It wasn't exactly like women were throwing themselves at me though. Nothing says sexy like rolling into a room. Sure, it had been a while, but even if I had just finished fucking my way through the female population of the city, I still would have gotten rock hard from watching her fold that rectangular stick of gum into her mouth. Something about the way she slowly pressed it against her tongue left my mind reeling with a million different ideas of what else I could put in that mouth.

"You want some?" she asked, extending the pack toward me.

As a matter of fact, yes. I do.

Clearing my throat, I turned back to face Quarry, who was staring at her with his mouth hanging open.

"No. I need you to get out," I lied. I needed her to get naked.

"Are you always this much fun?" she asked condescendingly, but again, she didn't bother to move toward the door—or remove her clothes.

"Oh, you have no idea!" Quarry exclaimed.

"Well, I bet a burger would fix you right up. They have the best milkshakes too. Oh. My. God. They make them with real homemade ice cream. You have to suck so hard just to get it through the straw." She looked up at me and blatantly licked her lips before raking her teeth across the bottom one.

Fuck. Me.

As she giggled, it was apparent that she was just fucking *with* me.

"Don't be a dick, Flint. I'm so fucking hungry. Mom has been starving me for the last week. She cooked every night," Quarry pleaded, causing Ash to laugh.

"He isn't lying. I've lost, like, twenty pounds since she married my dad."

"Excuse me?" I swung my head to Quarry.

"Yeah, I was shocked too. She does actually know how to operate an oven. It's the ingredients that she struggles with the most. I know you hate Till's ramen, but it's like a gourmet meal compared to the shit Debbie puts on the table."

"No. Asshole." I looked back at Ash, who was casually lounging in the backseat. "You're a Mabie?"

"Unfortunately, yes," she huffed. "I can see how you wouldn't recognize the family resemblance. Thankfully, I didn't get the receding hairline or his affinity for bacon grease as a styling tool. Don't worry. I also dodged the douchebag gene. So . . . burgers?"

Quarry busted out laughing.

"Fuck that. Get out of my car. *Now.*"

Ash completely ignored my demand. "Oh! Did I mention that they have those delicious waffle fries too? Come on. You drive and I'll whip you up a batch of my famous fancy sauce for dip when we get there."

"Get. Out," I growled again. "I'm not taking a fucking *Mabie* anywhere." I could see the words land on her face, but she quickly covered whatever effect they might have had.

Instead, her smile grew even wider.

"She's cool!" Quarry looked at me as if I'd lost my mind for being so rude.

And maybe I had, but I was in no mood to deal with a Mabie, no matter how hot she was.

"I'm sorry, Flint *Page.*" She put extra emphasis on my last name as she slowly sat up, crossing her arms over her chest with obvious attitude, but her sugary-sweet smile never once faltered.

I wasn't quite sure if I was about to get my ass handed to me or if she was going to burst into song.

"I was unaware that you come from such noble blood that you can judge others based on the family they were born into."

Yep. Definitely getting my ass handed to me.

"Since, obviously, you have judged me based on who my father is, I'm going to assume that it's only fair I do the same based on your parents? Is it fair to guess that you, too, are a selfish whore who would do damn near anything for a man as long as he tosses enough money at you to keep you high and your nails painted? Or perhaps you take after your father and have such a deep gambling problem that you would be willing to sacrifice your children to keep your own ass out of trouble. Or perhaps . . ." She paused to take a deep breath, making it apparent that there was no end to her rant anywhere in sight.

"I got it!" I shouted, not wanting to hear any more.

I knew all about my shitty-ass parents. I had grown up in that hell-hole. Never knowing if the power would be on or not, and peeling eviction notices off the front door every other week. It wasn't anything new. But knowing was one thing; hearing her throw it in my face was a totally different story.

It wasn't until that moment that I realized what a true hypocrite I really was. I hated her father almost as much as I hated my own. And because of that, I was casting the same judgment I'd been fighting my whole life to escape on her. I wasn't my father any more than she was hers. Or, at least, I hoped she wasn't.

"Really? Because I was just getting started," she snapped, holding my eyes until I sheepishly looked away.

No apology was issued, but I did put the van in gear and head to the burger place. It wasn't because I felt guilty as fuck though. I just wanted a milkshake. Well, that's what I told myself as I silently drove away.

CHAPTER

Eight

Flint

"YOU NEED HELP?" ASH ASKED as I settled into my wheelchair.

"Nope," I answered. I needed a lot more than help.

"You know this not-walking thing has its perks," Quarry said, stretching and cracking his back as if the drive over had taken hours instead of minutes. "Front-row parking."

"You are truly a dumbass," I snarked, rolling up the short ramp to join him and Ash on the sidewalk.

Using my remote, I closed both of the sliding back doors.

"See!" she squealed, clapping her hands. "Party. Bus. You don't even have to close the door behind yourself."

"Riiiight. I can see how you and Q have become such good friends now."

She burst out laughing, throwing her head back and howling loudly. I wanted to snap at her to keep it down, but it was an incredible sight to see her losing herself in a stupid, sarcastic comment.

She laughed with her whole body; it was both amusing and bewildering. It was so fucking honest that it made me uncomfortable, yet I couldn't tear my eyes away. She was a Mabie. I couldn't even imagine what she had lived through with that kind of asshole for a father. Her life wasn't great. I was positive of that. But in that second, I was so fucking jealous of her. Who in the world got to be that happy?

"Shit!" she yelled, tripping over her own feet and falling into my lap. She tried to jump up but stumbled back down.

"Uh," I mumbled, helping her upright, but she slipped through my grip as she floundered around like a fish out of water. Finally, I grabbed her arms and placed her back on her feet. I held her for a second longer than necessary to be sure she didn't fall again—or, at least, that's what I told myself.

"I'm sorry," she breathed, and while it was a sexy sound, I just wanted to hear her laugh again.

"So, I see walking isn't your thing, either?" I joked.

She erupted all over again. I looked away but only to hide the small smile that was growing on my lips.

"I didn't hurt you, did I?" she asked.

I continued to stare at the ground as I pushed past her. "Nope."

"Oh. My. God," Quarry gasped from behind me.

I glanced back to see what was wrong, but he was staring in awe at Ash. She had a huge smile, and her eyes were leveling Quarry in a very proud told-you-so glare.

"I bow to you." He praised her with his hands. "In-fucking-cred-ible."

"You two coming?" I barked for no particular reason other than it was what I did.

"Yep," Ash said, skipping my way.

We all walked to the counter and placed our order.

"I'll have the cheeseburger all the way with fries," I told the cashier.

"Make that two," Quarry added.

"Same for me. Oh, but add a small onion ring and a vanilla shake," Ash said, stepping up to the counter and pulling a wallet out of her pocket.

"No. I've got this." I wheeled myself forward and dug into the pocket of my hoodie for my wallet.

"No. It's fine. I've got it." She slid a twenty out and started to hand it to the cashier, but I tugged her arm down to her side.

"Look, I was an ass earlier. Just let me buy you a burger," I said, patting my pockets down. "Shit," I cursed when my search came up empty.

Where the hell did I leave my wallet?

"You don't owe me anything. It's no big deal."

"Well, it's a big deal to me. I hate judgmental assholes."

"And buying me a burger will somehow mean you're not one?"

"No." I twisted my upper body to the side to see if, for some insane reason, I had shoved it in my back pocket when I'd rushed from the house. "But it will make me feel better. Please?" I asked.

Her bright eyes and wide smile melted away. She swallowed hard and glanced down at the floor—only to look back up with a shy smile.

"Okay," she answered quietly. Holding my eyes, she lifted the twenty back up and passed it to the cashier.

Just as I began to object again, she extended her arm, offering me . . . *my wallet?*

"Uh . . ." I stumbled out, confused as I took it from her hand.

Quarry burst out laughing as the cashier gave her a few coins in change.

"Hey, Flint? What time is it?" Quarry asked.

Ash's smile actually slipped completely. For the briefest of seconds, she appeared almost ashamed.

I dragged my eyes away from her in order to answer his question, but as I looked at my wrist, I had no answer at all.

"Here," she said as she pulled my watch from her pocket.

What. The. Fuck?

Quarry howled with laughter, and Ash chewed on her bottom lip.

"Explain," I demanded, wrapping my watch back around my wrist and shoving my wallet in the front pocket of my hoodie.

Quarry filled in the blank. "She's a pickpocket, dude. You should have seen her when she fell on your lap. It was so fucking fast. She straight-up stole that shit from you, and you had no fucking clue."

"I didn't steal it! I was gonna give it back," she amended uncomfortably. "It was just a joke."

A joke.

A. Fucking. *Joke.*

And just like that, I remembered why I didn't laugh anymore.

"Was it funny? Stealing from the cripple? You get a good laugh out of that?" I snapped, spinning and rolling myself away. "You know, maybe my judgment of you wasn't all that off to begin with. Like father, like daughter, I guess." It was a low blow, but I felt completely betrayed by a woman I didn't even know.

"Flint, wait. I wasn't picking on the cripple!"

I fully realized that I had just used the term, but it enraged me that she'd had the audacity to repeat it back to me. Who the hell was this chick? I pushed a hand into my pocket, searching for my keys. Fuck the food. I'd leave her ass there. Hell, Quarry too if he didn't get his ass to the car.

"Get in the car, Q!" I yelled, only to close my eyes and drop my chin to my chest when my hand never made contact on the keys. "Son of a bitch," I said as I spun back around.

Quarry was laughing next to her, but Ash's cheeks were bright red.

"Keys." I snapped my fingers and opened my hand, palm up.

"Stop being a dick," Quarry said, casually tossing an arm around Ash's shoulders.

She didn't budge as she held my glare.

"Keys," I repeated, but she remained still.

"It was a joke." Her chin began to quiver.

For fuck's sake, I wasn't in any kind of mood to deal with bullshit from some girl I didn't even know and was quickly discovering I didn't care to know, either.

Quarry's eyes grew wide as she turned to him and buried her cries in his chest.

What the fuck, asshole! Q signed before rubbing his hands over her back.

Her shoulders shook as she let out a loud sob that shocked us both.

"Come on. Let's sit down." Q tried to guide her over to an empty table.

Ash refused to look up and tripped over one of the chairs.

"Shit," Q said, catching her around the waist.

I was just about to roll my eyes when she glanced my way. He was still trying to get her back on her feet and over to a table when her tear-free, bright-blue eyes pointedly glanced in my direction. My head snapped back in surprise, but a smile grew on her face.

Ash was about to put on a show, and with that one look, she had invited me to have a front-row seat.

As she floundered all over Quarry, her hands slid between his pockets and her own. Every noise she made and each time she flailed covered up a jarring movement. She was keeping his mind too busy for it to process all the places she was touching him. Hell, I was only watching her and I could barely keep up.

There was no denying that it was entertaining, but I wasn't willing to show her that. However, as she *accidentally* lifted her knee, catching Q in the balls, a laugh erupted from my throat. He cupped his crotch while she apologized profusely and pushed him toward the same chair he'd been dragging her to only seconds before. Just before he sat, Ash swung her arm out, unwinding Q's belt from around his body before tossing it at me.

"Oh God. I'm so sorry!" she said as Quarry held a finger up to ask for a second to recover. She didn't wait at all though. Instead, she walked over in my direction; her prideful smile grew with every step.

She pulled my keys out of her pocket and dropped them into my lap. They were quickly followed by Quarry's phone, wallet, and house keys. Then she snagged his belt off the floor and tossed it over her shoulder.

"It had absolutely nothing to do with you being in a wheelchair. It *was* a joke and it *wasn't* supposed to piss you off."

"Hey!" Quarry yelled. "That was messed up. You did not have to knee me in the balls to prove a point to him."

"Oh, that wasn't to prove a point. That was for bullshitting me. You knew good and damn well that he wouldn't find it funny," she said without ever tearing her gaze from mine. "Look, I'm sorry. I don't have a lot of friends. And I've mentally noted that pickpocketing might not be the best way to make new ones." She shrugged. "Consider it a lesson learned."

"Three burgers all the way, onion rings, and a shake?" the guy at the counter called out.

Ash arched an eyebrow. "You want it to go, or are we good?"

I didn't have to drop my attitude. Sure, she'd apologized, but while I might have had a short fuse, I also had a hell of a long burn. However, as she stood in front of me with her arms crossed over her chest and her blue eyes pleading for forgiveness, it magically fell away.

I swallowed hard. "No. We're good."

"You sure?" She leaned in, eyeing me warily, but her smile began to grow.

I swear to God it pulled at my lips as well. I fought it. But the harder I tried to keep it restrained, the bigger Ash's grew. She was stealing my smile. The chick was good! Finally, with an eye roll, I let out a quiet chuckle, which seemed to appease her.

"Good. Now, help your brother get redressed and I'll make the fancy sauce." She waggled her eyebrows.

Ash

"No! I dreamed about it. I swear to you, three months later, they won."

"You are so full of it."

"I'm not kidding. I totally predicted it."

"I'm calling bullshit," Quarry said, swiping a fry through my mayo-and-ketchup concoction.

"Well, I'm calling bullshit on your bullshit." I reached forward, snagging one of his fries since I had completely devoured all of mine.

He tried to swat my hand away, but he was way too slow. Unfortunately, he had been paying attention to the lessons I'd been giving him every night since he'd moved in. While I was preoccupied with his fries, he stole my shake.

"Germs!" I yelled as he pulled a long sip. I wasn't serious though. I didn't have any germs that I knew of, and even though Quarry probably had a slew, I didn't particularly care. I was having entirely too much fun to worry about catching a cold. "Stop! You're gonna drink it all!"

"Fine. I'll get my own." He stood up and headed toward the counter, leaving me alone with the definition of fun personified.

"So, Flint. I heard you used to be a boxer too. I bet that was fun, you and your brothers all hanging out in the gym together."

"Yep," he answered stoically, leaning back and folding his hands over his lap.

"Do you miss it?" I ripped the breading off the onion ring and popped it into my mouth.

He narrowed his eyes and tilted his head. "Sometimes."

"Quarry told me you used to be really good at it. You ever thought of doing, like, the Special Olympics or something? They have that, right?" I peeled another onion.

"The Special Olympics are for children with intellectual disabilities. I'm starting to think you might be a better suited for it than I am."

Whoa!

Flint Page was quite possibly the weirdest guy I had ever met. I mean, I wasn't exactly an expert on men or anything, but even I could tell he wasn't *normal,* so to speak. On the surface, he was fine-looking. His dark-brown hair was perfectly styled, but he had this weird patchy thing on his face that I assumed was supposed to be a beard. He had gorgeous, blue eyes, but they were always so angry. If he'd smiled a little more, he could have been attractive. Maybe. But what really boggled my mind was the fact that it seemed like he truly wanted to be a miserable asshole. And let me just tell you, he was good at it. Luckily, my father was a dick. I knew exactly how to handle it.

I pasted on a sugary smile and met his angry smolder. "Nah, I'm not all that athletic. I'm more of a dancer." I leaned back and propped my legs up on the table, crossing them at the ankles. "But hey, thanks for implying that I'm stupid. For a man in a wheelchair, you sure toss around stereotypes all willy-nilly."

He quickly looked away.

That was the other weird thing about Flint. He worked so hard to be a dick, but the second I called him on it, I could see the guilt physically wash over his face.

He let out a loud huff. "Sorry."

"No biggy," I replied, removing my legs from the table.

Using my teeth, I ripped a packet of ketchup open and squirted it into my fancy sauce. Out of the corner of my eye, I could see him watching me. I was relatively sure he was waiting for me to look back up, but I was still nursing the sting from our last interaction. I was in no rush to start round two.

"Flint!" Quarry yelled across the restaurant. "You want one too? They have peanut butter banana."

"Ew," I mumbled to myself.

"Yeah. I'll take one," Flint answered, and when I looked up, his eyes were still glued to me, and his expression appeared to be amused. "Not a fan of the banana?"

"Oh, I love bananas. Peanut butter makes me puke."

"Fair enough," he answered then went back to staring at me.

What the hell is with this guy and his staring?

I wiped my chin just to make sure I didn't have food on my face while wishing Quarry would put a move on it and get his ass back to the table. He was fun to talk to. Flint? Not so much.

"Soooo . . ." I started awkwardly, unsure what else to say, but Flint suddenly had more than enough of his own words to need mine.

"I don't like to think about the past. I would assume most people in my position wouldn't want to sit around and reminisce about everything they've lost. Yeah, I miss boxing though. A lot."

"Oh, sorry. I didn't think of boxing as something you lost. It's not like I said, 'Hey, don't you miss that feeling when you put on new socks?' Now *that* would have been rude." I shrugged. "Boxing's still there. Sucks you can't compete anymore, but punching bags don't discriminate, do they?"

Flint opened his mouth to respond but quickly shut it.

"Anyway. Quarry told me you didn't go to the gym anymore, and I was just curious why you'd quit something you loved."

"Jesus, how much has Q been running his mouth?"

"We're both talkers." I smiled. "Look, I wasn't trying to upset you or anything. Sorry if it came off that way. I've just never known anyone who was paralyzed before. It's kinda cool."

He barked out a laugh. "Cool is not exactly the word I would use to describe paralysis."

"Well, then maybe you're using the wrong words."

Flint didn't respond, but he did go back to staring, so I went back to uncomfortably pretending to be enthralled with my fancy sauce. After tearing the packet of mayo open, I drizzled a design over the ketchup and then swirled it together.

"Here." Quarry set two milkshakes down on the table.

Thank God!

"Dude, that bed at Debbie's is kicking my ass." He cracked his neck to the left, and even though I was only watching Flint out of the corner of my eye, I recognized the exact moment he saw it.

So fast that even I was impressed, Flint snaked a hand out and grabbed the front of Quarry's shirt, catching him completely off guard. Q toppled forward.

"What the fuck is that?" Flint boomed, pulling the neck of Quarry's shirt down to reveal his back.

"Let me go." Quarry fought to get on his feet.

It was magic, really. Flint might have been older, but Quarry definitely had him in size. But even as Q struggled against his grasp, Flint effortlessly pinned him as he inspected his neck and back.

"Tell me that's fake. I swear to God, Q. Tell me it's fake."

"It's fake!" he yelled.

Flint shook his head but finally released him.

Quarry straightened his shirt and glanced around the empty restaurant. "Yes. If, by fake, you mean a permanent tattoo, then yes. It's fake."

I giggled as Quarry jumped back a step when Flint's eyes almost bulged from his head.

"You're fourteen!" he hissed through clenched teeth.

"And?"

"And nothing . . . You're fourteen. You can't get a tattoo."

"Well, I didn't know that, Daddy. Guess I really shouldn't have gotten two, then." He took another step away, flashing Flint a mischievous grin.

I desperately tried to contain my laughter. The last thing I needed was Flint turning that scary gaze on me. I didn't have the force field Quarry so obviously possessed.

Flint suddenly rolled forward an inch, and it caused Quarry to flinch. That was it. I lost the battle with my lungs. I slapped a hand over my mouth as a loud laugh escaped.

Thankfully, Flint didn't notice—or he at least opted to keep the lasers he was shooting from his eyes from giving me a new haircut.

"Who the hell would tattoo a fourteen-year-old kid? Christ, Q. You probably have hepatitis now."

"Dustin Prince is eighteen, thank you very much."

Oh fuck.

Flint curled his lip. "Who the hell is Dustin Prince?"

As Quarry pulled his wallet out, I nervously looked around the room for some imaginary backup or, at the very least, an emergency exit door.

I jumped to my feet. "I'm gonna use the restroom."

And then enter the witness protection program.

Before I had the chance to walk away, Quarry dropped the bomb. "Ash got me a fake ID."

Flint swung his angry gaze my way. "Excuse me?"

"Uhhh . . ." I stalled, lifting my hand to fix my hair and flipping Quarry off in the process. "In my defense, I just thought he was going to buy lottery tickets," I lied, punctuating it with an innocent grin Flint seemed immune to.

"Who in God's name would actually believe he's eighteen?"

"Oh, they don't really care. They just needed the ID to make it look legit. And no hep C, either. The shop is really clean. They owed me a favor, so I made sure they took extra-special care of him," I tried to explain, but if Flint's reaction was any indication I had just dug myself even deeper.

"You. Took. Him?" he asked very slowly.

"Maybe," I squeaked and then followed Quarry's example of backing away.

"You took a kid to get a tattoo?" He moved toward me.

"Possibly." I once again stepped away. I didn't think I was in any real danger, but judging by the vein bulging on his forehead, his head was very close to exploding—and I didn't want to be in range when it did. Blood wasn't my thing.

"Calm the hell down," Quarry said, stepping between us. "This kid at school was going to do it for me, but Ash talked me into going to her place instead. You should see the sweet-ass design the guy drew for my back. This is just the start."

"I hope it was worth it. You're gonna look like Mabie when Till finds out."

"Nah. He already knows. Slate ratted me out after he saw me in the locker room. I gotta wait until I'm eighteen to finish the rest. It's Eliza I have to hide it from." Quarry laughed.

As if he had been slapped, Flint's head snapped to the side.

He stared into space for a few seconds before Quarry sighed and quietly said, "Come on. Don't be like that." It didn't take a rocket scientist to know he wasn't talking about the tattoo anymore.

"Whatever." Flint spun away, leaving an arctic breeze in his wake.

I looked over at Quarry for answers on what the hell had just happened, but he only offered me an exaggerated eye roll.

"Let's go," Flint bit out as he started loading our trash on the tray. "Ash, you done with your shake?" he asked, sans all attitude.

"Yeah," I replied, unbelievably confused. However, if he wanted to act like he hadn't just plotted mine and Quarry's deaths a few minutes earlier, I guessed I could do the same.

I could do normal. I was amazing at normal. It was my forte, really.

"Hey, would it be okay if I started calling you Wheels?"

He turned to look at me and quirked an eyebrow.

"What?" I asked as he closed his eyes and shook his head. "What?" I repeated, but he never answered.

Instead, he set the tray on his lap and headed toward the trash can.

CHAPTER
Nine

Flint

ASH POINTED OUT THE PASSENGER side window. "Take a left up here."

"Ummm . . . That's a right," I corrected, turning down a side street in what appeared to be the slums of downtown Indianapolis.

After dropping Quarry off at On The Ropes and luckily dodging Till and Slate, Ash had asked if I could drop her off at her friend's instead of taking her back home. With hopes of also avoiding my mom and Ray, I agreed. However, as I drove deeper into the city, I thought there was a strong possibility Ash was leading me into a gang setup.

"Where the hell are we going?"

"Just a little farther. Take your next right." She pointed across me.

"And that's a left," I mumbled, turning down an alley.

"Right here! Stop!" she exclaimed.

"Right where?" I looked around. There wasn't anything even remotely inhabitable. It was a vacant alley that served no purpose except to connect two busy streets.

With the exception of two bums leaning against the building, there wasn't a soul in sight.

"Right there." She slung her seat belt off and jumped from the car. "Hey!"

"How's it going, babe?" a gray-haired man replied.

"Get in the car, Ash," I called as the obviously homeless woman in dirty and tattered clothing stood up and walked toward her.

"You little tramp!" the woman said.

"Oh, shut up!" Ash yelled back.

I had no idea what the fuck was going on, but I didn't like it.

"Ash, get back in the goddamn car."

"What?" She turned to look at me, but the woman continued getting closer, and this time, her murderous gaze was aimed at me.

"Who the hell do you think you are talking to like that?" the woman snapped, and the man behind her pushed to his feet.

"Fuck," I hissed. "Look, we don't want any trouble," I told the woman, but my eyes were focused on the man. He might have been older, but as he strode toward the car, I realized he was also huge. "Ash, get the fuck in the car."

"Why? What's wrong?" she answered, leaning back into the van with her upper body.

She was insane, I knew that much, but she was also apparently fearless. I, however, had no way to protect her, and judging by the faces closing in on us, I was going to need to do just that.

Reaching out, I grabbed her wrist and yanked her back into the van.

"What the hell?" she yelled.

The man sprinted forward, capturing her around the waist and pulling her out of my grasp. My eyes went wide, and panic settled in my chest. I scrambled across the passenger seat after her, but my legs got stuck behind me and I fell out of the door, crashing to the pavement face first.

"Flint!" Ash yelled, but the man never released her.

I pushed myself upright so I could at least use my arms as defense, but with the exception of Ash's flailing to get free, no one moved.

"Max, put me down. He's my friend."

"Not touching you like that, he's not."

"Jesus Christ. Put me down. He's paralyzed. I need to make sure he's okay."

I wasn't sure what was worse: the fact that I was helplessly sitting on the ground while watching a stranger manhandle her or the fact that I was so weak and pathetic that she was worried about me while it happened.

"Damn it, put me down!" she shrieked.

The man finally relented.

After rushing forward, she dropped to her knees in front of me. "Oh my God. Are you okay?"

"We need to get out of here," I declared, watching the man and woman step even closer behind her.

"Flint, these are my friends, Max and Donna." She turned around to address them. "Back up. He's not going to hurt me."

Neither seemed convinced, but they did take a single step away.

"I don't care who they are. We're leaving." I started scooting toward the passenger's door, but the idea of actually pulling myself up, and into the van from the ground was daunting.

"Just hang on," Ash called, seeming to read my mind—or, more likely, my fear-filled expression.

After opening the sliding back door, she dragged my wheelchair out and pushed it in front of me. A rush of relief filtered through me. I'd never been so happy to see that damn thing in my life.

"You need help?" she asked.

"No, I don't need any fucking help," I snapped for absolutely no reason other than that my pride had suffered a serious hit.

"Oh hell no," Donna voiced behind us, causing Ash to roll her eyes.

"Can you two give us a minute? I promise I'm fine. You can watch me from over there." She pointed to where they had been previously situated against the wall.

"Ash," the man started.

"Please, Max," she whined.

His face softened. "All right." He tugged on the woman's arm and began leading her back to the wall.

Ash turned her attention to me. "Just let me help you."

"I've got it," I said roughly as I hoisted myself up to the floorboard of the van and then transferred myself back into my chair. It wasn't easy, but I had an audience, so I did my best not to look like a bumbling idiot.

"Get in the car," I ordered, rolling myself around to the driver's side.

"What? I'm not leaving."

"Yes, you are," I called out, dropping my chin to my chest as soon as I was blocked by the van. My hands shook as I pinched the bridge of my nose. I tried to get my pulse under control as the adrenaline left my body. God, I was such a fucking mess, and of course, Ash picked that exact moment to round the bumper.

"Hey, are you okay?" she asked, walking over and stopping in front of me.

"Can you stop fucking asking me that?"

She arched an eyebrow and cocked her head to the side with sudden attitude. "Can you start answering the question?"

I let out a resigned sigh. I desperately needed the entire fucking day to be over. I couldn't take much more, and I needed to reset my mind *and* body in the solitude of my apartment.

"Look, please just let me take you home. I can't leave you here. I'm sure you think those two are your friends, but there is no possible way I can leave you in a dark alley with two homeless people. It's dangerous."

She smiled widely. "I'll be fine."

"Maybe. But I can't in good conscience leave you here."

She opened her mouth to reply, but I put my hand up to silence her.

"Please don't argue with me, Ash. This has been one hell of a day, and I can't take it anymore. I'll be really honest here: If I don't get home soon, I'm going to lose my fucking mind."

Her smile widened.

Fantastic.

"Can we go tell Max and Donna goodbye?"

I blew out a breath. *Thank God!* At least she was rational.

"Yeah, go ahead."

"No. Come with me. I'm pretty sure they don't trust you any more than you do them. They're my best friends. I don't want them to worry." Her smile stretched even wider.

What the actual fuck is she smiling about?

"How the hell did you end up being friends with two middle-aged bums?" I asked incredulously. "You need to be more careful before you end up dead in a ditch somewhere."

"You're doing it again."

"Doing what?"

"Judging people and casting stereotypes." She reached her foot out and pointedly tapped one of my wheels.

"I'm not judging them," I defended, but even I knew that it was in vain.

"Yeah, you are. They're good people, Wheels."

My mouth dropped open at her actual use of the nickname.

"Difficult circumstances. But still good people."

"Wow," I responded, unimpressed. Or maybe I was crazy impressed at her flagrant insensitivity. Or *maybe* I was just annoyed at myself for not being able to join her as she burst out laughing at my reaction.

Instead, I lectured. "That may be true, but how well do you really know them? Ash, you can't go through life trusting everyone."

"Well, maybe you can't. But I can. I know there are bad people in the world. To some, I'm probably one of them." She reached into her pocket and pulled my wallet out, tossing it onto my lap. "We all deserve friends though." She shrugged.

"Stop stealing my fucking wallet."

But instead of returning my attitude, her face gentled and her eyes lit. "Thanks for trying to rescue me back there."

"Yeah," I scoffed. "Lot of help I would have been."

"You never know. Maybe just the trying helped the most." She looked down at her foot, which was drawing circles in the dirt.

I was annoyed.

Embarrassed.

Frustrated.

Exhausted.

But that was erased when she lifted her head up with a shy smile I didn't recognize at all. I'd known Ash Mabie for exactly two hours, but I was stunned into silence by the vulnerability on her creamy-white face. It shouldn't have been there. Mainly because it ruined every other smile she would ever be able to produce. *That* smile belonged there permanently.

However, just as quickly as it had appeared, it disappeared.

But I'd seen it.

God, did I see it.

Her typical wide grin replaced it, and even though she was still gorgeous, nothing could top that single second where she'd showed me something truly indescribable.

She'd showed me the real Ash Mabie.

And she is beautiful.

"Sooooo . . . ?" she questioned, nodding back toward Max and Donna.

"Okay," I huffed. "Let's go meet your friends."

One week later . . .

Unknown: What's your address?

Me: Who is this?

Unknown: It's an emergency.

Me: So I'll repeat. Who. Is. This?

Unknown: It's Ash. Quarry and I were out at the movies and suddenly he can't hear anything.

Sitting straight up in bed, I tossed my book to the nightstand and shifted into my chair, which was parked beside the bed. The genetic condition Till and Quarry shared was supposed to be degenerative, but this was exactly what had happened with Till. One day, he could hear, and an hour later, it was gone.

My heart began to race at the instant replay that was unfolding in front of me.

Me: Take him to the hospital. Now!

Ash: He says no hospital. He just wants to come to your house.

Me: I don't care what he says. Take him to a hospital.

Ash: Just let me bring him to you. He's trying to sign stuff but I don't know sign language.

Ash: Please Flint. I'm scared.

Me: All right, all right. Bring him here. 121 Broad Dr. Apt 113. Show it to Q. He'll know how to get here. I'll see you in a few.

Ash: K

I dropped my phone on the bed and then pulled a pair of shorts on over my boxers.

For several minutes, I stared blankly at my phone. I needed to call Till, but just the thought knotted my stomach. I hadn't spoken to him in months, and Quarry going deaf was the news I had to deliver? *Fuck.*

I couldn't waste any more time though. Clicking his name, I prayed for a miracle that he wouldn't pick up and I could leave a message.

Such was my luck, he answered on the first ring.

"Flint?"

"Quarry can't hear anything," I rushed out, not bothering with pleasantries.

"What?" he breathed in shock.

"Yeah, Ash just called. I don't know exactly what's going on yet, but she's bringing him over here. I'll take him to the hospital."

"Till? What's going on?" Eliza asked in the background.

"Hey, I have to go. I'll let you know when we leave."

"Flint, wait!" he yelled as I severed the connection.

But I couldn't. I just . . . couldn't.

After snagging a T-shirt from the drawer, I made my way to unlock the front door.

While I was still battling with a useless pair of Nikes, my front door swung open and Quarry sauntered inside.

"Holy shit! You moved into Eliza's old apartment?" He laughed. "You have serious problems, dude." He turned to look over his shoulder. "Ash, get in here!"

"Not until you tell him not to be mad at me," she squeaked from outside.

"Oh, right. Sorry. I borrowed Ash's phone and wrote the texts. It wasn't her. We were bored and I was curious about where you were hiding out." He winked.

My mouth dropped open. "Are you kidding me? You got bored so you decided to tell me that you were deaf?" I snapped, rolling myself forward.

"No. I asked for your address first. You didn't bite. So *then* I told you I was deaf."

"You son of a bitch. I was fucking worried!" I swung a fist as hard as I could, but Quarry easily dodged it.

"Well, then think of it as a miracle. I can still hear!" He threw his hands up in the air in celebration.

"You selfish little shit. Till's probably losing his mind right now, and you think this is funny?"

His laugh went silent and his eyes grew wide. "You told Till?" he gasped. "Why the hell would you do that?" He pushed a hand through his thick, black hair.

"I thought you were deaf!" I screamed so loudly that it echoed off all the walls.

"Shit," he groaned to himself.

"Yeah. Shit," I repeated, passing my phone in his direction. "Call him and explain. But don't you dare tell him where I live."

He dropped his eyes to the floor but took the phone from my hand. "I'm going outside to purgatory for this one," he mumbled as he walked out the door, dialing the phone.

Stupid kid.

"Soooo . . . is it safe to come in?" Ash said, peeking around the doorjamb.

"For you? Yes. For him? I'm not sure," I replied, grabbing the back of my neck.

"I swear I didn't know. He didn't tell me until we got here. For what it's worth, he wanted to keep up the act and mess with you, but I refused to play along."

"Thanks for that."

"No prob." She smiled.

And even with as pissed as I was, one pulled at the corner of my lips too.

CHAPTER
Ten

Ash

"SOOOO THIS IS A NICE place," I said, looking around Flint's apartment.

The building might have been shit on the outside, but it was obvious Flint had worked hard to transform it into something nice on the inside. It was simple, but everything was spotless. There were no decorations unless the bookshelves that lined nearly every inch of the walls counted. There was a cheap sofa and a chair squished together with a coffee table in the center of the room. As I watched Flint push himself past them, I gathered that their tight positioning was to allow more room for his wheelchair to pass.

"You want something to drink?"

"Whatcha got?" I asked, following him into a tiny galley kitchen just barely wide enough to fit the width of his wheelchair.

Pulling the fridge open, he said, "Milk, water, and . . . pineapple-banana juice."

"Shut up," I whispered.

"What?" He looked over his shoulder.

"I've never had pineapple-banana juice!" I squealed.

"Um . . . okay, then. Pineapple-banana it is." He backed up, unable to actually turn around. Then he removed a glass from the bottom cabinet and set it on the counter.

"This might be the greatest day of my life, Wheels," I announced, watching him fill the glass with sure-to-be-delicious fruity liquid. "First, Quarry took me to a 3D movie. Holy crap, it was ah-mazing. And now, you have pineapple-banana juice."

"I'm thrilled my juice selection has contributed to 'the greatest day of your life,'" he said dryly.

"And you should be. This is two newsies today."

"Newsies?" He slid the glass in my direction then motioned for me to move so he could back all the way out of the kitchen.

"Yep. I try to do something new every day. And today, I'm getting to do two! I can't wait to cross pineapple-banana juice off my list."

"You might be the weirdest person I have ever met. You have an actual list with pineapple-banana juice on it?" he asked with a slight smirk.

It was a rare glimpse at the man hiding under the patchy beard and angry, blue eyes, but amused looked good on Flint Page.

Really good.

"No, it's not technically on the list. But when I get home, I'm going to write it right below ride a roller coaster, and then guess what?" I lifted my eyebrows, tipping the glass to my lips. I held Flint's eyes as I took a gulp of the cool, fruity drink before setting it on the counter. "I'm gonna cross it off." I tossed him a smile, and much to my surprise, he returned it.

Now *that* was better than really good.

It was gorgeous.

And because I possessed absolutely no filter, I felt the need to inform him of that.

"You know, if you shaved that fuzz and smiled more often, you would be really hot."

Then it happened.

Something more elusive than the Loch Ness Monster and Bigfoot appeared in front of me.

Flint Page's lips parted and a real, honest-to-God laugh erupted from his throat. His shoulders shook and his blue eyes lit up so bright that I almost needed to look away.

I couldn't though.

I was mesmerized.

"Thanks, I think?" he said, rubbing his chin.

And for some unexplainable reason, my eyes drifted to his mouth. I regretted it the moment it happened, because even though his eyes heated, his smile fell. As sexy as that smolder was on him, nothing could top the laugh.

"Soooo . . ." I spun to face his bookshelves. "You like to read, huh?"

He cleared his throat. "Yep."

"Are you going to school?" I asked, dragging my fingertip over the dust-free shelf.

"Yeah. I'm starting my second semester. What about you?"

"Nah, not really. I'm just taking some classes online right now."

"Well, that's cool too," he said awkwardly, following me as I inspected each of his shelves.

"I guess. I'd rather be in an actual class every day. Sitting behind the computer can get pretty boring."

"Yeah, well, sitting in class can be pretty boring sometimes too."

"True." I suddenly turned to face him. "Hey, which one's your favorite?"

"Favorite what? Class?"

"No, I mean book. You have to have a favorite."

"Shit, I don't know. I've read so many that I wouldn't even know how to choose."

"Okay. You're stranded in a deserted train station during the zombie apocalypse. Quick, which book do you have with you?"

"Hopefully *The Zombie Survival Guide.*" He laughed again, and I'll be damned if my eyes didn't jump right back to his mouth.

What the hell was with my subconscious's sudden obsession with those two perfectly plump lips?

As if he'd read my mind, his tongue darted out, moistening them and magically drawing the slightest moan from me. Embarrassed, I glanced up to find that his eyes were sparkling with humor. *Perfect!*

No, really. It. Was. Perfect.

He was flirting. And it made my goal of seducing him that much easier.

Suddenly, Quarry stomped back into the room, interrupting our connection. "Well, that went over like a warm bag of shit."

Flint stared at me for a second longer before dragging his gaze over to his brother. I, however, wasn't quite ready for the moment to be over yet, so as he began talking to Quarry, I continued to watch Flint.

"Was he pissed?" Flint asked.

"First, he was relieved. *Then* he was mad, *and then* . . . he handed the phone to Eliza." Quarry stopped and blew out a loud breath. "*She* was pissed."

I should have looked away.

If I could go back in time, that might be the exact moment I'd go back to, and in that alternate universe, I would have immediately looked *away.*

At the mere mention of Eliza's name, I was forced to witness something utterly painful. I watched the gorgeous man I'd just been flirting with shut down. He didn't say anything or even flinch. But as if he had been hit by a massive wave of destruction, he disappeared right in front of my eyes.

His mask and attitude snapped firmly into place. "Well, good. You deserved it."

I wasn't a fan of this version of Flint, but I was determined to lure the other him back out.

I had to.

"Okay, Q's a jerk. Moving on. Since we're here, you wanna watch a movie?"

"No," he answered. "I want you guys to leave so I can go to bed."

Okay, so maybe luring him back was going to be a little more difficult than I had originally thought. But I was up for the challenge.

"Oh, so I had a dream that it's going to storm tonight. You wanna go outside and watch the clouds roll in? We can even make a bet on who feels the first raindrop. It probably won't be you since you wouldn't be able to feel it on your legs and half your face is covered with hair. Ya know, less surface area and all. So I'm going to put my money on Q."

Both Quarry and Flint turned to look at me as if I had suggested sitting at the base of a volcano.

"What?"

"Right. You had a dream or you watched the weather this morning?" Flint snapped.

"I had a dream, thank you very much," I sniped back, lifting my eyebrows to pointedly note his attitude.

"The rain better hold out for a while longer. We have over a hundred dollars' worth of spray paint in the car," Quarry said as he pushed the table out of the way so he could flop down on the couch.

"Spray paint?" Flint questioned, swinging his gaze between us.

Quarry propped his feet up on the table. "Tell him, Ash."

I was going to kill that kid. A long, torturous death where I squeezed lemons into his eyes and made him recite poetry. I shot him an angry glare he seemed immune to. Then I made a mental note to talk to him about getting one of those force fields it seemed I would need if I was going to pursue Flint.

And I was *absolutely* going to pursue Flint Page.

I'd made that decision about two point one seconds after he'd dived out of his van in an attempt to protect me.

Me.

A girl he barely knew, yet a girl he was willing to do anything for to ensure my safety.

He could be broody all he wanted, but I knew deep down that an amazing man existed.

I smiled tightly. "We . . . um. We were just gonna go tag a few buildings."

Flint narrowed his eyes and tilted his head to the side. I recognized that look. He was about to shift to full-fledged asshole.

"Quick! Take cover, Q. Incoming!" I yelled, diving behind the chair.

The room filled with laughter, but judging by the lack of my moan, none of it was Flint's. I peeked around the chair to find him sitting as stoically as ever.

"Oh, come on, Wheels. That was funny." I stood back up and walked toward him.

He cracked his neck, and the muscles in his jaw twitched. "Stop calling me Wheels."

"Maybe Legs, then? It doesn't really fit, but I like the paradox."

His eyebrows almost hit his hairline. "Paradox?"

"Yeah, it means contradictory to what—"

"I know what it means. I just didn't figure you did."

"Wow. Judgy McJudgerson strikes again," I deadpanned.

"I didn't mean . . ." he started only to stop and huff.

"Right. Well, anyway. Yes, I'm taking your brother out to tag a few buildings, but before you get all preachy on me, they are being torn down next week. No harm, no foul."

"No harm until you get arrested," he bit back.

"Oh please. No one cares about those buildings. Besides, Max and Donna said they'd pull lookout in exchange for some burgers. Don't you worry about a thing. I have it all planned out up here." I pointed to my head. "If you're worried, you could always come with us." I bounced on my toes and waggled my eyebrows. "You know, just to make sure we stay out of trouble. I mean, I totally understand that you're allergic to fun. But you could always pop an antihistamine or something." I tossed him a smile, which went unreturned.

When he didn't offer any kind of retort, I did what I did best: I kept talking.

"Also, I would like to formally retract my earlier statement. You can keep the beard."

His dim eyes perked the slightest bit, and a tingle traveled over my skin.

There *he* was.

"How generous of you."

"It really gives you a certain worldly, terrorist feel."

"Perfect. That is exactly what I was going for." He smirked.

Sarcasm wasn't what I wanted, but it was a step in the right direction.

"I now believe it's actually the bad attitude holding down your hotness. I think if you just stepped up your happy factor a smidge, you could really be a ten." I was trying so hard not to laugh, but a small giggle escaped before I could catch it.

His lips finally lifted at the corners, sending excitement thrumming through my body. I was winning the war he didn't even know we were fighting.

Victory was within my reach.

And *he* was my prize.

"Yeah? How much is a smidge, exactly?"

"Oh, I don't know. I'm not an expert or anything. Maybe like . . ." I paused, tapping my chin. "Maybe just increase it by say . . . ninety-nine percent or so?" I finished as seriously as I could.

"Really? Ninety-nine percent?" He busted out laughing.

I closed my eyes and sucked in a deep breath as if I could physically absorb the sound. I didn't need the extra laughs; I produced more than enough of my own.

But that one was *his.*

I wanted to keep it forever.

"I think you have problems," he teased when he sobered.

I absolutely did. And the newest one of them was sitting directly in front of me.

It was no coincidence that I was standing in his apartment. Sure, Quarry thought it was his idea, but I'd planted that seed days earlier. It had started out with subtle questions here and there about where Flint had disappeared to, but by that morning, I had talked Q into a full-blown conspiracy theory in which Flint was lying about his injuries in order to collect disability checks from the government. Sweet, naïve Quarry had fallen right into my trap. He'd no longer been able to resist knowing the truth about where his brother was really hiding out. It had taken a few days longer than I would have liked, but I'd patiently sat back and let Quarry lead me to Flint.

"Come on, Flint. Go with us. Just think about it. We can paint all of our troubles on that building then watch 'em knock it down." I crossed my arms over my chest, pushing my breasts up.

And like a moth to a flame, his eyes dropped.

Flint raked his eyes over my breasts and slowly up to my eyes. I gathered my long hair and twisted it, pulling it over my shoulder. Holding it with the ends just above my nipple, I led Flint's eyes right back down to my chest.

"Ash, if you think he is going to graffiti a building, you have lost your fucking mind. He once turned himself in to the principal at school for accidentally making a pencil mark on the desk," Quarry said, falling into hysterics at his own joke.

But I was focused on the guy in front of me, who seemed just as interested in my boobs as I was in him.

"You have to come," I whispered, and his lips twitched. "It can be your newsie for the day. And I'll even let you have first pick of the paint colors," I added.

"Seriously, give it up. He's not coming."

Oh, he was coming.

I innocently batted my eyelashes as I pressed my bottom lip out in a pout.

"You're ridiculous," Flint said, shaking his head.

My shoulders fell as I feigned defeat, but I was nowhere near done.

His eyes flashed wide as I took a step forward and leaned down. Stopping just a breath away from his mouth, I raked my teeth over my bottom lip before I whispered, "Please come."

"Ho. Lee. Shit," Quarry gasped behind us. "You told me you were a lesbian."

"Nope. Just didn't want you getting any ideas," I answered without tearing my eyes off Flint.

The side of Flint's mouth tipped up in a mischievous grin, and his eyes twinkled with something else completely. Leaning in even closer, he said, "Fine. I'll come."

Game over!

A huge smile spread on my face, and I started to back away, but Flint caught the back of my neck, dragging me forward.

"And eventually, Ash, you'll come too."

My breath hitched.

I was wrong. I might have conned Flint into hanging out with me, but as he backed away, holding my gaze with a sexy-as-hell smirk, I realized that Flint Page had just completely hijacked my victory.

Cheater.

CHAPTER
Eleven

Flint

THE DRY SPELL WAS OVER.

Thank.

Fucking.

Christ.

I had no idea what the hell Ash Mabie wanted or, better yet, why she wanted it from someone like me, but I knew with one hundred percent certainty that I was going to give it to her.

She was hands down the strangest woman I had ever met. The jury was still out on her sanity, and her social awareness might as well have been nonexistent. She simply said whatever-the-hell thought was passing through her brain at the moment her mouth opened.

But God, she was gorgeous.

She was terrible at flirting, and she'd more than proved that back at my apartment. But then again, that might have been the best part. Even as she licked her lips and awkwardly thrust her boobs at me, she was unbelievably confident. Watching her try to get me to go out that night had been as humorous as it'd been cock hardening. She was a woman with a clear mission and didn't give one fuck what she had to do to complete it.

Really, it worked out well for me, because I had full intentions of giving her that one fuck.

Which was exactly why I'd ended up in front of a brick wall, holding a can of spray paint while I listened to her argue with a middle-aged homeless woman over a pair of shoes.

"They were buy-one-get-one-free, Donna."

"Green though? You couldn't have gotten black or brown or something? I'm fifty-seven years old. Girl, these shoes are for kids. I'm surprised they don't have cartoon characters or some shit on the side."

"Oh, hush. You're only as old as you act," Ash sassed back.

"They're neon green!"

"Yep! And they match mine." Ash flashed her a grin. "Twinsies."

"Dear Lord, help me," Donna whispered, staring up at the sky.

Ash giggled, walking over to me. "Hey, you haven't painted anything yet."

"Yeeeeeah," I drawled. "Painting isn't exactly my thing."

"Don't think of it as painting, then. This is self-expression!" She snatched the can from my hand and sprayed a bright-yellow mark on the brick.

"Ah, yes. A line. Self-expression at its finest."

She laughed. "Shut up! I was just trying to get you started."

"Look, my artistic abilities are limited to diagraming molecules in chemistry."

"Don't worry about it. I'm not great, either. I just write words then decorate them with colors. But hey, it's fun. They are tearing this baby down. Let's help her go out in style." She lovingly patted the wall.

I chuckled to myself, and a bright smile spread across her mouth.

God, I wanted to taste that mouth. My cock thickened at the thought.

"Just draw anything." She picked the green can up off the ground and wrote the word *dream* in huge letters. "See? Easy."

"Uhh . . . Ash, can you come here for a second?" Max called out.

"Yep," she replied then looked back at me. "Just draw the first thing that comes to mind." She walked away, dragging the tip of her finger across my back and shoulders.

"The first thing that comes to mind," I repeated to myself, watching her ass sway as she disappeared around the corner.

But I had nothing.

My mind was absolutely blank.

There was no pain.

No ache in my chest.

No pity.

No hate.

No bitterness.

I was numb.

And it was *incredible.*

Ash Mabie was quickly becoming my own personal brand of lidocaine.

I stared at that wall for several minutes but never painted a single word. Instead, my eyes stayed locked on that single solitary line.

I drew in a deep breath, releasing it on a laugh.

"Shit. You're smiling," she cursed when she reappeared at my side.

I turned to face her. "It happens sometimes," I teased, but her eyes flashed to the ground in the most unlike-Ash way possible. It immediately set me on alert.

"Are you okay?" I asked, looking over her shoulder.

"Yeah, I'm fine, but I have something to tell you, but um . . . I'd really like to try something first." She began to chew on her bottom lip.

"Ash . . . what's going on?" I asked as I heard Max cussing around the corner.

"I really want to kiss you," she rushed.

My lips tipped in a smile. Oh, I had plans to be doing far more than just kissing her, but right then, I really fucking loved that she had ideas of her own.

"Okaaaay. Right after you tell me what has you all worked up, I'll see what I can do to make that happen." I caught sight of Donna peeking her head around the corner and jumping away as soon as we made eye contact.

"You're gonna be pissed though," she whined and then let out a loud huff. "I don't have enough time to make you laugh again. You have no idea how much work that is."

I narrowed my eyes at her.

"So, really, it's now or never." She took a step forward.

I leaned away. "Tell me what the hell is going on," I demanded when the way she was acting began to unnerve me.

Her shoulders fell. "Quarry's drunk. He and Max were playing cards and betting shots. Well . . . it appears Q sucks."

"What!" I exclaimed, backing up and knocking the cans of spray paint over.

"He kinda just puked . . . all over himself."

"We've been here an hour!" I yelled at her as if it were somehow her fault my brother was a raving idiot.

"Like I said, he's apparently *really* bad."

"Son of a bitch," I mumbled to myself as I pushed past her.

Sure as shit, I found my fourteen-year-old, tattooed brother covered in his own puke and laughing about it while he was sitting on a cardboard box with a homeless man.

I had two options.

As I looked up at Ash, who was nervously toying with her hair next to me, I realized I was really fucking sick and tired of my default choice.

"Ash, help me get some towels out of the van," I snapped. "Do not let him out of your sight," I said to Max, who was laughing at whatever the hell Q was slurring.

Max saluted then replied, "Not a problem."

I headed to where we had parked in the alley behind the condemned buildings.

"I'm sorry," Ash whined. "In Max's defense, Quarry does not look fourteen."

"He doesn't look twenty-one either!" I shouted over my shoulder.

She groaned, but her footsteps continued to crunch against the gravel behind me.

After using the remote to open the sliding door, I went to the passenger's side, maneuvering myself in the tight space between the door and the building.

"Little help!" I called out to Ash, who had absolutely no way of getting around me.

That was pretty much exactly why I had done it though.

"I'm coming." She turned sideways and tried to squeeze past me, her breasts brushing against my shoulder.

Just as she started to climb into the van in search of the nonexistent towels, I looped an arm around her hips and dragged her down. She squealed as she fell back, landing directly on my lap.

She looked up at me, surprised.

"Let's go back to the part where you said you wanted to kiss me."

A huge Ash Mabie smile spread across her face as if she had just won the lottery. It wasn't sexy. It was better because it might have been the best gift anyone had ever given me.

She absolutely wanted *me,* and what that gave me was immeasurable.

I was a miserable asshole in a wheelchair. I had no money. Nothing to offer her. She certainly was not winning any lottery when it came to being with me. Yet when Ash fell onto my lap, she was genuinely affected by the contact. It wasn't that sparks flew or our two souls bonded or any of that other shit people spout. It was a simple biological fact.

Her cheeks blushed.

Her eyes dropped to my mouth.

Her body responded to *me.*

In that moment, she reminded me that I was still a man.

And I had every single intention of showing her exactly how right she really was.

Without warning, I took her lips in a rough kiss. She bumbled it, opening her mouth too quickly, causing our teeth to clink, but I didn't allow it to slow me. I took control, deepening it and coaxing her tongue into a smooth rhythm she met stroke for stroke.

That fucking mouth would be the end of me. I loved it when she used it to smile—and even more when she used it to laugh—but it was so much better when it was moving against mine.

Her racing heart fueled me forward. After trailing a hand up her back and into her long hair, I gently fisted it just enough to urge her to move. She shifted to a better angle, and I groaned into her mouth when she settled against my straining cock.

At the noise, she pulled away. I tried to follow, but she stood.

"Hey hey hey. Where are you going?" I nabbed her hand and pulled her back toward me.

She rewarded me with a quiet giggle, but I took the back of her neck, silencing her with my lips. Our arms tangled as we both tried to find a way to get close without the separation my wheelchair required. It was tedious and entirely too time consuming for me.

"Get in the van," I ordered, releasing her.

"I can do that," she responded, licking her lips, but she didn't move.

"Tonight?" I urged.

Fidgeting with her fingers, she asked, "Front seat or back?"

"Your call. Just do it fast." I tossed her a wink, and she shyly looked away.

There was absolutely nothing shy about that crazy woman, so I figured the innocent act was for my benefit. I wasn't complaining, either. I fucking loved it.

When she looked back up, there wasn't a smile in sight.

There was desire.

Desire *I* had put there.

Desire I *owned.*

Desire *I* was absolutely going to fulfill.

Ash

I could have lived the rest of my life under Flint's dark and heated gaze. His lids were hooded, and I was relatively sure he had every intention of devouring me.

And I had every intention of letting him.

Sure, guys had checked me out over the years, but I was usually hustling them or groping them in order to swipe their wallets. But no one had ever looked at me the way Flint did.

I didn't have a ton of experience with guys, and by that, I mean I didn't have any—like none whatsoever. The kiss Flint had just pressed to my lips would actually go down as another "newsie" for the day. I was a chameleon though. I could fake it and make it so freaking believable that Flint would be none the wiser.

I had decided I wanted to be with him after he'd dived out of that van after me days ago. But right then, I wanted more.

I wanted him to look at me like that every day for the rest of my life.

"Come here, beautiful," he said as he moved himself from his chair to the floorboard of the van.

I went willingly, stopping between his legs. My stomach was at his eye level, and even with as confident as I was, I wasn't exactly sure what to do next. Thankfully, Flint was.

"You know, Ash, it's suddenly occurred to me that there are *a lot* of places I want to taste on you."

My eyes went wide before I could cover up the effect his words had had on me.

After pushing the edge of my shirt up, he placed a wet kiss on my stomach. His warm tongue snaked out, rolling against my skin the same way it had in my mouth. The combination of the memory and the feel of his touch forced a groan from my throat. Swaying, I became lost in the sensory overload.

Gripping my hips, Flint trailed his tongue along the low waistband of my jeans. I threaded a hand into his dark hair for balance, but as I gently tugged, he let out a loud growl that I swear traveled over every inch of my body.

"Fuck," he hissed, trailing a hand up to my breast and squeezing hard enough to send the moan flying from my mouth. "Please, tell me you're good with this?" he asked—even as I pressed my breast against his hand, pleading for more.

Oh, I was *good* with it.

I might not have responded with words, but I absolutely answered.

After gently guiding his head away, I crossed my arms and gripped the hem of my shirt. In one swift movement, the shirt was gone, and before he had the chance to react, my bra quickly followed.

I brazenly stood before him completely bare, and the way his eyes dilated confirmed that it had been the right move.

"Jesus Christ, woman," he cursed, looping an arm around my waist before lying down on the floor.

I fell with him, catching myself on my arms by his head.

"People can see you!" he scolded.

Okay, maybe it hadn't been *exactly* the right move.

I sheepishly looked away.

Using my chin to force my eyes back to his, he amended, "It's just that I want these to be mine for tonight." He gently rolled my nipple, causing me to gasp. "I'd have to fight off half the city if anyone else saw you." He leaned up, catching my mouth in another kiss. Once again using my chin, he turned my head to gain access to my neck. After teasing his way up to my ear, he whispered, "And if I'd had to do that, it would have taken time away from doing this." He raked his teeth over my earlobe, spreading chills over my body.

He pushed up on his elbows, gliding his rough hands up and down my sides.

"What's that?" he asked, stopping at the tattoo on my left side over my rib cage.

"A dream catcher," I answered breathlessly as he continued to explore my body.

"You and your dreams," he murmured.

I wanted him, and as I opened my legs to straddle his waist, I felt exactly how much he wanted me too.

And it scared the confidence right out of me, sending a sea of doubt washing over me.

Sitting up, he sucked my nipple into his mouth, and while it was amazing, I was unsure of the right reaction. What if I got it wrong? What if he thought my moans were annoying? What if he didn't want to be with me again?

"Um," I mumbled as he shifted to my other breast.

Leaning away to catch my eye, he asked, "You want me to stop?"

"No," I told him unconvincingly. What I really wanted was to go home, read a bunch of books, maybe look up some porn, and figure out exactly how to do this. Then I'd transport myself right back to that exact moment, owning all the confidence I was attempting to fake.

"Ash," he drawled in warning. "We can stop."

"Can we . . . just, maybe . . . kiss some more?"

One side of his mouth hiked in a grin. "Absolutely."

He grabbed the back of my head and reclined. My breasts pressed against his chest as he closed his mouth over mine. His soft tongue once again made its way into my mouth and rolled in a way that demanded mine to join it. He swallowed my sigh as my hips involuntarily rolled against his hard-on.

With one hand still on the back of my head, his other trailed down my back and over my ass, forcing me to groan all over again.

"Yessss!" was slurred from outside the van.

I sat up at the shock of being caught, completely forgetting that I wasn't wearing a shirt.

"And she's naked!" Quarry exclaimed as we made eye contact.

Well, I made eye contact—he made nipple contact.

"Oh Christ," Max cursed, dragging Q away from the window as Flint wrapped me in his arms to block the view.

"For fuck's sake, cover up!" Flint bit out, searching with his hand around the floor of the van to locate my shirt. "Put this on," he ordered when he finally found it.

While I pulled my shirt on, not even bothering with the bra, I tried to suppress my laughter at the whole situation. Flint didn't look like he was in the mood for it. However, it bubbled out before I could stop it.

He gave me an unimpressed glare. "I'm glad you find this funny, because Q's gonna be dreaming about you naked for the next six months."

I grabbed my chest over my heart, feigning injury. "Only six?"

"You're insane," he mumbled as he shook his head, but he did it smiling.

Just before I climbed off his lap, I kissed him. "You know, I'm more concerned with what you'll be dreaming about." I tossed him a flirty wink.

However, never one to be outdone, Flint one-upped me. "Oh, that's easy. Tomorrow night." He confidently returned my wink.

His was better.

Damn cheater!

CHAPTER
Twelve

Ash

Me: Coffee or soda?

Flint: It's seven in the morning.

Me: Uh, yeah. Hence the question.

Flint: Who drinks soda at seven am?

Me: Me. Caffeine is caffeine. Now answer the question. I'm on the way over to your place.

Flint: Right now? It's seven am.

Me: We've established the time already. Coffee or soda?

Flint: Coffee.

Me: I knew it! I'm totally clairvoyant. Open your door. I'm here.

Flint: Already?

Me: Yeah, I was already at your door when I worried you'd want soda. I like you and all but I wasn't willing to share mine.

A minute later, the door swung open to Flint staring up at me, shirtless in a pair of athletic shorts. I sucked in a fast breath as I openly gawked at him. His chest was thin but clearly defined, and a small amount of hair was dusted over it.

"Jesus, it's early, Ash."

"Well, good morning to you too." I extended the coffee toward him.

Using one hand to shield his eyes from the sunlight blazing into his dark apartment, he took the drink without so much as a thank-you. "What are you doing here?"

Hmm. Not exactly the welcome I was hoping for, but Flint was never easy.

Turning sideways, I squeezed past him.

"Well, by all means, come on in," he snapped.

Okay, maybe showing up uninvited wasn't the best idea.

When Flint had dropped me off the night before, he'd given me a toe-curling goodbye kiss that had me wishing I hadn't chickened out in the back of his van. It had also left me thinking about him pretty much nonstop for the rest of the night. Sleep had proved to be impossible. Each time I would start to doze off, a memory of our night together would flash through my mind, forcing a smile to my face. My cheeks had ached by the time the first ray of sunlight had peeked through my bedroom window, which, coincidently, was the same time I'd raced to my dad's car and headed back to Flint's apartment.

It had taken every ounce of self-restraint I possessed, but I'd made it to seven A.M. before giving in and texting him. I didn't want to look desperate or anything. Clearly, seven A.M. was the hour of cool and collected girls everywhere. Well, at least it was a hell of a lot better than five thirty, when I'd bought his coffee from the gas station.

"Cold coffee. Delicious," he snarked. "Jesus, did you get this last night?" He curled his lips in disgust.

Not quite. "I woke up early and decided to stop by and see if you wanted to go garage-saling with me."

"It's seven in the morning."

Suddenly, I felt like an idiot for being there. I was great at reading people, but Flint was a totally different story. He got me all flustered with those bright-blue eyes and his sexy smirk. I couldn't decide if I needed to work harder to get that smiling and laughing guy back or tuck tail and run before I made myself look like even more of a fool.

His eyebrow popped up when I didn't immediately respond.

Yep, tucking tail it was.

"Umm . . . You know, on second thought, you don't look like you are much in the mood for garage-saling." I pulled the coffee from his hands and turned to squeeze back past him.

"Hey! You can't take that back." He swung the door shut, plunging the room into darkness.

"Holy shit," I cursed, temporarily blinded.

Stumbling back a step, I felt him wrap an arm around my waist and drag me down into his lap. Coffee and soda sloshed in the cups as I landed on top of him.

"Where do you think you're going?"

I continued to blink while my eyes adjusted. "How the hell did you convert your apartment into a dungeon?"

"Blackout curtains. I hate being woken up early by the sun."

And stalkers too, I assume.

Spinning his wheelchair, he propelled us toward the hall.

"Um . . ." I mumbled, trying to climb off his lap, but his arm folded over my hips, locking me firmly in place. My hands were still filled with cups, so there wasn't a whole lot I could do to fight against his grip.

Not that I really wanted to anyway.

He continued pushing us toward the bedroom. "We're going back to bed. Then we can go to whatever garage you want to when we wake up."

"But we'll miss all the good stuff. You have to get there early or everything will be gone." I turned to look at him over my shoulder, pouting my lips and batting my eyelashes.

He leaned forward and pecked my lips. "Yeah, but if you go late, you get the best deals when they start marking shit down to almost free."

My eyes lit. "You've been garage-saling before?" I squealed in delight.

"Are you kidding? I used to take Quarry every weekend. I might as well be the king of yard sales."

I smiled then returned his peck. "Look at us! We have common interests and everything."

He released my hips in order to use both hands to maneuver his wheelchair around the tight corner into his room. "Is one of your interests sleeping in my bed? Because that is my favorite at seven A.M."

I had never slept in Flint's bed, but I could say with absolute certainty that it was my favorite interest of all. However, judging by the bulge that had grown in his pants, Flint didn't really want to sleep. And if I crawled into his bed, I probably wouldn't want to sleep either. Familiar nerves from the night before flooded me all over again.

After jumping off his lap, I set both cups on his nightstand. "Come on. I need some new jeans, and I want to find some stuff to spruce up your boring apartment. We need to hit 'em early."

"I'm not letting you decorate my apartment. I'd end up with neon curtains and sequined throw pillows."

"Well, clearly, not all of our interests are the same, because that sounds fabulous."

He shook his head. "My apartment's just fine the way it is."

"Okay, okay. But you can't stop me from at least getting you a welcome mat."

He tilted his head. "A welcome mat? So I can wipe my feet before I come inside?"

I burst out laughing. "Oh, don't look at me like that, Wheels. Dirty feet or not, a welcome mat would go a long way in making this place a little more inviting."

"Who exactly am I supposed to be welcoming?" he teased, intertwining our fingers.

"Uh. Me. I need to feel welcome or I'm gonna stop coming back. The resident isn't exactly warm and fuzzy." I tilted my head, mirroring his. "Well, that's not true. He's kinda fuzzy."

A toothy grin formed on his mouth. "Fine. Let me get dressed. Then we'll find you a welcome mat."

"Yay!" I clapped. "Be quick about it. A neon, sequined welcome mat is going to be difficult, but I bet, if we get a move on it, we can beat the rush and at least find one with kittens or puppies."

"Dear God," he breathed, rolling himself over to his dresser.

As much as I wanted to stay and watch Flint get dressed, I opted to warm up his coffee instead.

"Six for a dollar." Flint haggled with a woman behind the small folding table at our last stop for the day.

"They are basically brand-new books on sale for a quarter apiece. I can't go any lower than that," she responded.

"Right. A quarter each would have been fair, but the previous owner had a nasty habit of dog-earing the pages instead of using a bookmark. They also apparently only read one page at a time, because every. Single. Page. Is turned down. That severely decreases the value." He leaned back in his chair and extended two dollars over the table, engaging her in a stare-off. "Six for a dollar. Final offer."

I giggled to myself, watching him out of the corner of my eye while pretending to be busy looking at the picked-over knickknacks.

Flint wasn't lying. He was, in fact, the king of yard sales. He'd been wheeling and dealing all over the city. Pun intended. I loved a good haggle, but Flint was an animal. I had two full tote bags in the back of his van and had spent less than half of the ten bucks I'd brought with me.

The woman finally relented, snatching his money. "Oh Lord, just take them. Saves me from having to move them back inside."

"Excellent," he replied, stacking his twelve books in his lap. "Ash, you ready to go?"

"Yep." I walked over, sparing a tight smile for the woman he had all but hustled.

After opening the tote bag on my shoulder, Flint filled it with his newly acquired books. Side by side, we headed back to his van.

"Sorry you didn't find any welcome mats."

"Yeah. I guess you'll just have to make me feel welcome until next weekend." I looked down in time to see him glance up with a gorgeous grin. "I have to say, even with the scruff and bad attitude, the hotness factor went up today."

He took my hand as he glided down the sidewalk. "Oh yeah? Why's that?"

"I don't know. It was sexy watching you talk people in circles. Let's just say I'm glad I'm with you instead of against you."

"You're with me, huh?" he teased.

"Well, yeah. Who knows when I'll need to negotiate jeans for a dime again. I'll keep you around for that alone." I smiled down at him, but his fell.

Flint suddenly became engrossed with the ground. I tried to follow his eyes, but with the exception of our shadows cast out in front of us, nothing was even remotely enthralling about the asphalt.

Once he'd released my hand, he pushed ahead of me.

"Hey, slow down," I called, speed-walking after him. "Jeez, you in a rush?" I asked, out of breath, when I caught up to him at the van.

"Come on. I'm gonna drop you off," he snapped.

"My dad's car is at your apartment. You can't drop me off anywhere."

"Fine. Then let's go. I have shit to do today."

I narrowed my eyes at him. "Uhhhh . . . okay? Ya want to tell me what the hell just happened to turn you back into an asshole?"

"Nothing happened," he said, but I was never one to be dismissed.

After taking the bag from my hand, he slung it into the backseat. Then he made his way around the bumper of the van, but I rushed around the front, stopping him before he reached the driver's side door.

"Look, I have no idea what I said back there, but whatever it is, I'm sorry." I bent at the waist and forced his eyes to mine, but I wasn't ready for what I received. I could have dealt with his attitude, but for the first time, insecurity was brewing in Flint's eyes.

"You didn't say anything. Now, move."

He reached for the door, but I stepped forward, blocking him from opening it.

"Then why are you acting like an ass? We've had a great day, and suddenly, I feel like we are right back at angry seven A.M."

"Move," he repeated on a growl.

Crossing my arms over my chest, I propped myself against this door. "Nah. I'm good. Thanks."

"Ash, I'm not in the mood."

"I got that. What I don't have is the why? You completely just shut down on me for no reason whatsoever."

His Adam's apple bobbed as he swallowed hard. "I don't want to do this anymore. I just want to take you home and be done with it."

The initial sting of his words hurt; there was no doubt about that. But while I hadn't known Flint for very long, I knew for sure he was lying.

"Nope. Wrong answer. Try again."

"Excuse me?"

I bent over, catching enough attitude to match his. "I said try. Again."

"You're insane," he mumbled.

I let out a loud laugh. "Maybe, but I'm not the one with multiple personalities. Pick one, Flint. Either be sweet or an asshole, but I'm going to need a neck brace pretty soon if you keep this up."

"Pick one? Pick. One?" he repeated in disbelief.

I confidently held his stare. "That's what I said. No need to repeat it."

For several seconds, I could physically see this unknown truth waging war with his body. His breathing sped up, and his eyes flashed from the van back to mine, finally landing on the ground again.

"Why the hell are you here?" he finally gritted out.

"Well, it's not for the cheerful company. That's for sure," I snarked back.

He looked up, his angry façade melting away. "I'm serious. Why are you here? You're gorgeous, and smart . . . and funny. What the fuck are you doing here with *me?*"

I shrugged. "I like you. Wait." I dramatically lifted a finger. "I like the sweet personality. That other one is a real dick."

"I am that dick though. I'm a bitter asshole who stands at six foot four, yet you will always be looking down at me."

My head snapped back. "Are you kidding me? Who the hell am I to look down at anyone?"

"You don't get it. I have nothing to offer you. *Nothing.*"

"Okay," I drawled. "I guess the good news is I'm not asking for anything. I just like hanging out with you. Wait." I dramatically lifted my finger again, causing him to roll his eyes. "The sweet one," I clarified before flashing him a smile.

He sucked in a deep breath and then admitted, "I hate that you're taller than I am."

"I'm only five nine. You've got me by, like, seven inches."

"You know what I mean."

"No, I really don't," I replied, turning to follow his eyes down.

Two black silhouettes stretched out across the asphalt in front of us. Just as to be expected, mine towered over his.

"Oh, hey! I can fix this!" I exclaimed, walking backwards until our shadows were level with each other.

"Don't be a smartass," he snarled.

I took two giant steps backwards until his seated shadow was notably longer than mine. "And look, you're six four again." I laughed.

Flint, however, didn't find it amusing. "You're ridiculous." He yanked the van door open.

"Am I? Because I just gave you exactly what you wanted and it still isn't enough. Maybe you could try to just be happy with what you do have instead of focusing on what you don't."

He froze.

"Flint, don't get so caught up on the shadow that you forget the man who casts it. You might not be able to walk, but that's the extent of your disability."

I watched him for several seconds until he eventually became unstuck. He didn't even spare me a backward glance as he climbed into the driver's seat. After collapsing his wheelchair, he slung it in the back door.

"Get in the van, Ash," he ordered roughly, starting the engine.

When he shifted into gear, I didn't have much choice but to obey or be left in the middle of the road.

We drove home in silence. I wasn't sure what else to say. I thought my inspirational speech had been pretty freaking awesome; obviously, Flint didn't share my feelings. For ten excruciating minutes, he blankly stared out the windshield without even acknowledging I existed.

As we pulled into his parking lot, nerves started to flutter in my stomach. I wasn't ready to leave him yet, especially when I didn't know if it was for the last time.

"Flint—" I started when he put the car in park, but that was all I got out.

He plucked me out of my seat and dragged me over the armrests until his mouth collided with mine. My knees banged around and my feet became painfully tangled behind me, but that wasn't why I moaned.

"You," he accused against my lips before sealing his mouth over mine. His tongue swirled greedily, and I met him stroke for stroke.

After scrambling the rest of the way into his lap, I settled my ass on the steering wheel and squeezed my legs into the tight spaces on either side of his hips. His hands sifted through my hair as he continued to hold my mouth against his own.

I was an all-too-willing victim though.

"I'm assuming you're not trying to get rid of me anymore." I teased, but he took my mouth again, transforming my words into a moan.

"You," he repeated.

I didn't quite understand how that was an answer to my question, but I can't say that I didn't love it.

Me.

For over a half hour at noon, Flint and I made out in the front seat of his van. He never attempted to take it any further. Rather, he seemed content with ravaging my neck and mouth, and I was more than content with letting him do it.

Finally, he released my swollen lips. Holding each side of my face, he tipped his forehead to mine. "I'm going to follow you to drop off your dad's car. I want you to spend the day with me. I'll bring you back home later tonight."

"Okay," I breathed.

"And, Ash."

I looked up at him as I crawled off his lap, smoothing down my hair.

"I'll get whatever welcome mat you want as long as you just promise to keep using it."

My smile was unrivaled, and my heart soared. "I can do that."

I could do that.

I could *so* do that.

CHAPTER
Thirteen

Flint

FOR THE NEXT THREE WEEKS, Ash became part of my daily routine. Every day, she either showed up at my apartment after I got out of class or I would pick her up on my way home.

We hadn't worked our way up to sex yet. Or really anything below the waist. And it was getting harder and harder—literally. I'd had blue balls more in those weeks than I'd ever experienced in my life. I didn't press her though. We were having fun—something my life had been seriously lacking for a long time.

I didn't have the money to take her out on big dates, but she didn't seem to care that we usually drove around aimlessly or talked and made out on my couch. She just acted like she wanted to be around me. Which, in turn, made me desperate to be around her. She made me laugh, and while I had no idea what I did for her, I was selfish enough that I didn't care. I just needed her to keep coming back.

She never did stop stealing my wallet, but I started to enjoy trying to catch her in the act. She'd always straddle my lap and kiss me apologetically. This usually ended with me missing my watch or my phone, but I wouldn't have traded those moments with her for all of my possessions in the world. And that was probably a good thing, because gradually, they all started disappearing anyway. At first, it was random

T-shirts and the occasional hoodie, but then she worked her way up to my books. Every day when Ash left, I would notice an empty hole on one of my shelves. I had no idea when she took them or why she didn't just ask, but I didn't actually care. By the next day, it was back and a different one was missing.

Until one day, I guessed she found what she was looking for.

Somewhere around the two-week mark, my absolute favorite book, *A Heartbreaking Work of Staggering Genius* by Dave Eggers, had vanished. I'd checked every day to see if she had returned it, but it hadn't made its way back to its spot on my shelf.

"You planning to bring my book back?" I asked as we were lying in the grass outside my apartment. It was actually a small patch of weeds between two buildings, but Ash loved to lie there and stare up at the stars, and though transferring myself from the ground back to my wheelchair was difficult and sometimes embarrassing, I quickly learned to love it too.

"What book?" she asked innocently, twiddling her thumbs that were folded over her stomach.

I had known for a while that Ash was odd, but I'd never met a woman who wasn't a cuddler. Sure, she touched me and kissed me, but she always moved away when she was done. I couldn't tell if she liked her space or if she just didn't realize there was another option.

"The one you stole." I quirked a knowing eyebrow.

Her lips twitched before she looked back up at the stars. "I have no idea what you're talking about."

"Right," I said following her gaze.

A few unbelievably *comfortable* moments of silence passed before I spoke again.

"So, where's your mom?"

"She killed herself when I was five," she answered nonchalantly.

"Shit," I breathed, pulling an arm from under my head to take one of her hands.

"Yeah. I don't remember her," she said without elaborating, so I decided to once again change the subject.

"Was Q at your dad's when you left?"

"No. He went to the gym. Debbie was pissed, but giving a damn is pretty low on Quarry's list of cares."

I laughed at her assessment.

"Hey, can I ask you a question?" she asked, pulling her hand away.

"Yeah. Go for it."

"What's your problem with Till and Eliza? Quarry told me they basically raised you guys and how you got shot and stuff, but why don't you talk to them or anything now?"

I let out a loud huff. Of course she would ask that question. The one question I honestly didn't have an answer to. Well, I did—but it wasn't one I wanted to explain to her.

"I don't know. Just some family shit, I guess."

"Are they, like, total assholes?" She pushed up on her elbows and turned to look at me. It was the oddest thing I had ever seen. She appeared downright hopeful.

I tilted my head curiously. "Not at all."

"Did they, like, hit you and stuff when you were growing up?"

"What? No way!"

"Oh," she said, deflated, as she reclined again.

"What gave you that idea?"

She sighed. "I don't know. Q always talks about them. He mentioned that you avoid them at all costs. So I was thinking maybe they were pricks and Quarry just didn't see it yet."

"No. Till's . . ." I started, but the words lodged in my throat. "Great. He's like a father to me."

"Is Eliza a bitch? I know you don't like her very much."

I barked out a laugh. "What? Why do you think that?"

"I don't know. You get all weird and cranky when Q mentions her."

I looked away.

The moments that followed would later become one of my biggest regrets with Ash. No matter how many times I'd try to rationalize my actions that night, they'd never add up. The only thing I'd figured was that Ash always made things lighter for me. Gravity didn't keep me pinned to my wheelchair when I was with her. She freed me, and back then—when it came to Eliza—I needed that more than anything else.

"No. Eliza's pretty incredible." I paused and turned my head to face her.

She was still staring up at the sky, and her long, strawberry-blond hair fanned out beside her. The bright moon illuminated her white skin.

She was so beautiful.

She deserved to know what the hell she was getting into with me.

So, for some incredibly ridiculous reason, I admitted, "I've been in love with Eliza for years. It's just easier to avoid her."

Only the second the words were spoken, it didn't feel like an admission at all.

It didn't feel like anything actually.

Not the truth.

Or a lie.

They just felt like *words.*

"Ewwww!" Ash cried. "You're in love with your mom?"

"No. She's not my mom," I defended.

"You said she and Till raised you guys."

"I mean, they did. But . . . she's *not* my mom."

"Whatever you think." She laughed and went back to staring at the stars.

She didn't speak again for several minutes, and it began to unnerve me. I regretted my decision to tell her. I mean, what the actual hell had I possibly thought I could gain from sharing something like that?

Hey, look. I'm disabled and in love with another woman. Please be with me?

"I mean, it's not like I'm trying to be with her or anything," I clarified. "Really, it's no big deal."

"Nah. I get it. You have an Oedipus complex?"

"I don't have an Oedipus complex! She's not my mom!" I yelled, and she burst out laughing.

That conversation with anyone else would have sent me into a fit of rage, but watching Ash roll around in some dirty weeds while she laughed so hard that tears spilled from her eyes did the opposite.

I didn't even feel numb.

I felt *everything* for the first time in as long as I could remember.

Probably too much, actually.

Maybe Ash wasn't a thief at all.

Because she had given me back far more than she could ever take.

Ash

Every single word of his confession was like a jagged knife to the heart.

I tried to keep my reaction locked away, but when the tears fell from my eyes, I covered it with a large dose of artificial laughter. I could con Flint into thinking it was funny, but there was nothing I could do to con myself.

I was in love with Flint Page.

And *he* was in love with someone else.

I didn't have much experience with relationships. As far as I was concerned, fairytales were real and love only came once in a lifetime, and I had just used mine on a boy who had already given his to another girl.

It didn't matter that he could never have her. Or that he was watching me with a warm, content smile unlike anything I'd ever seen. All I'd heard in his admission was that I would never truly have *him.*

I wished I had never asked him about Eliza. I could have lived a thousand lifetimes without knowing how he felt about her. Or, better yet, how he didn't feel about *me.* But I hadn't once expected that to be his answer. I'd just wanted some dirt on her and Till. Dirt that would make me feel better about allowing my father to take Quarry from them.

Only hours earlier, I'd overheard—or, more accurately, recorded—a conversation between Ray and Debbie. It should be known that I'd seen my father do a lot of despicable things, but Debbie had taken it to a whole new level. She knew precisely how much Till loved his brothers and exactly how far he would go to keep his family together. Till probably would have paid them a hefty sum of money to disappear or sign the custody paperwork. However, what Debbie had masterminded had guaranteed a whole lot more than just a hefty sum. The plan was simple. Get custody of Quarry, move him across the country, and cut Till off completely. Then, after a few months, once Till and Eliza got desperate, basically sell him back to them.

They were both aware that getting actual custody of Q wasn't going to be an easy feat. No judge in his right mind would place him with loser Debbie Mabie over celebrity "The Silencer" Till Page. But just last week, a judge and a date had been assigned to Quarry's custody case. My father had called in some favors, and within twenty-four hours, he'd had more than enough pictures of that judge with his mistress to secure a win for Team Mabie. With part one done, I knew that part two would be moving. And while I had already decided I wasn't going with them this time, I knew that Q wouldn't have that choice.

My conscience had needed Till and Eliza to be assholes who deserved that.

Unfortunately, I'd gotten far more than I'd bargained for.

He was in love with her.

"Thank you," Flint said as I finally got my emotions under control and was able to give up the show of laughter.

"For what?"

"Being weird. And making me lie under the stars on a pile of weeds." He brushed a hair off my face. "And for calling me Wheels."

My head snapped to his. "You hate that nickname."

"Yeah. It's really fucking rude." He laughed. "But it's also a truth that doesn't necessarily have to be taken as an insult. You've never pitied me, Ash. Not even for being a sad bastard with an Oedipus complex."

"I have a freakish toe," I announced.

Flint bit his lip to stifle a laugh. "Oh yeah?" he asked, amused. Then he slid an arm under my neck and pulled me against his side, shifting me awkwardly until my head rested on his chest.

"Yep. It's, like, way shorter than the others. I would hope you wouldn't pity me for it."

His shoulders shook as he kissed the top of my head. "Maybe I should start calling you Toes." His foot gently tapped on the sole of my shoe.

"Oh my God! Flint, you moved your legs!" I screamed, suddenly sitting up. My eyes must have been huge, because he looked at me like I had transformed into a maniac. "It's a miracle!" I proclaimed.

He laughed, shaking his head.

"You want to get up and try to walk?" I asked in all seriousness. "Come on. I'll help." I grabbed his arms and started pulling.

"Ash, stop. I can't walk."

"Would it help if I start singing 'Eye of the Tiger'? You're a boxer.

That's a *very* inspirational song."

He barked out a loud laugh and yanked on my arm, forcing me back down. His mouth landed on mine before his smile even had a chance to disappear. Holding me against his lips, he breathed deeply for several seconds. I kept my eyes open, but his were reverently closed. I wasn't completely sure what was going through his mind, but I had a feeling it was something big, a fact that was confirmed when his eyes opened and stared so fiercely into mine that I felt as though he were branding me from the inside out.

It was a moment I would remember for the rest of my life.

He could love her. I could learn to be okay with that. Because as his eyes held mine, I knew I'd never belong to anyone else, something I needed more than any love he could ever provide.

Releasing my mouth, he whispered against my lips, "I can move my legs."

"Oh," I breathed, still reeling from our moment.

"I mean, a little bit. It takes a lot of concentration, and they don't do much, but . . ." He paused, and his foot lifted an inch before falling back to the ground.

"Oh," I repeated.

"But I do appreciate your offer to sing," he teased.

I started to roll back to my spot on the grass, but Flint held me tight, forcing me to lie tucked against his side—something I loved so much that I instinctually avoided it at all costs. I simply couldn't allow myself to get used to the way my whole body warmed or the feeling of security he gave me with the simple drape of his arm. I knew that, if I ever lost it, I'd never be able to enjoy my life in the cold world that was left behind. I didn't need to know how truly amazing life could be at his side.

Rolling away, I asked, "Do you think you'll ever be able to walk again?"

He let out a groan that I thought had more to do with me moving than the question. "I don't know. I hope so, but I'm not sure. I mean, my doctors say it's promising that I can move my legs. But I try not to get my hopes up. Disappointment's a real bitch."

"Yeah, I get that," I answered, remembering his little revelation about Eliza.

"It is what it is," he said, dismissing the topic as he scooted over an inch and pulled me back against his side.

That time, I didn't move away. Instead, I gave myself a minute to dream of a future with Flint. It was the best dream I had ever made up—and a dream that would later turn into a nightmare, haunting me for years to come.

CHAPTER
Fourteen

Flint

Me: What are you doing today?

Ash: Sitting on your couch?

Me: Excellent answer.

Ash: I'm glad you approve.

Me: You want to go to a birthday party with me?

Ash: Oh. My. God! I've never been to a birthday party!!!!!!!!!!!!!!!!!!

Me: Wow! That's a lot of exclamation points!

Ash: !!!!!!!!!!!!!!!!

Me: You done yet?

Ash: !!!!!!!!!!!!!!!!!!!!

Me: Should I wait for an answer or just assume the exclamation points are a yes?

Ash: !!!!!!! Ok. I'm done now. !!!! Sorry those just slipped.

Me: So . . . party?

Ash: Yes, I'll go! Q told me there was going to be a clown and

a bounce house.

Me: Probably.

Ash: Pick me up at 12:30. We need to stop so I can get a present.

Me: Cool. See you then.

Ash: <3 <3 <3

I tossed my phone on counter and stared at the invitation to Blakely Page's first birthday sitting on the table in front of me. It seemed my secret whereabouts weren't all that secret anymore. I wasn't sure if Quarry or Slate had finally spilled my address, but earlier that morning, I'd opened the front door to find Till standing on my welcome mat. He hadn't said a single word as he'd handed me the invitation, but the muscles in his neck had strained, letting me know he'd had a ton of pissed-off words to say and was struggling to keep them under wraps—a fact I immensely appreciated.

He'd slowly backed away, pausing just before he turned toward the parking lot.

"I know for a fact that fucking door works. Use it," he'd gritted out before disappearing.

I'd sat there staring at the pink envelope in my hand while Till's old truck rumbled away. He was a millionaire and he still drove that hunk of junk everywhere. Eliza drove a top-of-the-line SUV, and even the van he'd bought me had every possible bell and whistle imaginable. Yet Till still drove the same truck that had already been a piece of shit when he'd bought it years earlier.

That's my brother.

And for the first time since the accident, thinking about Till actually stung.

Well, that's not totally true. Thinking about Till used to do far more than sting. It used to devour me. However, this time, it stung in a different way.

The pain I felt was from guilt instead of resentment.

Even the idea of seeing Eliza didn't send me into some sort of panic.

It was time.

I was finally going back.

And *she* was going with me.

When I arrived to pick Ash up, my mouth gaped open as she sauntered out of the house. She had always been a jeans-and-T-shirt kind of girl, but that day, she had clearly stepped it up a notch. She was wearing a short, red sundress that exposed a tasteful amount of cleavage. Well, tasteful in the sense that it guaranteed I would, in fact, be tasting it again that night—and hopefully other places as well. Instead of her usual flip-flops or flats, she was wearing tall, strappy wedge sandals that immediately hardened my cock. The front of her hair was twisted back, and bright-red lipstick painted her lips, making her look like she had stepped off the front of a 1950s pinup calendar.

She looked incredible.

And as a wide smile spread across her face, she made me *feel* incredible.

After a long stop at the toy store, where Ash had insisted on asking a mother carting around a toddler to help us shop for Blakely, we finally arrived at Till and Eliza's house.

Ash's eyes all but popped out of her head as we drove through the security gate. But the second I saw that house, my nerves hit in full force.

"C'mere," I said to Ash as soon as I parked. Pulling her into a hard kiss she enthusiastically returned, I traced up her long legs and under the edge of her dress. "You look beautiful," I murmured.

"So you've mentioned." She giggled, and my nerves started to fade away.

"Just making sure you heard me." I released her, and she grabbed a wipe from her purse and cleaned the lipstick from my mouth for approximately the twentieth time since I'd picked her up.

I took a deep breath, and with Ash at my side, we headed toward the party.

When we got to the backyard, I ran into a myriad of familiar faces.

"Did the world end and I somehow missed it?" Slate said dryly, walking over from where Erica was watching their kids in the bounce house.

"Hey," I replied, embarrassed, remembering how I'd spoken to him that day in my apartment.

"I'm glad you came, son." He squeezed my neck.

"Hey, listen, I'm really sorry about—" I started, but he interrupted me.

"Who's this?" he asked, extending a hand over my shoulder.

"Oh sorry. This is my . . ." I stalled, trying to figure out what to call her. *Oh, fuck it.* We all knew who she was. "This is my girlfriend, Ash. Ash, this is Slate Andrews. He owns On The Ropes with Till." I looked up to find her staring down at me in absolute awe. I tossed her a puzzled expression, but she didn't explain.

"Hi! So nice to meet you." She took Slate's hand.

Judging by the slight tip of his head, he had witnessed her strange reaction. Whatever. I could worry about that later, because suddenly, as if a ring announcer had just spouted my introduction to the entire party, dozens of eyes all flashed my way.

I could feel them watching me, but my attention was homed in on a pair of dark blues boring into mine from only a few feet away. Her eyes instantly pooled with tears, and an ache grew in my chest.

But it wasn't my *heart* that hurt.

And it *wasn't* agonizing.

It was just *there*.

Lingering.

Then, with my eyes still focused on the object of my obsession for most of my adolescence, Ash's hand closed over mine, and I was hit by a sudden rush of that same ache ebbing from my body—freeing me.

Eliza warily approached, repeatedly glancing down to where Ash's hand covered mine. She didn't attempt to say anything as she stood there with tears streaming down her cheeks.

A small smile tipped my lips. "Stop crying. I promised I'd come back, didn't I?"

And that was it. She launched herself forward, wrapping her arms around my neck. She held me for several seconds, half crying, half laughing. I took a deep breath, filling my lungs with the ease and relief I felt from her embrace.

Till appeared and attempted to peel Eliza off me, but she was crying so hard that it was almost comical. Well, that was until I saw the utter devastation covering Ash's face.

Shit.

Ash

I had been wrong.

I couldn't handle it at all.

I didn't care that Flint had more than shown that I belonged to him, that he was proud to have me on his arm. And I didn't care that he would never in a million years have Eliza as anything more than a sister-in-law. I knew how *he* felt, and that was more than enough to shatter whatever childish dreams I had invented and replayed every single minute of every single day.

Watching him breathe so deeply, as if he could inhale her. That was mine. And if I'd had to witness the branding blaze of his eyes when he opened them, I would have more than self-destructed.

Thankfully, Quarry chose that exact moment to offer me an escape.

"Ash!" he yelled from several yards away. He was waving his hands and pointing at the clown making balloon animals for the kids. "Told you!"

"Excuse me," I addressed the group, and then I hurriedly clomped away.

The one fucking day I wore heels, I had to march across what might as well have been a football field of grass. Although I only actually *marched* for about three steps before my ankle rolled and sent me crashing to the ground.

"Ash!" Flint shouted, chasing after me.

"Fuck," I hissed, quickly pushing back to my feet and wiping the dirt from my dress. "I'm good," I said with a smile that should have won me a goddamned Oscar nomination.

"Stop," Flint said, taking my wrist.

"Stop what?" I snapped, trying to pull it from his grasp.

"Getting upset."

I looked up to find a group of people curiously watching us, so I pasted on a grin and replied, "Don't be silly. I'm just going to see the clown."

Flint didn't buy it for even a second.

Before I could utter another excuse, his arm folded around my hips and dragged me down onto his lap. "I swear to God, Ash. I will not have this conversation with you out here on the lawn, but you will not fucking run away without allowing me to explain, either. So you have two choices. You follow me inside and talk to me. Or I will tie you to this chair and *carry* you inside to talk to me. One is tedious, time consuming, and embarrassing. But I am more than willing to give it a go for you."

"What the hell? You got a spool of rope in your pocket?" I snarked.

"I have a belt," he retorted.

Normally, I would have sassed back, but I could tell by the determination in his eyes that he wasn't kidding. While being tied to Flint didn't seem like a bad option at all, I decided against the embarrassment factor.

"Lead the way," I bit out, pushing myself off his lap.

He nodded toward the huge house. "After you."

I walked a little more carefully through the grass, smiling as we passed the onlookers.

"I'm gonna take Ash inside to get cleaned up," Flint called out, following closely behind me.

Instead of going to the front door, he directed me around back toward a long ramp that led inside. A huge room nicer than anything I had ever seen greeted me on the other side of the automatic door. Everything was new, and there was more than enough space for Flint's wheelchair to maneuver around. It was obvious, based on the empty bookshelves that lined the walls, that it used to be his room. He must have had it really bad to be willing to leave that place in exchange for his tiny apartment.

Yeah, bad . . . In love with *her.*

"Talk," he demanded as I continued to take in the room and expansive connecting bathroom.

"I don't have anything to say." It was both a truth and a lie. I had tons to say, but the thoughts and feelings were so jumbled in my head that I couldn't pinpoint where to start.

"Ash, don't do this. I know that made you uncomfortable out there."

"Maybe just for a minute. I'm okay now." Now *that* was definitely a lie.

"Liar," he whispered, stopping in front of me and taking my hand. "You don't have to be jealous of her." He kissed my knuckle.

"Yeah, I know," I replied without meeting his gaze. "Come on. Let's go back out. I've never seen an actual clown before."

"Wait. Look at me."

My traitorous eyes followed his order.

"I shouldn't have told you what I did about her. It's not a big deal anymore."

And with that, all of my thoughts finally aligned.

And they were *pissed.*

"How exactly is it not a big deal that you're in love with her? Because it's a really big freaking deal to me!" I snapped with entirely more attitude than I had anticipated.

"Listen to me. It doesn't matter anymore—"

"It matters to me!" I shouted before closing my eyes, wishing I could magically transport myself out of there. Although I wasn't sure where I would go, because the only place I truly belonged was sitting in front of me. "I love you," I admitted with my eyes still squeezed shut. I'd wanted to say it, but I didn't want to see the absence in his own eyes when he was unable to return the sentiment.

"No, you don't. You barely know me," he whispered.

I guessed it was his turn to lie, because I knew enough about Flint to have fallen in love with him within twenty-four hours of meeting him.

I continued talking but never opened my eyes. "I do. I love you a lot."

"Ash—"

"No. Don't. I know what you're thinking. Max told me it's too soon and I'm way too young. But it may have only been a month and I might only be sixteen, but I know without a shadow of a doubt that I love you. And it hurts so much to know that *you* love *her.*"

The proverbial record stopped.

"Wait. What?" He suddenly dropped my hand.

I pried an eye open to gauge how hard I needed to keep trying to disappear, but when I saw his ghostly white face, they both popped open.

I had known he couldn't return my feelings, but I hadn't expected them to horrify him.

CHAPTER
Fifteen

Ash

"YOU'RE HOW OLD?" HE GASPED.

"Sixteen." I twisted my mouth in confusion. *What the hell is his problem?*

His eyes raked over my body in a way that usually sent tingles down my spine, only this time, his eyes never heated. Instead, they became cold and distant.

"How?" he asked incredulously, only confusing me more.

"Ummm . . . how old did you think I was?"

"Not sixteen!" he roared, shoving a rough hand into the back of his hair. "This is not happening." He began to glide his chair around the room in a nervous pattern.

"What's the big deal?"

"You're sixteen!" he repeated as if they had become the sole words in his vocabulary.

"So what?" I crossed my arms over my chest.

His eyes automatically dropped. I would have smiled at the small victory, but we had far bigger issues to deal with. Like him being in love with another woman.

It was clear that Flint was still obsessing about my age though.

"You have a tattoo," he stated as if that would magically alter the year of my birth.

"So does Q."

"You take college classes online," he continued to argue.

"Uhhh . . . no. I take high school classes online."

"Oh my God." He pinched the bridge of his nose.

"What the hell are you freaking out about?"

"Everything!" he yelled so loudly that it forced me back a step.

"Okay, you need to calm down."

"I need to calm down? Are you fucking kidding me?"

I wasn't kidding. I wasn't even smiling.

I actually had a horrible feeling in the pit of my stomach, and judging by his murderous glare, I had every reason to feel that way.

"Get out," he bit out, and while it hurt, I could gladly give him some time alone to get his attitude in check.

"Fine. Let me know when you're ready to talk about the real issue instead of this bullshit." I turned to stalk away, mentally high-fiving myself for not taking the brunt of his hissy fit.

"The real issue, Ash?" he said behind me. "Exactly how is you lying to me for the last month not the real issue?"

"Lying to you?" I spun back around to face him. "How the hell was I lying?"

"What the fuck is wrong with you? You didn't think the fact that I could go to jail for being with you was need-to-know information?"

"I'm not jailbait. Sixteen is the age of consent. Besides, it's not like we were having sex anyway."

"Thank fucking God for that."

I flinched at his words. *That hurt.*

But Flint was just getting started. "You're a goddamn child. This explains so much about you."

"You're three years older than I am. It's not exactly robbing the cradle or anything." I laughed to cover my fear, which was multiplying with his every word spoken. Or, in the seconds that followed, his every word *not* spoken. "Flint, let's just calm down here. It's still me. So I'm a little younger. Age doesn't matter. I love you," I reminded him. I didn't give a damn if he felt the same way or not. I just needed him to know that I loved *him.* That was enough.

No one had ever loved me. I didn't need it. I just needed *him.*

He stared blankly across the room; his eyes never even bounced to mine.

Suddenly, he blurted, "I want you to get the fuck out of my life and never come back."

"You're breaking up with me because of my age?" My voice quivered.

"No, I'm breaking up with you because I can't have you."

"What are you talking about? I'm right here. I'm yours. I belong to you."

"Bullshit! Sixteen-year-old girls belong with their parents. They giggle in homeroom with their friends and talk about hairstyles and trying to score the high school quarterback. They don't tie themselves down to a guy in a wheelchair."

"Well, maybe you don't know the right girls, then. Because I'd give anything to be tied down to *you*. Wheelchair or not. Walking or not. Just you."

His infuriated eyes softened as he looked up. "Why?"

"I can't describe it. You're smart. And you're kind of an ass, but I love the challenge of making you laugh. I feel safe with you. No one's ever tried to protect me like you did that first night. You're my hero, Flint." My heart swelled from the memories.

Flint barked out a laugh. "And this is exactly our problem. That right there is how sixteen-year-old girls think. They have dreams and fairytales about how life is going to be. I'm no one's white knight. I'm just a bitter guy who has to relearn to walk like a fucking baby. I have no money." He opened his arms and signaled around the room. "This is my brother's. Not mine."

"What are you talking about? This is the first time I've ever seen your brother's house. Do you think for a single second I care about money?"

"Well, you *are* a Mabie," he sneered.

"That is not fair! I'd lie in that dirty patch of grass with you for the rest of my life if that's all you had."

He swallowed hard and looked away.

"What is this fight really about, Flint? Because I have to admit I'm pretty lost right now. You keep changing the topic. I was upset earlier by the whole Eliza thing, but obviously, you have far bigger issues than

I do." I paused and took a step toward him. "Is this because you think I want your brother's money? Flint, I've shoplifted groceries for the majority of my life. I wouldn't even know how to go through the checkout line. I don't want money. I want *you.*"

I took another step to close the distance between us. "Or is this about you being in a wheelchair? Because I have never known you without it. I. Don't. Care. If you never walk again. Your legs are not the part I fell in love with." With one last step, I finally reached him. "Or is this because I'm sixteen? I'm sorry you thought I was older, but I don't see for one second how that changes what we have together. If you had never found out how old I was, this wouldn't even be an issue. You aren't pissed because I'm some immature little girl. You're pissed about a number."

Flint

There were a million different reasons why I was mad, the biggest one being how deceived I felt. Not just about her age, but about the future I hoped we could start making together. I wanted things from Ash.

A *lot* of things.

I might have only been nineteen, but my situation was truly unique. My age did not represent the point I was at in life. I wasn't a normal college kid who went out drinking and partying on Friday nights. Rather, I wanted to stay at home and lie on the couch, reading a book—or, actually, lie in the weeds with *her.*

There was a reason I was fast-tracking college. I wanted to be done with it. I loved school, but the big picture at the end was what motivated me. I didn't want to be a teenager anymore. I wanted my life to start. One where I had a house and a wife of my own. Maybe, in a few years, toss in a kid.

Basically, I wanted exactly what Till had.

A family.

It was sad. I would have figured that walking again would have been my main priority. It wasn't though. Having somewhere I truly belonged was.

For a brief moment, I'd had high hopes that that was with Ash Mabie. Hopes that had all come crashing down with one little number.

Sixteen-year-olds didn't settle down.

I'd always been mature for my age because of the way I had grown up, but who I was at nineteen was completely different than who I had been just three years earlier. I had already been in love with Eliza back then, but girls were still girls, and I had gone through them faster than I had condoms. There were always stupid fights and drama, breakups followed by tears and false confessions of love. Girls were freaking crazy when they were young, but that was part of the game—one I'd played hard for several years in high school.

A game I never wanted to play again.

In my perfect world, Ash and I would have dated for six or so months. Fallen irrevocably in love. I would have asked her to move in. We would have lived together for another six or so months, and then I would have proposed. Six months later, she would have been walking down the aisle in a white dress. And one year later, I would have taken my very first step as I was handed my college diploma while my pregnant wife was beaming with pride from the audience.

That was *my* game.

Two and a half years and I'd be done trying to make a life and ready to start living it.

It had seemed impossible after I'd been shot, and there was that little issue that I hadn't been able to move past Eliza. But the moment Ash had barged her way into my life, it suddenly hadn't seemed so hard anymore.

Sitting around while waiting for Ash to grow up and praying that she didn't up and leave me during those crazy years of adolescent self-discovery was definitely not part of my plan. It actually scared the shit out of me.

I'd already fallen for one unattainable woman.

I couldn't make it two.

Not even for Ash.

"I'm still your girlfriend. Nothing has changed!" she cried, attempting to take my hand.

I snatched it out of her reach. "You're not my girlfriend," I announced. She was so much more—which was exactly why I'd never be able to keep her.

"What?" she whimpered in a broken voice that absolutely gutted me.

I needed her to go.

I needed to be alone.

I *needed* her to crawl into my lap and tell me that she'd never leave and she'd love me forever.

"This thing . . . whatever the hell it was, is bullshit. I just brought you here today to make Eliza jealous." The lie burned my lungs.

With that one childish statement, it became blatantly obvious that I wasn't the mature one of the two of us. But I needed her out of my life before I begged her to stay.

"You're lying. You didn't even know about this party until today."

"Yes, and you've served your purpose. You can leave."

"You are so full of shit, Flint. I'm not leaving until you tell me the truth about what the hell is going on."

"I don't want you!" I yelled, and her whole body tensed at my outburst. Or maybe it had been the words. I couldn't tell. "That's your truth, Ash. You're a criminal whose only future is behind bars. You happen to have a nice set of tits, so I was hoping you'd put out, but children aren't exactly my thing. So now that Eliza has seen us together, I'm gonna need you to get the fuck out of my life."

Her eyes went wide, giving her away, but a fake smile stretched her mouth, attempting to cover the pain I had just inflicted. I hated that fucking smile. It was all wrong and I wanted to erase it from existence. And the sooner she got away from me, the sooner I could do just that.

She didn't budge, and neither did her smile, but her chest heaved as she desperately tried to hold it together.

With shaking hands, she squared her shoulders. "You . . . You told me once that I couldn't go through life trusting everyone. Thanks for proving that." She tried to laugh, but it came out as a sob. "You're wrong about me though. I'm a good person. I'll prove *that*." She pulled her heels off. Tears were streaming down her face when she looked back up. "Since that's what you really think of me, don't worry. You'll never have to see this *criminal* again."

I apologized profusely in my head, but anger and self-preservation never allowed the words to leave my mouth as I watched Ash, barefoot and with her head hung low, walk out my life.

CHAPTER
Sixteen

Flint

I DIDN'T EVEN MAKE IT a full four hours before I regretted all the things I'd said to Ash. I wasn't sure how anything could work between us, but I had dismissed the idea of even trying entirely too quickly. I just needed a few days to logically work it out in my head. Develop a new strategy for slowing things down between us but still keeping her in my life.

I couldn't lose her.

I was told that Slate had driven her home from the party. Quarry texted me late that night to tell me that something was seriously off. Ash had cooked dinner that night for everyone and sat at the table with a huge smile, telling her father that she loved him and how much she had loved getting to know Debbie and Quarry. She had hugged them all then spent the rest of the night in her room.

I gave Q strict instructions to keep an eye on her. I had too much pride to actually call her, and part of me was a little scared too. I was positive she needed some time to cool off.

My phone rang the following morning at seven A.M. I was exhausted, and if it weren't for Quarry's name showing on the caller ID, I would have sent it to voicemail.

"What's up?" I answered, wiping the sleep from my eyes.

"I need you to come get me. The cops are here arresting Ray and Debbie."

I sat straight up in bed. "What!" I yelled, settling the phone between my shoulder and ear so I could transfer into my wheelchair.

"I have no idea what the fuck is going on. About four cars arrived at the house. Cops stormed in and hauled them out. Till's not answering. I need you to come get me."

"Where's Ash?" I rushed out as I headed to my dresser to pull some clothes on.

"I don't know. She's not here, and most of her shit has been cleared out."

"Where the fuck did she go?"

"I don't know! Just come get me!" he responded.

"Okay. I'm on my way." I hung up and started dialing Ash's number.

I put the phone on speaker and tossed it on the bed then struggled to get dressed, pausing every few seconds to hit redial when it went to her voicemail.

"Come on, Ash. Where the fuck are you?" I mumbled, tugged my shoes on.

She still hadn't answered when I left my apartment, and I had to regretfully give up calling in order to find Till.

After the third time calling, he finally answered.

"I'm headed over there now. Cops just left here," he informed me without so much as a greeting.

"What the fucking hell is going on?" I asked, weaving though traffic.

"Good ol' Debbie and Ray were blackmailing the judge to get custody of Q. Federal offense. Cops assume they were going to try to use him to extort money from me."

"Oh, fuck!"

"Anonymous blonde dropped off a box full of evidence last night. Pictures, recorded conversations—you name it, the cops have it. Ray and Debbie are going to *prison*."

I was vaguely aware that Till kept talking because I instinctually held the phone to my ear, but my mind was stuck on two words: anonymous blonde.

I knew.

I *fucking* knew.

"I'm a good person. I'll prove that."

Suddenly, an all-too-familiar pain settled in my gut.

"You'll never have to see this criminal again."

"Oh God," I breathed, dropping the phone into my lap.

"Ash Mabie!" I yelled at the detective, slamming my fist on the table.

"Chill. That's not helping," Till scolded from beside me.

"Neither is sitting here, answering seven million questions, when we could be out looking for her." I turned my head back to the detective. "When *you* could be out looking for her."

"Calm down, son. Her picture and the plates have been distributed to all the officers in the city. We really just need to figure out who this girl is. As far as we can tell, Mabie doesn't even have a daughter."

"Yes, he does! She's not a fucking figment of my imagination."

"And you're sure this is her?" he said, pushing a grainy surveillance photo in front of me.

"Yes," I snarled, shoving it away.

I didn't need to look at that picture again. Once had been more than enough. I didn't need to see her usually bright eyes absent of all emotion or the way her confident shoulders rounded forward in defeat. But what killed me the most was that pain-filled grimace that didn't deserve to be anywhere near her beautiful face. However, even with all of that . . . it was still Ash.

"Get Mabie's ass in here," I barked.

"He's asked for an attorney. It's going to take a little while before we can get in there to find out who she really is."

"I swear to fucking God . . . I just told you who the fuck she is. Now, get up off your ass and find her! She's only sixteen. She can't be running the streets alone." I huffed out a hard breath as my anger momentarily slipped, revealing the true anxiety. "Please. I'm begging you."

I had never exactly been an optimist, so my mind began to spiral out of control with scenarios—none of which brought her back to me.

I dropped my head into my hands as I tried to get myself under control, but I couldn't even catch my fucking breath.

"Can you give us a minute?" Till asked the officer when I began to break down.

"Sure. And you guys can head out whenever. I'll give you a call with any information we receive."

"Thanks," Till replied.

But I kept my head buried in my hands.

With a loud sigh, he squatted down in front of me and grabbed the back of my neck. "All right. Let's pull it together. You're the logical one, remember? I'm the emotional one." He tried to lighten the mood, but it was useless. My mind was trapped in the dark and vicious pits of worry.

"You don't understand. She's . . . different than we are, Till. She's the smartest person I've ever met, but she's so fucking naïve. And now . . . she's out there alone. She'll trust damn near everyone she comes in contact with. If something happens to her—"

He quickly interrupted me. "*Nothing* is going to happen to her."

"Please help me . . . I don't deserve it, but please," I began to plead. I was looking at my brother, but my words were aimed at each and every greater force in the universe that could possibly exist.

"You love her?" he asked, temporarily snapping me out of my downward spiral.

"She's sixteen. At this point, I'm just—"

He interrupted me again. "I didn't ask how old she was. I asked if you love her."

"I've only known her a month," I answered.

Only Till didn't think it was an answer at all. "Again, not what I asked."

Was I in love with Ash Mabie? I could have sat there for a decade and never given an adequate answer.

"I don't honestly know. I think I'm a little fucked up in the whole love department." I shook my head at my own assessment.

"You mean because you think you're in love with Eliza?"

Oh. God.

My eyes jumped to his then, just as quickly, bounced away.

"Uh . . ." I stalled nervously. "I'm not sure what you mean."

"I'm not stupid, Flint. I've always known you had a thing for her."

Fuck. Shit. Damn. Multiplied by infinity.

"I'm sorry." I looked away, embarrassed.

"What? Don't be sorry. I get it. You forget I spent years pining over that woman. It fucking sucks." He laughed. "We had shit for a mom. Then Eliza showed up one day, doing everything for you boys that a real mother should. It's not hard to figure out how those lines got crossed for you. It never really bothered me until you moved out. Then it killed me because there is nothing in this world that I wouldn't sacrifice for you . . . *except her.*"

"I never—" I started, but he kept talking over me.

"I knew you'd eventually get over it when you met someone. So I let it go. Probably for too long."

"I'm over it," I rushed out.

"Why? Eliza not good enough for you anymore?" He quirked a teasing eyebrow.

"Ash—" I started, and I swear to God he interrupted me again.

"But she's only sixteen?"

"Yeah, but—"

Interrupted. Again.

"In a month?" He glared at me, unimpressed.

"I guess—"

Inter-fucking-rupted.

"You love her?" he asked again.

I was so frustrated by his constant disruptions that the word escaped my mouth without a conscious thought. "Yes!"

Yes?

No.

No?

Maybe?

Fuck.

Yes.

A world of hurt faded away with such a simple admission. I didn't understand how, in such a short time, that crazy girl had sauntered in and twisted my life into something unrecognizable—but on the other hand, that was probably exactly how. With Ash, it didn't matter that I was being smothered by gravity. I was more focused on her than I was on how impossible it felt to breathe. Air in my lungs wasn't a priority when she was laughing beside me.

God, I'm such a dumbass.

Till watched me intently. "What was that? I didn't hear you. Can you repeat that for me?"

"I said yes."

"Yes what?"

"Yes. I love her!"

His signature one-sided grin popped up. "Then I'm gonna find her."

"That easy, huh?" I asked sarcastically as the reality of my feelings continued to settle in my chest.

"No, it's gonna be expensive as shit, but I owe you for saving Eliza."

"You don't—"

He cut me off.

Again.

Son of a bitch!

"Yes I do. And if you love her, then she's family. You know how I feel about my family."

God, did I know how Till felt about his family. Just the fact that he was standing there after the hell I'd put him through over the last few months spoke wonders.

"I'm sorry." I paused, waiting for his response.

When it appeared that he had no plans to interrupt me, I opened my mouth to continue my apology, but my asshole brother, who I equally wanted to punch and hug, got there first.

"We'll call Leo. Get a referral for a good PI firm." He smiled again, proving that he was, in fact, fucking with me.

His words were reassuring, and the levity of his attempted joke helped soothe my nerves.

Momentarily.

"What if . . . we can't find her? Or what if . . . we do find her and I can't fix this? I said some really shitty stuff."

"We'll deal with that when we get her somewhere safe. Besides, I have big plans to hold you down and shave that shit off your face. Not a woman in the world will be able to resist you. Well . . . except my wife." He winked and punched me on the shoulder.

He was such a dick. It was easily one of the worst days of my life, and Till was cracking jokes at my expense.

I loved him for it.

"Thanks," I whispered.

"Thank me when she's home." He held my gaze for several beats in an unspoken promise.

A promise he more than kept.

CHAPTER
Seventeen

Flint

FOR THE FIRST WEEK AFTER Ash had disappeared, I spent every waking moment driving around the city looking for her. Even Max and Donna got in on the action, toting a picture of her around and showing it to anyone they could find. I knew she wasn't in the city anymore, but it was either keep busy looking for her or allow my head to implode while sitting at home and worrying about where the hell she was.

Finally, Ray Mabie admitted that Ash was actually his stepdaughter. Her last name was Carson, but she had elected to use Mabie even before her mother had taken her own life. While he'd never formally adopted her, he'd been a father to Ash since she was two. That was pretty much all the information he was willing to provide. With the knowledge that she had turned him in, he was reluctant to offer any possible guesses to her whereabouts. I plotted that man's death enough over those first two weeks to secure myself a place on death row—even without committing the crime.

After two weeks, the car Ash had been driving was found abandoned at a truck stop an hour away. Bile had risen in my throat at the thought of her climbing into a random trucker's cab. She was young and gorgeous—it wasn't like she would've had a difficult time convincing some perverted scum to drive her out of town. Visions of her being taken advantage of led me to destroy my apartment until my upstairs neighbor called the cops. Not convinced that the paralyzed maniac shredding books and splintering furniture was mentally sound, they refused to leave me alone until Till showed up.

Unfortunately, he brought Eliza with him. The instant she walked into her old apartment, she burst into tears then begged me to move back into their house. But I couldn't leave that place. I might have moved into that shithole because of the memories of Eliza, but I refused to leave because of the memories of *Ash.*

My life became a perpetual cycle of ups and downs. The day they found Ash's car was really low for me. I was terrified something had happened to her. Then, two weeks later, I experienced one of the highest highs when surveillance video of her shoplifting from a convenience store turned up.

She wasn't home, but she was still okay.

Still smiling.

Still laughing.

Still dreaming.

The private investigators Till had hired had more than proved to be good at their jobs, but Ash had proved to be better. It seemed they were always one step behind her. Luckily, she hadn't gone far. Every time they managed to track her down, she was always within a two-hour radius of the city.

It gave me hope that she had plans to come back.

It also made me a little neurotic, because every single time I left my apartment, I unconsciously searched for her face. Every blonde I passed and every laugh I heard was always her.

It was never her.

I slept on that patch of weeds outside my apartment more times than I cared to admit over those first four weeks. She loved those damn weeds.

I just loved her.

I knew the investigators were costing Till a fortune. Though he never acknowledged that, nor did he seem to care—even as the weeks turned into months. Each time they popped up with some sort of information on the elusive Ash Mabie made them worth every penny.

Suddenly, at the one-year mark, Ash disappeared all over again.

We received a final video of her stealing clothes from a department store, narrowly escaping security. After that, she seemed to completely fall off the radar. I was devastated. Then I got pissed. *Really fucking pissed.* Sure, I'd said some mean shit to her, but no worse than the crap most people spouted in a fight. And there I was, using my brother's money to stalk my ex-girlfriend.

I went to Till around the two-year mark, begging him to call the search off. He smiled and nodded, agreeing with me. He'd said all the right things, validating my feelings. Then, one month later, I received the usual "no news" e-mail update from the investigating firm. It infuriated me that he hadn't stopped the search. We got into a huge fight that night, in which numerous punches were thrown, and it ultimately ended with us rolling around on the floor while Quarry acted as ref. Coincidentally, it was also the loudest I had laughed since Ash had taken off.

A lot of things happened over those years spent searching for Ash.

I couldn't find *her,* but the most amazing thing happened: I found my fight for life again.

In desperate need of distraction, I threw myself into the gym and physical therapy. If and when I saw her again, I wanted to do it standing so I could tell her to fuck off eye to eye.

Or strip her naked and lose myself inside her.

Or send her packing without so much as a backward glance.

Or lock her in my bedroom so she could never leave again.

Or walk away, showing her exactly what she had been missing out on.

Or lie in that patch of weeds while listening to her laugh for all of eternity.

Like I said: *lots* of ups and downs.

I also got really serious with school, graduating from college in just two and a half years.

I added my diploma to the list of things I could throw in her face, proving how well I had done without her.

Or that I could use to provide for her forever.

One of the two.

Definitely one of the two.

But regardless of the reason, positive or negative, Ash was always my motivation.

Moving on was hard, but the world kept spinning and time never stopped.

I got older; I assumed she did too.

I got stronger; I prayed she didn't need to.

I built a life; I hoped she did too.

I never stopped wishing she would come back; I didn't even care if she wanted me to.

Then, on a cool Friday morning, the world stopped spinning.

And time came to a screeching halt—at least, for me.

Three years, four months, one week, and five days after Ash Mabie had taken off, I brought her home.

"Wake up, sunshine," Till said, sauntering into my room, kicking the foot of my bed.

"Jesus Christ, I knew I shouldn't have given you a key," I grumbled, clearing the sleep from my eyes.

"Like you had a choice. I made the down payment on this baby."

"It was a gift, and I said I was gonna pay you back, asshole."

He lifted a silver boxing glove keychain in the air and jingled it at me. "Yeah, but until then . . . I get full access."

"Why are you here"—I rolled over to look at the clock—"at six A.M.?"

"Well, I would have been here at three, but Eliza made me wait. She also made me feed and change little Slate since I was already awake. That took forever. That boy has entirely too much of Quarry's attitude in him."

"Did he flip you off and tell you to fuck off like this?" I asked, giving him the finger as I sat up, only mildly amused by the conversation.

"He might as well have. The kid's only four months old, but I swear to God he said 'shit' the other day."

I let out a loud chuckle, shaking my head. "Seriously, why are you here?"

"Oh, right. You need to get dressed. We're going on a road trip."

"If this has anything to do with scouting another fighter, it can wait until I clock in at nine." I rested my elbows on my knees, cradling my head and wishing I could go back to bed. I still had two hours before my alarm clock went off; I was in no mood to go on any impromptu road trips.

He didn't say anything for several seconds until I glanced up to find him watching me warily.

"What?" I growled.

He took a giant step back, well out of my reach, before he said the words I'd both dreaded and dreamed about for over three years.

"We found her."

My stomach dropped.

My heart stopped.

Flames shot through my veins only to be iced by the nerves that immediately collided against them.

"What?" I repeated on a whisper.

"She's about ninety miles away. Someone at Willing Hearts homeless shelter started digging around on Victoria Mabie. It pinged on our end, and when the guys got there, they found out she's been living there for over a year."

Chills spread over my body as rage brewed in my soul. I blankly held Till's eyes while anger, relief, and hope all warred inside me.

He pulled his phone from his back pocket and passed it to me. Sure enough, there was a picture of Ash smiling, huddled between two elderly women at what looked like some sort of office Christmas party.

Same hair.

Same eyes.

Same face.

Completely wrong smile.

Before Till could even object, I hurled his phone as hard as I could, shattering it and denting the wall.

"Well, okay, then. We're gonna need to make another stop now."

"Fuck her," I said, pushing to my feet and grabbing my forearm crutches, which were leaning against my nightstand.

"Flint—"

"Get out," I snapped, limping my way to the bathroom.

"Flint, don't do this."

Oh, I'm doing it. "I need to get dressed. Have the coffee ready," I snapped.

Till loudly clapped his hands. "Now *that's* what I'm talking about."

Less than two hours later, Till and I arrived at Willing Hearts. It wasn't the hellhole I had expected, but it still infuriated me that she'd lived there—just within my reach—for so long.

"We're here to see Judy Jenkins. My name's Till Page. I believe she's expecting us," Till said into the small intercom at the front door.

"Oh hi, honey. Come on in," the friendly voice replied as the door buzzed, allowing us entry.

The smiling face of a gray-haired woman in her late sixties greeted us.

"Hi, I'm Judy. So nice to meet you." She extended a hand toward Till.

"I appreciate you seeing us today. This is my brother, Flint."

Her eyes flashed to mine, growing wide before filling with tears. "Of course it is." She grabbed her heart and continued to watch me with gooey eyes usually reserved for twelve-year-old girls, not elderly women.

"Where is she?" I barked, causing Judy's warm smile to fall.

Till kicked the foot of my crutch out from under me, sending me stumbling forward. Just before I crashed to the ground, he grabbed my arm and stepped in front of me.

"Whoa, easy there," he said. Then he snarled into my ear, "Less abusive ex-boyfriend, more long-lost love."

I gave him the side eye as I got my crutches positioned on my forearms again. Taking a deep breath, I pasted on a smile I was positive looked no more authentic than it felt.

"So, where's Ash?" Till asked when he turned back around.

Judy was still eyeing me as she answered his question. "Tori . . . I mean Ash is out on a breakfast run. Every morning, she delivers food to the people we can't take on at night. There's just so many of them, and our space is really limited."

For a brief second, my smile turned genuine.

Yeah, that sounds like Ash.

"She'll be back in about an hour. Listen, I did a lot of research on you two before I agreed to this. Leo James spoke very highly of both of you. I even had Kathy, our volunteer accountant, look you up on the computer. I'm sure you two are nice young men." Her eyes flashed to mine. "But if she doesn't want to see you, I will have you escorted out." She lifted her eyebrows and pointedly glanced over her shoulder to an overweight, elderly security guard sitting at a desk in the corner.

Till began to quietly chuckle while nodding. "We completely understand."

"Good. Now that we're clear on that"—she took a deep breath before rushing out—"I'm really happy there are people who care about her. She's such a sweet girl. We didn't realize until recently how young she was. She was a minor when we first took her in, and we had absolutely no idea. She told us she was nineteen, and Lord knows she looked older than that, so we didn't even question it when she asked if she could volunteer." She motioned for us to follow her down the hall. "It wasn't until one of our regulars found her sleeping on the streets that we found out that she was homeless too."

My whole body stiffened as I froze in the middle of the hallway.

She was sleeping on the streets.

I might not have grown up in the lap of luxury, but I'd always at least had a roof over my head. I chewed on my bottom lip as I became lost in the visions of Ash at sixteen, resting her head on the cold concrete. My heart began to race, and guilt overwhelmed me.

I should have been there for her.

I wasn't.

I'd sent her packing into that world.

Alone.

"Hey," Till said, stepping in front of me, reading my anxiety. "Never again. We're here. That life is over for her."

I nodded absently, but I couldn't escape the thoughts.

"Much better," Judy whispered before releasing a sigh.

Till urged me forward with a squeeze on my shoulder. My legs might have followed, but my mind was stuck reeling in the middle of that hall.

Judy continued. "We didn't have much to offer her, but she was so good with everyone who walked through the doors that we knew we needed to keep her." She stopped at a door. "So we made her a room, and Tori . . . erm, Ash moved in."

She pushed the door open to what could only be described as a small closet. The walls were bare, and the floor was covered in old, faded linoleum. There was a small pile of clothes in the corner situated beside a worn-out pair of neon-green Converse. A cot and a nightstand were wedged into the tiny space.

And on that nightstand sat *my book.*

I roughly pushed past both of them and scooped it up. I could tell by the tear on the cover that it was, in fact, my copy, but I continued to search for further proof just to be sure. As I started to flip through the pages, Dave Egger's heartbreaking words were barely visible. Each and every page was filled with her handwriting. It started in the margins then eventually ran between his words as if his typed letters were nothing more than lines for her to write above. Then there was the highlighting. Random letters were highlighted in green, pink, and blue. Never a whole word, just a random 'a' here then an 'n' a few lines down. Sometimes, there were multiple colors in each word. Then, other times, one of the colors would disappear completely for several pages.

Even as strange as it was, the biggest smile I had ever felt formed on my mouth—even bigger than any she had ever put there in the past.

I was so fucking pissed at her. So angry that she'd left and never given me a chance to apologize. Frustrated that it had taken me so long to find her. But deep down, most of that was because I'd been terrified that, even if I'd found her, I'd never truly get her back.

As I looked down at *my book,* which she had held on to for all of those years, even going so far as to turn it into a some sort of diary, I realized that Ash had never let go of me, either.

Hope filled my chest.

And time started all over again.

I shoved the book into the waistband at the back of my jeans.

"Pack her shit. I'm taking her home." I turned around to find Till sporting a one-sided grin, and much to my surprise, so was Judy.

CHAPTER
Eighteen

Ash

"HEY, JUDY," I SAID, DROPPING my basket on the front desk. "Dude, I'm exhausted. I had to hike halfway across the city to find Betty. How that old woman walks so far, I'll never understand. I had to stop and take a break halfway. I was lucky I took water this morning. Well, sort of lucky. That just turned into me having to pee every two blocks." I giggled. "I gave her double breakfast just in case I couldn't make it back out there tomorrow."

"Oh good, honey. That's just great." She reached out and rubbed my arm.

I quickly moved away. "So, anyway. I'm gonna go take a shower and get started on lunch."

"Um, well. Dear, there's a new guest in the conference room. Would you mind giving him a warm welcome?" She smiled tightly.

"Cranky old asshole?" I asked with a laugh.

We had a lot of those, and for some magical reason, I was always in charge of welcoming them. It worked though; they really weren't rude with me. People were my forte. Well, that and the Dewey Decimal system.

She didn't reply as I backed toward the door. I straightened my shirt and my name tag before smoothing my hair down.

"Where the fuck have you been?" a man's voice growled as soon as I entered the conference room.

My eyes flashed to his for only a single second before I recognized them. The door had barely clicked behind me, but I already wanted nothing more than to bolt. My heart raced, and my mouth dried.

I have to get out of here.

"Um . . ." I stalled, giving myself time to formulate a plan.

"Sit. Down," he ordered, pushing out the chair next to him, but there was no way I was getting that close.

"I'm good," I said, taking a step backwards toward the door.

"Don't even think about it," he snapped. "I swear to God, if you so much as open that door . . ." His words might have trailed off, but the threat had been clearly stated.

I swallowed hard and slowly walked to the chair farthest away from him, perching on the very edge—waiting for the right moment to escape.

He looked down at the name badge around my neck and quirked an eyebrow.

"Victoria?"

"You can call me Tori if it's easier." I tried to fake a smile, but it only seemed to infuriate him.

He took several calming breaths, which did nothing to dampen the blaze brewing in his angry eyes. "I've been looking for you, *Ash*." He snarled my name.

"Oh, yeah? Well, mystery solved. Here I am." I pushed back to my feet, but I was halted when his fist pounded against the table. My whole body flinched from the surprise.

When the room fell silent, I slowly looked back up to find him staring at me with a murderous glare. Even while he was sitting down, I could tell he was huge, and as he held my gaze, the tense muscles in his neck and shoulders strained against the cotton of his grey henley. He blinked at me for several seconds before finding his voice again.

"You live in a homeless shelter," he stated definitively, as if the words told a story all of their own.

And maybe they did.

"I *work* at a homeless shelter," I quickly corrected.

Only he corrected me just as fast. "In exchange for a permanent place to live . . . in. A. Homeless. Shelter." He enunciated every single syllable.

I looked away, because it was the truth.

A truth I hated.

But the God's honest truth nonetheless.

Tears welled in my eyes, and I battled to keep them at bay.

My life was hard, but his being there made it infinitely harder. If I could just escape that room, I could disappear again. It wasn't ideal, but neither was his showing up.

"I want you to leave," I lied with all the false courage I could muster.

"I can't do that. You stole something of *mine.*"

"Look, I don't have your book anymore."

A knowing smirk lifted one side of his mouth. "Liar," he whispered, reaching into the chair beside him, revealing the tattered book, and unceremoniously dropping it on the table.

My eyes widened, and without a conscious thought, I dove across the table after it.

That was *mine.* Not even he could have it.

Just as quickly as the book had appeared, he snatched it away and grabbed my wrist.

I slid off the table and tried to pull my arm from his grasp. It was a worthless attempt though, because even if he had suddenly released me, his blue eyes held me frozen in place.

"Three fucking years," he seethed.

"I had to," I squeaked out as the tears streamed down my cheeks.

"Three. Fucking. Years, Ash. You took something that belonged to me." He let go of my arm and pushed to his feet.

My mouth fell open and a loud gasp escaped as he took two *impossible* steps forward.

Pinning me against the wall with his hard body, he lifted a hand to my throat and glided it up until his thumb stroked over my bottom lip. Using my chin, he turned my head and dragged his nose up my neck, stopping at my ear.

After sucking in a deep breath, he released it on a gravelly demand. "And I want *her* back."

My breath hitched.

I'd waited three years to hear those words.

If only I could trust them.

"Flint, please."

"Don't you dare 'please' me. I have spent years of my life looking for you." He leaned away to catch my eyes, but I was looking anywhere but at him.

Tears rolled down my cheeks, and in an unexpected show of gentleness, he used the pads of his thumbs to dry them.

"Why are you here?" I whined, dropping my chin to my chest.

He scoffed at my question. "To take you home."

My head snapped up, and the tears slowed. "I am home."

Then the most amazing thing happened; the angry man standing in front of me melted away. His entire face softened, and his voice lowered. "Not anymore. Your home is with me now."

He wasn't wrong. It always had been.

I had been back to Flint's apartment no less than a thousand times over the years—never physically, but always in my dreams. And not the ones I made up, either.

A week after I'd left, as I'd slept in my car at a truck stop, I'd had my very first dream. It was the most amazing thing I had ever experienced.

Until I'd woken up.

Then it had been *agonizing*.

But each night as I'd laid my head on whatever makeshift pillow I'd had, those dreams kept coming—louder, stronger, and more painful every time. They were never the same, but they always started in his apartment and ended with him *walking* away.

Despite all the years I had wished for those late-night fairytales, I would have given anything to get rid of them. For those hours of slumber, Flint and I were perfect. We had a life together. One where he was walking and I was laughing. One where he touched me every opportunity he got and I snuggled into his chest just for fun.

One where we were in love.

Then, when I would open my eyes, those dreams made the empty reality of my life that much harder. Which was why his being in that conference room scared me to death. I'd survived losing him once; I wasn't sure I could do it again. He might have been searching for three years, but I had been running and carrying the staggering weight of my memories of him with every step. I couldn't make any more memories with him. Not even that one, where his hard body touched mine and his every exhale breezed across my skin. I couldn't bear to add it to my already overflowing burden.

No matter how deeply I enjoyed it.

"Please leave," I squeaked out, ducking under his arm.

He pushed off the wall and staggered back two steps, roughly sitting as if he couldn't possibly have stood there any longer. *Interesting.* But I didn't have time to focus on it right then; that would have to wait until I lay in bed after he'd left and cried for days.

"Ash, stop. Just hear me out."

"Listen, I don't know what you expected when you came here today, but I'm not the same girl you remember. I have a life, Flint. Sure, we had fun for, like, a month or so a while back, but I've really moved on. I have a boyfriend. Things are just starting to get serious."

He flinched, but I continued.

"Yes. I live in a homeless shelter, but I love it here. The people are great, and I feel like I'm really making a difference." I smiled, and it was real—not because I was telling the truth, but rather because it was aimed at *him.*

The hopeful expression in his eyes when he glanced down at my smile barely covered the pain my lies had carved on his face.

His beautiful, beautiful face.

Flint was even more gorgeous than I remembered. His thin frame was covered with layers upon layers of muscles I could have touched for hours without feeling them all. Gone was that crazy wannabe beard. His strong jaw was covered with a five-o'clock shadow I was dying to feel brushed over my skin while his mouth trailed kisses over my breasts. I envisioned thrusting my hands into his jet-black hair, which was so neatly styled that James Dean would have been jealous.

Not everything was different though. Those piercing, blue eyes were exactly the same as I'd envisioned every single time I had ever touched myself.

He wasn't a nineteen-year-old boy anymore.

He was Flint Page, the man.

And I was still Ash Mabie, the criminal who wasn't good enough for him.

"I have to go," I whispered and then bolted for the door.

"Stop running from me," he growled.

"I can't do this." I pushed down on the handle only for it to remain in place.

What the hell?

I jiggled it again but achieved the same result.

"Judy!" I yelled, knocking on the door. "Judy!"

Her muffled voice spoke from the other side of the wood. "You're lying to him. You don't have a boyfriend."

"Shut up, Judy! Open the door." I looked over my shoulder to find Flint donning a pair of black crutches that wrapped around his forearms. "Open the door!"

I continued to fight with the worthless handle, and Judy continued to spill all of my secrets.

"I read that book you are always writing in. You're not happy here and you do love that boy. Stop lying to him and hear him out."

"Shut up!" I screamed as Flint closed in on me.

"Show him the tattoo," she added loudly enough for half the state to hear.

Oh, I was killing Judy fucking Jenkins. She might have been my best friend for the previous year and a half, but her life was over. She was old. It would be okay.

"I swear to God, when I get out of this room, you better run."

She giggled.

Then I felt him.

His chest brushed against my back as I flattened myself against the door. I moved as far out of his reach as possible. Unfortunately, it was only about an inch, and really unfortunately, he followed me forward, crushing me with his hard body.

That stubble I so desperately wanted to feel scrubbed up my neck, and his smile was so wide that I could feel it on his lips as he murmured, "Yeah, Ash. Tell me about the tattoo."

"Fuck you," I snapped when a witty retort failed me.

"Soon enough," he purred, and my entire body heard his promise. Instinctually, my back arched, pressing my ass into his hips.

Foiled by my own body!

It was at that point that I believed I must have had a small sei-zure—or perhaps a stroke? Because there were a full three seconds that I had absolutely no recollection of. One second, I felt Flint shift to my side. Then the next thing I knew, I was flat on my back on the ground with Flint on top of me.

He must have swept my legs with his crutch and caught us both on an arm before we crashed into the tile. However, with my luck, it could have been that my brain had suddenly figured out the miracle of teleportation and wasted it on moving me to the nearest horizontal surface. It didn't really matter either way though, because ultimately, I was on the *ground.*

With Flint.

On top of me.

"Tell me about the tattoo," he repeated.

His mouth was entirely too close to mine . . . But really, it was only entirely too close without actually touching mine. Now that would have been just the right amount of close.

"It's nothing. You've already seen it," I breathed, trying to shake off the desire to throw consequences to the wind and take his mouth in any and every way he was willing to offer it.

"Show. Me," he ordered.

"It's just a rock. It's silly. I was sleeping with a guy who owns a tattoo shop—"

"She's lying!" Judy's voice once again entered our conversation. "He's a volunteer. She wasn't sleeping with him."

"God damn it! Shut up, Judy!"

Flint chuckled as I dropped my head back against the tile floor and stared up at the ceiling.

This was not going as I'd planned. Although there'd never really been a plan for when Flint showed back up into my life. It was the one thing I'd never allowed myself to even consider.

The whole thing with Flint had been an adolescent, childish fling I'd had for one month when I was sixteen. He'd been completely right all of those years ago—I couldn't love him. I was just young and stu-pid.

Unfortunately, I must have still been young and stupid, because I was still in love with Flint Page.

Defeated, I scooted over a few inches and lifted the hem of my shirt. Unwilling to see his reaction, I stared at the ceiling as he traced his callused hand up my side to my dream catcher tattoo.

He blew out a hard breath then asked, "When?" He cleared his throat. "When did you get this?"

I didn't even have it in me to lie anymore. "About six months ago."

That time, the breath was sharply drawn into his lungs. "Look at me," he urged gently.

I shook my head while biting my bottom lip.

"I'm gonna kiss you. This is your only warning."

"Flint," I objected to the ceiling, but even to my ears, it came out as a plea.

Closing my eyes, I darted my out my tongue to moisten my lips and waited for his mouth to find mine.

However, that's not what it found at all.

CHAPTER
Nineteen

Flint

I PLACED AN OPENMOUTHED KISS to her side just below her tattoo, sealing a promise I was wholeheartedly making to both of us.

That tattoo.

That fucking tattoo.

Ash had made a few additions to her dream catcher since the last time I'd seen it. Hanging from the bottom were two black feathers. Fitting and simple enough. However, in between them was what looked like a simple rock at first glance, but the grey teardrop piece of flint wasn't formed with lines. The tiny letters of my name were painstakingly repeated over and over to create and fill the entire design. Even the shading used to produce the curves and contours that gave it dimension were done within those tiny letters. The stone wasn't any larger than the palm of her small hand, but the amount of detail was unreal.

Ash had marked herself as mine even when I hadn't been there to do it myself.

I dragged my tongue across her flat stomach, sending chills over her pale skin.

She moaned as I pushed her shirt up to just under her breasts. I had a lot to say to her, but I also had an insatiable need to feel every inch of her that I had been missing.

I'd have to multitask.

"You don't know me anymore." I trailed kisses down to the waistband of her jeans and teased my fingers just underneath. "But we'll fix that. We'll start over."

"I can't," she breathed, lifting her hips, encouraging me further.

"I'm taking you home, Ash. We're giving this thing a real try."

"I can't try." She suddenly sat up, but I was nowhere near done yet.

I had just gotten my first taste of Ash in three years; there was going to be an all-out feast before she was going anywhere. Pushing up on my arm, I used the other to grab the back of her neck and drag her down to my mouth. She stiffened in surprise, but it was short-lived. The moment my tongue swept hers, Ash proved that she was in the mood for a feast of her own.

One of her hands flew to my hair, tugging roughly in a needy attempt to take the kiss impossibly deeper as she reclined again. She was suddenly frantic, but even as her fingers made their way under the edge of my shirt, gliding up and down my back, she mumbled, "I can't."

"I wasn't giving you the choice," I replied, pulling away from her mouth long enough to peel the shirt over her head—an action she quickly returned, tearing mine off as well.

"I can't be with you again." She rolled over, pressing me down on the cold tile and swinging a leg over my hips.

"Well, that's too bad, because it's happening." I reached up to unsnap her bra while she raked her teeth over my neck. "Fuck," I hissed when her core settled against my straining cock.

"You don't understand," she said, letting her bra fall down her arms. "I can't try. Not with you."

"Then don't try. But you're still coming home with me," I told her chest, unable to drag my eyes away.

Her long hair flowed over one of her shoulders, and I brushed it away. Nothing should have obstructed that view. Her creamy, pale breasts were much fuller than I remembered, and those small, pink nipples were screaming my name, pleading for me to take them in my mouth.

A plea I could more than oblige.

Sitting up, I grazed my teeth over the flesh before repeating the process on the other breast. She moaned, dropping her chin to her chest to watch as I laved in circles. Her fingers once again threaded into my hair as she rocked against my cock. Dropping a hand to her ass, I guided her into an agonizing rhythm that had us both whispering reverent curses.

Why in God's name are there two pairs of jeans between us?

"Fuck," I groaned.

As I reached down to her button in order to remedy the situation, Judy's voice came from the other side of the door.

"Um, Tori, I'm not sure what you're doing, but please be mindful that I eat my lunch in that room."

Then Till said, "Would you leave them alone? Get away from the door."

I dropped my head to her chest, furious that I finally had her and we were being interrupted. And even more frustrated that we were on the cold floor of a homeless shelter.

Just as I started to let out an angry curse, a laugh bubbled from Ash's throat.

It was real.

And beautiful.

And so much better than I remembered.

It was everything.

But really, it was just *her.*

"I need to get you home and into my bed." I laughed, folding my arms around her and tugging her down on top of me. Her naked breasts pressed against me as she continued to laugh in my ear.

A wave of nostalgia crashed over me, only soothed by the promise of a future where Ash would laugh every day. A future I would give her and, in turn, selfishly keep for myself.

Her laugh slowly faded away as she picked our shirts up before dropping mine on my chest.

"Soooo . . ." she drawled awkwardly.

"Soooo . . ." I mimicked, tugging my shirt on.

"It was really good seeing you again," she said dismissively.

She really was a funny girl, because if she thought for one second after that little sample of us together that I was letting her go, she was kidding herself. She was coming home with me. Of that I was sure.

"Yeah. You too." I chuckled, using one of my crutches to climb back to my feet. "So Till packed your stuff. I'll give you a few minutes to say goodbye."

She twisted her mouth and smarted off. "Umm . . . okay. Goodbye, Flint."

I ignored her. "Let me know when you're ready to leave."

"I'm not leaving. *You* are leaving."

"Right. So, yeah . . . Not happening. Here's how this is going to go down. Tonight, we're finishing what you just started."

"I didn't start that!"

I gave her a knowing smirk. "You got my name tattooed on your body."

"No. I got a piece of flint tattooed on my body." She crossed her arms over her chest in a show of attitude that had me growing hard all over again.

I stalked toward her, fully expecting her to back away, but she held her ground. She just didn't understand that it was my ground she was standing on.

I brushed her hair off her neck, carefully dragging the tips of my fingers over her skin. "Oh, I'm gonna give you more than just a piece of Flint, Ash. In my bed. Tonight. I'm gonna show every inch of that body how much I've missed you. Then, when we wake up in the morning, I'm going to fuck you until I'm done being mad at you. Then I'm taking you on a date, and *then* we are figuring out the getting-back-together part." I winked.

Her mouth gaped open. "I should really take off right now," she whispered, but she swayed toward me, dropping her head to my chest.

"You're leaving with me."

"You don't understand," she whined.

"So you keep saying." I kissed the top of her head. "Just give me a few days. Let me apologize and explain the things I said to you. If you want nothing to do with me, I'll bring you back."

"I don't know." She wrapped her arms around my waist.

"Well, I do. I can make this right, Ash. You just have to trust me."

"I, um . . ."

"Just try." I leaned away and looked down into her innocent, blue eyes. "And stop stealing my fucking wallet."

Her arms fell away, and she let out an exaggerated huff. "Fine. You have two days." She backed up, slapping the wallet against my chest. "But I'm still calling you Wheels. I don't care if you are walking."

"I can live with that." I laughed.

She was back.

And suddenly, so was I.

CHAPTER
Twenty

Ash

I COULDN'T DECIDE IF LEAVING with Flint was the best or worst decision I had ever made. On one hand, I couldn't deny the fact that I wanted him on practically every level. On the other, I didn't trust him to feel the same way. And I had so little in life that even trust wasn't something I could afford to give away. But back on that first hand, I wanted him so much that I could give him two days then torture myself with the memories for years to come. I'd figure out a way to survive.

After voicing my displeasure that he'd replaced the party bus with a charcoal-grey SUV, we headed toward his apartment. Or, according to Flint, his bed. I secretly cried for the first thirty minutes for reasons that were lost even to me. I just knew I had never been more scared of anything in my life—and that was saying a lot. Eventually, I fell asleep, only to wake up when we dropped Till off at On The Ropes.

"You guys coming to Q's fight tomorrow night, right? We'll all go out to dinner afterwards, Doodle's treat. She sold a painting yesterday." Till smiled, poking his head in Flint's window. "It was good to see you, Ash. Take care of this asshole." He slapped Flint on the back of the head then jumped away before Flint could retaliate.

"Jackass," Flint mumbled, smoothing the back of his hair down. "We'll be there," he replied, rolling his window up.

Instead of walking away, Till started laughing and lifted his hands to continue the conversation in sign language.

"Jesus Christ." Flint shook his head, quickly backing out of the parking lot.

"What'd he say?" I asked.

"Nothing," he rushed out, his eyes nervously flashing to mine.

I would have questioned him further, but as he stared out the windshield, a grin tipped the side of his mouth.

I'd missed him so much.

Unable to restrain myself, I reached across the center console and rested my hand on his thigh. He never acknowledged the subtle gesture, but his simple grin spread across his face, transforming it into a full-blown smile. It was probably awkward as hell that I was staring at him, but I couldn't tear my eyes away. It was so surreal that he was sitting next to me. And it was so amazing that my fears began to melt away. Maybe I didn't have to trust him. I could just steel myself for the worst and embrace every second of the good I got with him.

Maybe I never had to leave at all.

That was until Flint turned into a quaint subdivision I didn't recognize. Then I realized I couldn't even stay for the originally promised two days.

Rows of new houses lined the streets. Flawlessly manicured lawns butted up against the unmarred sidewalks, illuminated by old-timey streetlights, while shiny, new minivans and SUVs filled the driveways.

"Um . . . where . . . where are we?" I stuttered, taking it all in.

"Home," he answered. The garage door lifted as he turned into the driveway of a small, two-story, brick house complete with blue shutters.

"Whose house is this?" I asked as I looked around the perfectly organized garage.

"Mine."

"Where . . . I mean . . . you moved?"

"Yeah, a few months ago. Till gave me the down payment as a graduation gift, but I'm paying him back." He smiled proudly, but my gut wrenched.

"Graduation?"

"Yeah. I finished school. I'm running the business side of On The

Ropes for Till and Slate right now, but I'm trying to become a sports agent. I just recruited a fighter who's about to go pro. He moved to the gym and agreed to let me represent him. There is a lot of money to be made if you get the right clients."

"Oh God," I breathed.

"What?"

"Oh God." Panic began to ricochet in my chest.

"What?" he repeated, reaching out to grab my hand.

"I can't do this. I'm sorry." I scrambled out of his car then darted from his garage.

Once my feet hit the sidewalk, I realized that things were even worse than I'd thought. He had flowerbeds, with bushes that were trimmed to . . . well, perfection.

"Shit," I cursed as I saw the basketball hoop in the driveway across the street.

"Ash!" Flint called as he followed me out.

I turned back to look at him and caught sight of the scariest thing I had ever seen in all of my nineteen years.

There was a wreath.

On his door.

And it wasn't even Christmas.

"I have to get out of here," I told myself.

"What the hell is going on?" he asked, suddenly stepping in front of me.

"I can't," was all I said before taking off at a sprint.

"Ash!" he yelled, but I didn't bother to stop. I couldn't even if I'd wanted.

And God, did I want to.

I ran until my legs wouldn't carry me any farther, which ended up being approximately two blocks. (I noted that track and field was decidedly *not* my forte.) Out of breath, I sat on the concrete sidewalk, not daring to touch the plush grass, then hugged my knees to my chest.

"This was such a bad idea." I tucked my head low, praying that I could disappear.

It didn't take but a minute or two before I saw the headlights of his car as they rounded the corner. I heard the creak of his car door open before he grumbled, "I am sick and fucking tired of chasing you."

"Can you please take me home now?" I told my knees.

He let out a frustrated sigh. "Jesus Christ, what is going on?"

"I have to leave. Like, now. I need to go home."

"Fuck, Ash. Is that what you really want?"

"Yes," I lied. Swallowing hard to mask the emotion, I looked up into what I fully expected to be his angry eyes. Only they weren't at all; they were soft and sincere. And it made my decision hurt that much more.

"All right." He loudly exhaled. "Get in the car."

"Thank you." My heart began to slow in relief even as dread filled my stomach.

I slid into the passenger's seat, and Flint grudgingly climbed behind the wheel.

"I'm so sorry," I whispered, dropping my head back against the headrest and closing my eyes as he started to drive off.

"Yeah. Me too," he mumbled, breaking my already shattered heart.

I kept my eyes closed as I felt him do a U-turn, beginning our journey back to Willing Hearts.

Back to my home.

Or so I'd thought.

"You are fucking insane if you think I'm taking you back to a homeless shelter," he boomed as the car bumped over the curb of his driveway.

My eyes flew open as he once again drove into his garage. Grabbing my wrist, he restrained me while waiting for the door to seal us in.

"You liar!" I screeched.

"No, I didn't lie at all. I already told you this was your home now," he said smugly.

I wanted to slap that stupid look off his face. Or kiss it. I wasn't sure which.

"Flint, you can't tell someone where to live."

He lifted his eyebrows and leaned in closer before whispering, "Watch me."

Yep, I definitely wanted to slap him.

And maybe still kiss him a little.

"I think you're the insane one." I snatched my arm away and swung the car door open. Frantically, I tried to figure out how to open his garage as he lumbered out of the car.

"You can try to run, and I may not be able to chase you physically, but we need to be clear on one thing, Ash. I will *not* let you go again."

I froze.

"You belong with me. And I will do whatever I have to do in order to keep you. I fucked up the first time. I won't do it again. You can walk out that door, but know that I will find you. I will chase you for the rest of my life if that is what it takes to be with you."

I'd waited my entire life to hear someone say those words to me.

Anyone to say those words to me.

My mom. My dad. Hell, I would have even been okay if Quarry had said them when he was fourteen.

But Flint saying them was almost too much.

Slowly, I turned to face him. I had no idea how to respond, but if he was going to be honest, so would I.

"I can't stay in this perfect house in this perfect neighborhood where I'm the dirtiest thing in it." I shrugged and offered him a tight smile that served no purpose because I knew it was transparent.

"Jesus." He immediately made his way over to me. Supporting himself on one hand, he dropped a crutch to the ground and folded an arm around my waist, pulling me against his chest. "Don't say shit like that."

"I'm sorry. I just wasn't expecting you to live here. I thought we were gonna go back to your old apartment, where dirt lined the streets and people like me lived upstairs."

"Stop." He kissed the top of my head. "What did I do to you?" he asked rhetorically.

I answered anyway. "Nothing. You didn't do anything to me, Flint."

"And that's exactly the problem."

I didn't understand his response, but I didn't have time to harp on it.

"I want to show you something. Can you promise not to run?"

I couldn't promise that at all. Running was what I did. Still, I said, "Yeah. Okay." I wiped away the single tear that had somehow managed to escape. Attempting to hide my eyes, I bent over to pick up his crutch. As I straightened, offering it to him, he took my mouth instead.

Tipping my head back, he whispered a dozen apologies against my lips, sealing each one with a gentle kiss. His mouth never opened the way I wanted it to, nor did his tongue find mine. To be honest, I wasn't positive what he was apologizing for, but I accepted them all the same.

How could I not?

They were *his*.

After a final chaste kiss, he led me out to the stone patio of his small backyard. Looking down at the precisely manicured grass and elegant, wooden privacy fence, I felt no better.

He must have followed my eyes, because he whispered, "The grass was like this when I bought the place. I put the fence up though. The neighbors are nosy as hell."

"Right." I swallowed hard.

He nodded toward the small fenced-off area on the side of his house. "This way."

"Oh my God," I gasped, covering my mouth. "It's beautiful."

He barked out a laugh. "I'm not sure about that."

He was right—it was more than beautiful.

Thick weeds covered the ground of the eight-by-eight area. I could tell they weren't wild or unkempt because they had been trimmed to an even length that didn't even meet my ankles, but I couldn't have cared less that they were *perfect* weeds.

They were still *weeds*.

I hurriedly slid my shoes off and headed into them. The dirt clung to my feet as I paced a pattern. While I looked for the right spot to lie down, Flint decided to tell me a story.

"For the first month after you left, I spent a lot of time in that patch at the old apartment. Then, as months passed, I got really pissed and just wanted to forget you'd ever existed. So I ripped them out of the ground."

I stopped pacing as I watched him use his crutches to lower himself to the ground.

"Of course, they grew back." He laughed, patting the dirt next to him, asking me to join him—an offer I couldn't refuse. He continued as I settled at his side. "So then I sprayed them with weed killer." He tossed an arm around my shoulders and reclined back, dragging me with him and then manhandling me into that position on his chest that

I remembered he loved so much. "Seriously, weeds are resilient. No matter what the hell I did, I couldn't get rid of them. Eventually, I gave up and went back to spending my nights there. So when I moved a few months ago, I took the only thing I had left of you with me. Some of them died in the move, but for the most part, they've done pretty well." He ran his hands through the green bristle.

"Wait. These are the weeds from your apartment?"

"Some of them. I had to add a bunch." He looked down, catching my gaze. "You should have seen the faces at the lawn and garden center when I walked in asking to buy weeds." A hearty chuckle rumbled in his chest, warming me.

For several minutes, no words were spoken but Flint repeatedly kissed the top of my head and stroked his fingertips up and down my arm. I was in heaven as the world momentarily disappeared.

He finally broke the silence. "I was in love with you too."

Past tense.

I rolled away, remembering all too quickly why I hated that position on his chest.

CHAPTER
Twenty-One

Flint

I *DIDN'T* TRY TO STOP her as she settled on her back a few inches away. I fucking hated the distance she'd always put between us, but I needed her to hear me out.

Turning to my side, I propped myself up on an elbow. "I'm going to give you that space while I say what I have to say, but do not get comfortable. This conversation ends with you back at my side. You got it?"

"Mm-hm," she hummed unconvincingly.

"Okay, so listen. I was in love with you back then too."

"Right. Got that," she noted, folding her hands over her stomach. "You know, I really don't feel like having this conversation anymore. I get it. You didn't mean the stuff you said. It's in the past. Let's talk about something else."

"It's not in the past if you feel for one fucking second that you aren't good enough to live in my house."

"Oh, I was just being funny." She waved me off but never once looked at me.

"Damn it, Ash. Stop lying to me. That was probably the only honest thing you have said today."

"Great. Now, I'm a liar, too?"

"Okay. Clearly, space isn't work*ing. "* I snagged her arm, trying to pull her back toward me, but she didn't budge.

"Can we just talk about something else, please?"

"No. We absolutely cannot talk about anything until you hear me out. Ash, I'm so fucking sorry for the shit I spewed before you left. None of it was true. None."

"Apology accepted."

"Please don't shut me down like that."

"Flint, I just accepted your apology. I didn't shut you down."

"You just sprinted out of my house like I was some sort of serial killer. I'm thinking this is going to take more than just a simple 'I'm sorry.'"

"Fine. I'll amend my statement. I accept your apology tonight. We only have two days together. Let's talk about something else. We can come back to the depressing stuff later."

I rolled my eyes at her stupid imaginary time constraint. There was a lot to be said, but maybe she was right. As long as she didn't try to run again, it could wait.

"Fine. What do you want to talk about?"

She rolled to face me. "When's your birthday?"

"June first. You?"

"Shit," she cursed under her breath.

"Is that a bad day for you?"

"We have a big problem. Mine's April eighteenth. Gemini and Aries are not compatible at all. It would be a disaster."

I rested my hand on top of hers, intertwining our fingers. "I'm willing to chance it."

"Disaster," she whispered to herself.

We sat in silence for several minutes until I asked, "Anything else you want to know?"

"Yeah. Tell me about your first step? Was it amazing?"

"Meh, not really."

"What?" she shrieked in disbelief.

"Seriously, the first one wasn't a big deal. I was at physical therapy. No one except the therapist was even there to witness it."

"That's depressing."

"It was just a step, Ash. Then it became two steps. Then it became ten. It was cool, but it was still a long way from my goal of functionally walking again."

"Well, that's a lame story. You should never become an inspirational speaker."

I barked out a laugh. "I'll keep that in mind."

"I'm serious. My version is so much better."

"You have a version of my first steps?" I questioned.

She cleared her throat dramatically. "It was a warm day, and you were out picking strawberries."

I tucked a stray hair behind her ear. "Picking strawberries in my wheelchair?"

"Yep, and you weren't wearing a shirt."

"Where exactly was my shirt?"

"I don't know. Maybe some of the strawberry juice dripped onto it."

"Oh, well, that makes sense. Can't have that poison touching my skin," I teased.

"Agreed," she answered seriously, making me laugh all over again. "So there was a small kitten who suddenly came limping past."

"There was a kitten in a strawberry field?"

"Shh . . . My version. Anyway, you leaned down and picked up the kitten only to notice that his legs were badly damaged."

"Was I at all concerned that it would be rabid and claw up my beautiful naked chest?"

"Nah. You were more worried about your manly bits."

I choked on my laugh. "My manly bits? Where were my pants?"

She shrugged. "Strawberry juice."

"Ah, yes. Please continue."

"You were inspecting that poor kitten when you realized that it had to have walked hundreds of miles to get to such an isolated area. As you stared deep into that tiger-striped kitten's eyes, trying to figure out where he had come from, words filtered through your head that affected you so profoundly it sent sensation back to your legs. So much so that you were able to rise up and rush the kitten to a vet."

"Sweet Jesus," I whispered when I realized where she was going with the story.

Suddenly, she sat up and asked, "Do you know what those magical words were?"

"I'm gonna go out on a limb and guess the lyrics from the song 'Eye of the Tiger'?"

"Exactly," she breathed before bursting out into hysterical laughter.

"That was quite possibly the worst version ever."

"Did you miss the part where you were naked? That alone was better than your pitiful story."

She rolled around, laughing, and I watched intently, drinking it in.

I had missed that crazy woman so fucking much.

As *much* as I hated and regretted all the time apart, I couldn't even find it in myself to be angry anymore.

I just wanted to be with her. To show her who I truly was—not the jaded asshole she probably remembered. I wanted to find out who she had become and, even more than that, who she wanted to be. And then I wanted to be the one to give her that.

I draped an arm across her hips then pulled, forcing her to roll over on top of me. Her laughter abruptly stopped when I grazed a soft kiss over her lips.

"No more running. Give me time to fix this."

"I already—"

"And not two days. I've spent years dreaming about having you back. Swear to me you'll give me a shot to make that a reality."

"You dreamed about me?"

"Ash, you tortured me on a regular basis. I didn't even have to be asleep."

She smiled. "You too."

"Good. Then we're even." I kissed her again, letting it linger.

After pulling away, she whispered, "I'm scared. I don't know how to trust anyone in my life, much less you."

"Then I'll fix that too."

"I just don't understand why you're trying so hard. It was a *really* long time ago."

"Because, when I was nineteen years old, I fell in love with a girl who changed my life by showing me that even the darkest nights still had stars and it didn't matter one bit that you had to lie in the weeds to see them. We were kids and I barely knew her, but I loved her. I should have been there while she grew up, but I was a fo*ol*. Now, I have the woman back and I have every intention of making her fall in love with me again, and this time . . . I'm never letting go." I took her mouth again, but it wasn't gentle.

It was deep and needy.

Strong and firm.

Bold and assuming.

It was the way Ash had always kissed me.

And fortunately for both of us, it had the exact same effect on her that it always had on me.

She straddled my hips and folded her arms around my neck, pressing her chest down against mine. I have no idea how she did it, but I swear, every time Ash kissed me, she managed to squeeze herself flush against me as if she were attempting to meld our bodies into one—an idea I *was* completely okay with.

Palming her ass, I rubbed her against my hardening cock.

I needed to get inside her. She had marked the outside of her body as mine, and I desperately needed to mark the inside.

"Tell me you'll try. Give me a chance to show you how right we were—how right we are."

"I'll try," she moaned into my mouth.

"Good girl," I purred, grabbing the back of her head for another deep kiss.

She sat up enough to grab the hem of her shirt, but I stilled her hands before she had the chance to pull it over her head.

She searched my eyes with a puzzled expression.

"I'm not risking any more interruptions with you. I want you on my bed, where I can take my time and explore every curve of you that I've been dreaming of touching since you first dove into my van. My neighbors are nosy as fuck, and I will be damned if I'm willing to share the sound of you crying my name when I make you come with my hands, tongue, and cock." I pointedly rolled my hips against her core.

"All three?" she smarted back on a moan.

"All three," I confirmed, catching her mouth again. "Now, get up. We're going to bed." I slapped her ass, fully expecting her playful giggle to follow, but like music to my cock, she hissed a, "Yes," that quickly morphed into a cry of ecstasy.

I mentally noted the fuck out of that cry as visions of turning her creamy-white ass various shades of pink caused my dick to twitch.

"Now," I ordered.

She quickly popped to her feet. Then she handed me my crutches and stood awkwardly as I pulled myself up.

"What?" I asked when she started knotting her hands.

"So, um, I really want to . . . um . . . be naked in your bed."

I tilted my head, unsure what to make of this flash of insecurity from such a confident woman.

"But I need to tell you something first, since I think you are assuming something else. Last time you assumed something, it ended with me turning my father in to the police and then running from you for three years. Sooo . . ."

I tried to *close* the distance between us, but before I got close enough to touch her and soothe whatever worry she had, Ash dropped a bomb.

"I've never had sex before."

My crutches became rooted to the ground, and my entire body went rigid—which included my already impossibly hard cock.

"You've never?"

"Well, no. Not exactly."

"Are you serious?" I asked in disbelief.

"Uhhh . . ." She stalled in embarrassment before blowing out a loud frustrated breath. "Don't hold it against me. I'm sure I'll be great. I'm a fast learner."

"A fast learner," I repeated incredulously.

"I shouldn't have even mentioned it, but I was worried it would piss you off when you found out."

"Damn right it would have pissed me off!" I snapped.

"Great," she huffed, folding her arms across her chest. "You're pissed."

"Oh, I am so far from pissed you can't even imagine."

She rolled her eyes.

"Okay, so you've never had sex. What exactly have you done before?"

"Well, you were my first kiss."

"I was your first kiss!" I shouted with an undeniable laugh.

I fucking loved that I had her all sexually frustrated and nervous. I truly wanted to keep up the angry façade, but there was no possible way I could have hidden the huge shit-eating grin that spread across my face.

"See! I told you I was a fast learner. You had no clue."

I headed toward her. "What else have you done?"

"I'm not sure what you would consider what we did on the floor of the conference room, but that about sums it up. If I haven't done it with you, it hasn't happened."

My mouth fell open in stunned silence. I searched her eyes for lies but only found the truth.

"No one else?" I clarified.

She shook her head.

I dropped my head back to peer up at the stars. "I am so fucking sorry, Ash."

"Why?" she asked timidly.

"Because now that I know no one else has ever touched you, the things I am going to do to you tonight just multiplied . . . and not in your favor." I shifted all of my weight to one arm and looped the other around her waist, roughly pulling her against me. "They aren't going to be gentle the way you deserve." I glided my hand down to her ass and squeezed, using it to grind her against my very angry cock. Then I dragged my nose up her neck to her ear and whispered, "But I *swear to God* you will beg for more." I nipped at her earlobe. "Most of all, I'm sorry because I won't be able to fulfill that angry fuck I promised to give you in the morning."

She whimpered as I raked my teeth across her skin.

"We may have to postpone that now, but make no mistake. It will happen. Ash, baby, I have three years' worth of frustration to work off inside you. And that's the part where your begging becomes fun." I lifted my hand before swiftly landing it against her ass.

"Fuck," she breathed, tilting her hips into mine.

"Close your eyes. We're going to bed and I'm not risking another freak-out about the inside of my house. We'll deal with that in the morning. Tonight, your only worry is how deep you can take my cock."

"Jesus. Stop talking already." She caught my mouth with her own.

"Not a problem. I can't talk with my tongue occupied by that sweet pussy."

"Flint."

"And that's just the first time you call my name tonight." I stepped away from her and proffered an elbow. "Eyes closed."

"Yes, sir," she replied, linking her arm through mine.

"Even. Better." I laughed.

CHAPTER
Twenty-Two

Ash

FLINT'S FOUR-BEAT STRIDES LED ME blindly through his house. I heard him close a sliding door, and some sort of hard surface, which I immediately recognized wasn't carpeted, welcomed my feet. I wanted to open my eyes and take in every nook and cranny of where Flint dwelled, but he was right. It would have done me no good. In the weeds on the side of his house, he had managed to convince me that I belonged with him—that I deserved him, even. But convincing and believing were two separate issues. However, I was more than happy to ignore that for a night spent in his arms.

"Okay. Open them," Flint said after a door clicked behind us.

I peeked my eyes open, and a simple, clean bedroom lay in front of me. Everything was neat, and bookshelves lined the walls. I felt at ease. While everything was a hell of a lot nicer, the room was reminiscent of his old apartment.

I glanced over my shoulder to find him warily watching me—purposely positioned in front of the door.

"I'm fine."

"You sure?"

"Yeah. I really am." I smiled, and he let out a relieved breath. "Can I . . . um . . . use your bathroom to . . . maybe freshen up?"

Using his crutch, he pointed to a closed door adjacent to his bed.

"Thanks." I walked away.

Flint called out from behind me, "Don't get too excited. There's no window in that bathroom."

"Ha. Ha," I deadpanned, closing and locking the door behind me.

I looked around his modest bathroom. It had a large garden tub with a glass stall shower at the foot, complete with a glass bench inside. The double vanity made me smile, and I was so much more than pleased to find that the stone countertop was faux.

I took a deep, calming breath.

Then freaked the fuck out.

"Shit shit shit!" I started rummaging through his drawers. I need a shower, razor, and toothbrush—stat. I was about to have sex with Flint Page and I had spent the morning sweating my ass off on breakfast deliveries.

I knew for a fact that my legs weren't clean-shaven, and I had never had sex, but I knew that men liked a smooth palette to work with in the lady regions as well. The electric trimmer resting next to the sink explained how he kept that sexy stubble so neat, but it did me little good. After starting the shower, I continued my search until I found his linen closet, where I hit the ultimate jackpot. Towels, razors, and shaving cream were all meticulously organized, complete with printed labels to assign their location.

God, he's anal.

I suppressed my smile, nabbing the necessities, including his toothbrush, off the counter and got in the shower.

Twenty minutes later, I stepped out a new woman—or at least a clean and hairless version of one. I would have given anything for some sexy lingerie or, at the bare minimum, a clean bra and panties, but my two small bags were still in Flint's SUV. Really, what was the point though? He had made it more than clear that they would be coming off—a fact that excited me.

After finger-combing my long locks, I wrapped myself in one of his plush, white towels and took one last glance in the mirror.

I should have been nervous.

I wasn't.

I was ecstatic.

Once I'd allowed myself a final silent schoolgirl scream, I collected myself and headed out to *him.*

"I told you there wasn't a window," he joked.

He was lounging on the far side of the bed, shirtless, and judging by the way the covers showed off the sculpted muscles just above his hips, he was pantsless as well. His hair was no longer styled but rather appeared to still be damp. A book sat in his lap, and a sexy smirk played on his lips.

I wasn't nervous at all—regardless of the way my heart began to race.

"Well, aren't you presumptuous. Showered and naked," I quipped.

"I could say the same to you." He winked. "Drop the towel, Ash," he ordered, closing the book and setting it on his nightstand.

Mayday! Mayday! I lied. Totally nervous!

"Um . . ." I stalled, but it was only for a second.

I had wanted this with Flint since the day I'd first laid eyes on him. Nerves had stopped me the first time all of those years earlier, but I wouldn't allow that to happen again.

So, while staring into the bright-blue eyes that had haunted me, I brazenly released the towel.

"Fucking hell." His gaze raked over me from head to toe then back again.

I sauntered to the foot of the bed. "Sooo . . . I owe you a razor."

I leaned down on my hands and began to prowl up toward him, but I didn't make it very far. As soon as I got within arm's reach, he grabbed my shoulders and dragged me on top of him. Then his mouth slammed over mine and a hand thrust into my wet hair.

"Goddammit." He roughly tugged at the blanket between us, failing in his frenzy. Within seconds, he gave up and tossed me to the other side of the bed, tearing the blanket away before rolling to cover me with his muscular body.

I was right. Flint was very, very naked. I didn't have a chance to fully check him out, but I felt every hard inch of him pressed against me.

"You are fucking beautiful," he whispered against my skin as he trailed kisses down to my breasts.

"So are you," I answered awkwardly—but it was the truth.

Flint's body was gorgeous, and even as I looked down over his shoulder at the numerous scars that covered his back, it didn't change that in the least.

I felt his lips tip up, but just as quickly, his tongue circled my peaked nipple.

"Shit," I breathed, arching off the bed.

His mouth shifted, capturing my other breast and shooting sparks to my core.

"Flint, please," I begged wantonly.

I couldn't say exactly what I wanted him to do; I just knew I needed more.

More of his hands.

More of his mouth.

Just more Flint.

"Oh God," I prayed when his fingers brush over my folds. My hips lifted, urging him forward.

After cascading kisses down my stomach, he settled between my legs on an elbow.

"Slow down," he murmured.

"No. You speed up." I threw my head back against the pillow with a groan as his hand disappeared. Well, that was until the warmth of his tongue laved over my clit. "Yes," I hissed.

"Have you ever gotten yourself off?" he asked before licking me again, sending my head spinning.

"Yes," I admitted on a breath.

"You think about me?" he questioned, pressing a finger inside me.

I couldn't have uttered words if I'd tried; a nod was my only reply.

Twisting his hand, he adding another finger. A sharp sting flashed over me before it faded into overwhelming pleasure.

"I didn't hear you, Ash. Say it out loud. Tell me how you thought about me every time you touched this tight pussy."

His fingers deliciously twisted again, and my hands tangled in his short hair, urging his mouth down.

"I especially thought about how you would feel inside me," I said boldly, and he rewarded me with another flick of his tongue.

"Soon. First, I want to taste you." Without removing his fingers, he sucked my clit into his mouth.

My hands flailed, knocking everything including the lamp off his nightstand, before slamming down on the bed, fisting the sheets. The tension was building already, my muscles clenching with every swirl of his tongue, but just as I reached the highest peak before the euphoric fall, he backed away.

"No, don't stop," I begged, opening my eyes.

He rolled to the side, settling next to me on his back. "I need to feel you come, and not on my mouth and fingers. You aren't the only one who has been using their imagination to get off for the last three years. I want you to come while wrapped around my cock," he replied, his voice husky with desire.

"Stop talking," I said even though I loved every syllable out of his dirty mouth.

Judging by the smirk that formed on his lips, he knew it too.

He began stroking his long, thick cock. "Get on top. It'll be easier this way."

"Easier for who?" I asked, rising to my knees, but my eyes stayed glued to his moving hand.

He caught my wrist and guided my hand to join his. "There you go," he moaned, releasing his cock as I continued gliding long strokes up and down his shaft.

The sight of Flint's smooth length sliding through my grasp enraptured me. I was vaguely aware of him rifling around in the drawer of his nightstand.

Suddenly, Flint sat up, grabbed the back of my neck, and hauled me down to his mouth. My hand fell away while he kissed me deeply. Gripping my hips, he shifted me to straddle him. His cock settled between us as he held me to his mouth in a deep and sensual kiss. My arousal still lingered on his lips.

Turning his head to break the connection, he growled, "Sit up."

As always, when it came to Flint, my body obeyed. He made quick work of rolling on a condom as I watched his skilled hands in awe.

The nerves began to creep back up at the thought of finally having him, something I had fantasized about more times than I could count. There was no question that I wanted to be with him. I was just terrified of what would happen after we finished. I wasn't sure I could ever go back from a moment when I belonged to him in every possible way.

And because of that, he would belong to me too.

I wasn't sure that, if I ever truly had him as my own, I'd ever be able to let go.

"Look at me," he ordered.

My gaze immediately lifted to his.

"I have waited so long to have you, Ash. I have so much to apologize for, but this . . . tonight . . . with you . . . will never be one of those things."

My eyes flashed away as insecurity and doubt clouded my vision.

Or maybe they were tears.

Whatever they were *sucked.* I was naked and in bed with a man who had literally been the star of every single dream I had ever had. Insecurity had no place in the equation.

"Be with me, Ash. Tonight, tomorrow, a decade. Just *be* with me. No more running."

I swallowed hard, pushing the paralyzing fear of tomorrow out of mind. "I can do tonight."

I want to do eternity.

I leaned back down, resting my arms next to his head. Nose to nose with him, I inched my hips forward to hover above his straining erection. His hand slipped between us, poising himself at my entrance. Without giving myself another second to reconsider, I slowly sank down on his cock.

I wished we were frenzied by passion—all hands and mouths— because then I wouldn't have seen the moment his face softened.

Or felt his breath whisper across my skin as he gasped.

But especially because I wouldn't have heard his possessive growl. "All mine."

I stilled. The biting pain from him stretching me was nothing compared to the vise he had twisted around my heart.

Who I belonged to had never been in question.

Flint, on the other hand . . .

He nipped at my lips, gliding his hands up and down my back. Rocking his hips ever so gently, he began moving inside me. I may have been on top, but Flint took charge. After several minutes of coaxing, the ache between my legs subsided, leaving something very primal in its place. My body overrode my chaotic mind, allowing me to forget about the searing pain in my chest.

"I know I need to be gentle, but fuck," he groaned, planting himself inside me then roughly taking my mouth again. His hands squeezed my hips and guided me into a rhythm he met thrust for thrust.

The familiar climb began building inside me. I lost one of Flint's hands as he lifted it to his mouth before licking his index finger and dropping it to my clit.

A cry escaped my throat as I tossed my head back. I was unable to even concentrate on kissing him any longer.

"God, you are so fucking tight," he whispered in my ear. "No one else will ever experience this with you, Ash."

With his finger circling my clit, I was dangerously close to stepping off the edge. But before I gave him that, I needed to give myself something first.

"*You're* mine," I demanded, suddenly sitting up.

His lips twitched as his tongue darted out to dampen them. I held his gaze, searching for affirmation.

But I got so much more.

His eyes were burning with emotions I had never been given but prayed I could earn.

"Always," he breathed, gripping my hips and roughly burying himself to the hilt.

"Flint," I moaned as the orgasm tore through my body, ravaging me physically while the echo of his promise soothed me emotionally.

Not even a full minute later, he found his own release with the hiss of my name flowing from his lips.

He might have done all of the work, but I was exhausted. I collapsed on top of him as he began to soften inside me.

"You okay?" he asked.

I nodded against his hard chest.

He drifted his fingertips up and down my back. "You want to take a shower?"

I shook my head.

"You ready for round two?"

My head popped up in a weird combination of "no fucking way" and "abso-fucking-lutely."

"I'm kidding." He laughed, pressing a chaste kiss to my lips. "Let me get rid of the condom and clean up. I'll be right back."

I rolled off him and settled facedown on the bed. I didn't even bother getting under the covers. It had been one hell of a day, and sleep was threatening to consume me with each passing second.

Flint rejoined me in bed, sliding in behind me and dragging the covers over both of us.

As per usual, he shifted me in his arms until he found a position for me that suited him.

As per usual, I played limp and giggled the whole time he jostled me around.

I smiled to myself when he tangled his legs with mine. Once I'd wrapped my arms around his stomach, I squeezed him tight.

"In my dreams, you were walking," I whispered, kissing his chest.

"In mine, you stayed," he replied on a deep, content sigh.

Sated and smiling, I drifted off in his strong arms, reveling in the culmination of every fantasy I'd ever had.

CHAPTER
Twenty-Three

Ash

FLINT GROANED AS HIS ALARM clock started screaming through the room at what felt like an obscene hour.

"Oh God." I folded the pillow over my head in a worthless attempt to block it out. "Turn it off!"

"I can't find it!"

"Why the hell would you hide your alarm clock?" I cried in response.

"I didn't hide it, smartass. Someone who shall remain nameless knocked it off the nightstand in a fit of ecstasy last night." He laughed, pinching my nipple before snatching the pillow off my face and throwing it across the room.

"Just unplug it," I whined, slapping my hands over my ears.

"I can't. It has a backup battery."

"Who in God's name puts batteries in their alarm clock? That defeats the whole point of praying for a power outage before you go to sleep." I'd rolled off the bed and begun searching the floor for the blaring disturbance when a second distinct tone joined the chaos.

My too-early-in-the-morning glare swung to him.

"What the hell is that?"

"Backup alarm."

"You have got to be kidding me."

"I hate being late." He laughed, flipping the blankets off and nabbing his crutches off the ground.

I dropped to my hands and knees, following the noise. "Got it!" I shouted, stretching my arm under the bed and barely catching it with the tips of my fingers.

I quickly turned it off, and he had apparently found the second alarm, because the room fell blessedly silent. Well, that was until I heard Flint breathe, "Fuck," from behind me.

It was then that I remembered I was naked and kneeling with my chest to the carpeted floor and my ass sticking straight up in the air. I glanced over my shoulder to find him standing, staring down at me, his already large cock thickening between his legs—a sight that had me returning his curse.

"Don't move," he commanded when I started to sit up.

As Flint's heated eyes leveled me, there was a part of me that felt as though I should have covered up. But I didn't feel insecure at all. Under his gaze, I felt more secure and wanted than I had in my entire life, and for that alone, I pressed my ass even higher into the air.

"I lied. Get on the bed, but right back in that position."

First, I had other plans. I sat up but didn't push to my feet. Instead, I spun on my knees and slowly crawled over to him.

"Don't do that," he warned, but his eyes said otherwise.

"I have a few apologies to make." I licked my lips.

"On the bed, Ash."

"No," I responded.

He arched an admonishing eyebrow, which I ignored.

"You did a lot of things to me last night—things I loved. But there was something I wanted to do." I wrapped my hand around his hard-on, steadily gliding to the tip and back again. "I'm going to suggest you sit down."

And for once, Flint didn't have a retort. He backed up to the edge of the bed and dropped his crutches to the floor. I smiled in victory as I followed him forward, running my hands up his thighs until I reached the base of his cock. Then I lowered my head to kiss the tip.

"Wait," he urged.

But I was done taking his orders. I slid his length as deep as possible into my mouth. "Fuck," he hissed.

"Wait," he repeated as I glided back up his shaft. He pulled me upright before bending forward to kiss my shoulder. Using my chin to tip my head, he forced my eyes to his. "I said wait." He chastely kissed my mouth and teased his hands down my sides to rest on my hips.

Then the ground below my knees disappeared and the entire world turned upside down.

Literally.

A loud laugh escaped my throat as Flint flipped me onto the bed to join him. He juggled me like a rag doll until he until he found a position that suited him—kneeling over his face.

I stopped laughing immediately when his mouth sealed over my clit.

Then I cried out as his long finger found my opening. His other hand darted between us and lifted his cock toward my mouth.

With a swirl of his tongue, he dropped his head to the bed long enough to say, "Now, apologize all you like while I have breakfast."

I gasped as his fingers began a rhythm inside me that left me unable to focus on anything else.

"Are you sore?"

"A little." I managed to pull myself together long enough to find his cock again. But I instantly regretted my answer when he removed his finger.

"Then you come on my mouth, but you better get busy." He swatted my ass deliciously hard before using each cheek to pull me down to hover only a centimeter from his mouth. "Because I'm coming in yours too." He pulled me down until I completely covered his face, licking and sucking in a deep and greedy way I should have been embarrassed by.

But embarrassment would have required thoughts, and right then, every single brain cell I possessed had abandoned me in the hunt for climax.

I came on his mouth, all right. Then, when I finally got my act together, he came in mine as well. And Flint being Flint, well, he was such an overachiever that he insisted on showing me exactly how much he accepted my sexual apologies. So, before I fell asleep on his chest, I came one last time with his hand between my legs.

I decided I could live with two alarm clocks if that was the wake-up call they provided.

Flint

Ash slept naked in my bed for most of the day. If it had been up to me, I would have gotten her off at least a dozen more times, but as much as I loved watching her come, I loved feeling her come while I was inside her that much more. She needed time to recover from the night before, because I had plans for that evening. And every evening of the foreseeable future.

After she dozed off, I snuck out of bed and drank my coffee with the memories of her swallowing my release as my only company.

It quickly became my favorite company.

I knew that Ash and I were a long way from being fixed or back together, but knowing she was mine, and only mine, in every possible way sexually made me that much more determined to claim the rest of her. I had already been pretty set on keeping her in my life before, but after having heard her come calling my name, I vowed not to let anything stand in my way.

At around three in the afternoon, a knock at the door forced me to finally pull some clothes on. I quietly closed the door to my bedroom and tugged my shirt down as the knock repeated.

"I'm coming," I called, limping over to the door.

Cracking it open, I rolled my eyes. "Three P.M. I'm impressed. I figured you'd be here as soon as Till left for the gym."

"The sitter didn't show." Eliza laughed, pushing past me, carrying a stack of glass baking dishes. "Where is she?" she asked, spinning in a circle.

"Asleep."

"Still? Flint, what did you do to that poor girl?"

"You want the honest answer?" I smirked.

She puffed her cheeks and pretended to gag. "Dear God, no."

"What's that?" I followed her to the kitchen.

She turned the oven on. "Pot roast and twice-baked potatoes. Well, only once-baked potatoes right now. Give them about twenty minutes and they'll be twice baked."

"Woman." I grunted like a caveman before lifting the edge of the tinfoil to sniff inside.

"I figured she'd be hungry, and Lord knows you can't feed her."

"I love the way you assume I'm worthless in the kitchen. However, if it means you show up with twice-baked potatoes, you can keep that assumption up for as long as you want."

She giggled, slapping me on the chest. "I don't assume you're worthless in the kitchen. I know you're worthless in the kitchen. The last thing any of us need is you trying to cook her lunch and send her running for another three years. Broody, crybaby Flint was a real drag."

"Crybaby Flint? You seriously have to make girlfriends and stop hanging out with Quarry so much." I laughed.

"No, Q would have called you a fucking crybaby. I edited."

"This is true." I snagged a slice of the pot roast with my fingers and popped it into my mouth.

"Are you two coming to dinner after Q's fight?"

"Yeah. I heard you sold a painting. I'm ordering the lobster."

"I did! My *Dream Window* is now hanging in the Museum de Coffee Shop downtown. I only made, like, a hundred bucks, so you might have to order off the children's menu."

"That's still pretty awesome though. You're a legit artist now." I took a fork from the drawer and scooped another slice of meat before Eliza pulled the dish away.

"Don't eat without her," she scolded.

"No. Let him eat. It's okay," Ash said, suddenly appearing behind us.

She was wearing her jeans and one of my hoodies that all but swallowed her. Ash was tall—a fact I'd loved even when I'd had to look up at her—but she was so thin that it hung well below her ass. An ass that, after this morning, I knew every curve of.

"Mm." I pointed to my mouth as I hurriedly swallowed the roast. "Hey." I dropped the fork in the sink and headed her way.

"Morning," she greeted shyly, which made me narrow my eyes as she wrapped her arms around my waist.

Eliza chimed in behind me. "Hi."

Ash leaned away, and her eyes flashed from mine to Eliza's and back to mine before she replied with a cold, "Hi."

Oh hell.

Eliza didn't catch the frigid air in the least. "We met once a while back. I'm Till's wife, Eliza. It's so nice to meet you again." She tossed out a warm grin that did nothing to stifle Ash's passive-aggressive chill.

"Yeah, I remember when we met." Ash grinned, something so fake that I almost believed it.

Almost.

I stepped in front of her. "Hey, can I talk to you for a second?"

"Of course, baby," she answered sweetly, but it was clear that talking was very low on Ash's agenda.

Her hands glided up my chest and over my shoulders. Standing on her tiptoes, she gave me a sensual and completely indecent kiss. I took it, even knowing Eliza was watching, but only because I could tell exactly what Ash was doing.

And.

I.

Fucking.

Loved.

It.

Begrudgingly, I broke the kiss just before her hands slid down to my ass. "Excuse us for a minute, Eliza." I turned my attention back to Ash. "Bedroom," I ordered.

Eliza giggled and wiped her hands on the towel hanging from the stove. "I actually have to go. I just wanted to drop off the food. The potatoes will be ready in fifteen minutes. Eat them while they're hot. Quarry's the main event tonight, so it will probably be after nine before dinner." She walked over to Ash, who was still possessively clinging to my waist. "You have no idea how happy I am that you're back." She squeezed her arm. "I'll save you a seat at the fight?"

Ash was glowering, but when she caught me watching her, she quickly covered it. "Yeah. Um. Sure," she replied.

"Okay, see you guys tonight," Eliza called out when she got to the door.

No sooner had the door shut behind her than Ash's shoulders fell in relief.

"Up," I barked, causing her head to tip back to look at me.

"Huh?"

"Put your ass on my counter so we can have this conversation eye to eye."

"What conversation?"

"Up," I repeated, and with the exception of a huff, she didn't argue. Jumping, she pushed herself onto the counter.

I settled between her legs and spread my crutches wide enough to wrap her legs around my hips. "You don't like Eliza?"

"She's fine," she chirped.

"Bullshit." I crushed my mouth to hers.

Fisting the front of my shirt, she pulled me even closer as she glided her tongue against mine. I shifted her to the edge of the counter until my cock found her denim-covered core.

"You have no fucking idea how hard I got watching you claim me," I mumbled into her mouth, rolling my hips against hers.

She leaned away to talk. "If I'm going to try with you, then Eliza—"

I shifted my weight to one side then caught the back of her head, forcing her mouth against mine. Her hands roamed my chest.

"Changed my mind. We're not trying. We're doing."

She smiled and reached down to the button on her jeans. "I won't argue."

"No. I'm talking about *us*. This time yesterday, you were running from me, and not five minutes ago, you were ready to mount me in the middle of the kitchen just so Eliza knew that I was yours."

"You *are* mine," she added defensively.

I smirked. "It's good to know we agree. Which is exactly why we're *doing* instead of *trying*."

She gently stroked my cock. "Whatever. I don't want to talk about this anymore."

I swayed out of her reach. "Too bad. I gave you last night. Now, you're talking to me."

"Oh God." She started to shift off the counter.

I blocked her. "Hear me out."

"I don't want to hear you out! Not about her. I'm sorry. I know she's your family and all, but part of the reason I left in the first place is because I'll never be Eliza. *Never.*"

"You are absolutely right."

Her mouth gaped open in shock.

"I was a fucking fool when I told you I was in love with Eliza. And not because it broke us up. I was a fool because it was a load of shit." Using her chin, I tipped back her head, forcing her gaze to lock with mine. "I was *never* in love with her—at least, not in the way I thought. But it wasn't until I fell for *you* that I realized that."

She rolled her eyes, but I kept going.

"Ash, I was really fucked up back then. Even before the accident, I was angry about everything. Life was a struggle. Every single day was an absolute fight. Before my mom left, I would wake up in the middle of the night and clean the house because I was panicked that social services was going to show up. Till moved out when I was twelve. Sure, he came back and took care of us as much as he could, but on a daily basis, I was a seventh-grader raising a seven-year-old. I was terrified I was going to fuck something up and lose the little stability I actually had. Then, when Eliza entered our lives, she took a lot of that responsibility off my shoulders. She and Till gave me real security for the first time in my entire life. I was desperate to hold on to that feeling no matter what. And somewhere along the way, I confused that desperation with love." I stopped talking and held her empty stare, begging her to truly hear my confession. I needed her to understand why I had acted the way I had. Maybe then we could start over without the shadows of the past fracturing the possibility of a future.

Finally, after several beats, she shyly admitted, "That's how you made me feel."

"Ash—"

"You made *me* feel safe and secure." She looked back up, squaring her shoulders and fearlessly meeting my gaze. "You know, you don't understand my life, either, Flint. I didn't exactly have it easy. My father used to send me out on the streets to hustle. Sometimes they were nice guys who were clueless as to what the hell I was doing. But sometimes they weren't. I got caught lifting a wallet once. The guy threw me down, kicked me in the ribs, and then spit on me before he walked away. It wasn't anything huge. I ended up with a busted lip and a bruised side. It was mainly my self-worth that took the brunt of the attack, but my own father inflicted those wounds. When I got back to the pickup location, he gave me a ten-minute lecture on how I hadn't brought him back enough money. He couldn't have cared less that I had been hurt."

"Son of a bitch," I cursed. Kissing her forehead, I plotted Ray Mabie's death all over again.

"That day when you tried to save me from Max meant more to me than you could ever imagine. I think I fell in love with you right then. Not because of who you were, but because of how you made me feel. After that, I opened myself up to you, which made everything you said to me that much harder. I could have dealt with that shit from anyone in the world—anyone but you. I trusted you, and look what it got me."

"I am so fucking sorry, Ash. That day was like the perfect storm of triggers for both of us, because when I found out how old you were, I panicked all over again. You were *sixteen.*"

Her eyes turned angry as she snapped, "I'm only *nineteen* now."

"Bullshit. You're not nineteen any more than I am twenty-two. Ash, you didn't spend the last three years partying it up. You were hanging out with elderly ladies and cooking lunch at a homeless shelter. We've both experienced enough *life* to last an eternity. I'm really ready to just sit back, relax, and *enjoy* it." I dropped my forehead to hers. "Preferably with you."

It was meant to be a reassuring statement, but it seemed to set her on fire.

She suddenly jumped to her feet, knocking me to the side before I caught my balance. "I don't know how to be with anyone! It's been me my whole life, Flint. Just me. Even when I was with my dad, I was still alone." She began pacing the room. "And now, you show up and not only want me to be with you, but live in your perfect house with your perfectly labeled cabinets. I don't fit in this life! I can't be your happy little wife in your happy little home."

"Okay. Slow the hell down. Ash, I'm not asking you to marry me."

She froze and looked over at me. Disappointment showed on her face even while her cheeks heated in embarrassment. It made me an asshole, but that disappointment made me happier than any smile she had ever tossed my way.

"I didn't mean—"

"Yet," I amended, and her head snapped back. "I don't know you anymore. I remember the girl that I fell in love with, and if I'm being honest with you, I still love her."

Her chin began to quiver, but my smile grew.

"I want to fall in love with the woman now. I want to know who Ash Victoria Mabie really is. I mean, I know she's gorgeous and great in bed," I teased, causing her to choke out a laugh. "But I want to know all of her. And while we're at it, I want her to get to know me too.

"I'm not the same guy you remember. The years have changed me too—in some ways for the better, and some for the worse. Hell, you might hate me in two weeks, but at least give me the chance. I want to make you fall in love with *me,* not the memories. And if and when that happens, I *will* make you my wife. And I *will* make this your home. And we can make each other safe and secure for the rest of our lives."

I walked over, stopping in front of her. Her eyes bounced around the room, but they weren't dim anymore. Something I had said had changed her. I just needed to figure out whatever-the-hell part it was she needed to hear so I could reassure her on a daily basis.

"Ash, all of that will come with time. Right now, I just need you to stop running and maybe start by going out on a fucking date with me."

She swallowed hard, and her blue eyes sparkled with unshed emotion. "I don't know."

I was so fucking sick and tired of not knowing though. I'd spent entirely too long living with uncertainty.

I knew.

I fucking knew.

And I was going to make her know too.

"Damn it, Ash. Give me a fucking chance. I can do this! I swear to God. I can do *this.*"

"It's just . . ." She trailed off, flashing her eyes down at the floor. She stared at her feet for several seconds before slowly looking back up with a huge grin. "I've never been on a date."

My lips twitched. "Well, now that I know that, I'm going to have to start you off easy. Can't pull out the big guns on the first night. I'd just set myself up for failure on the second date."

Putting her hands on her hips, she tilted her head. "Is that what you did last night in bed? I thought you were holding out on me."

"What the hell, Ash!"

She burst out laughing.

"That is not what you are supposed to tell a man! Repeat after me: I ruined you for all men, all the while fulfilling your every fantasy."

She continued to laugh as I tugged her against my chest. "See? I told you I was new at this."

"You also just like to fuck with me."

She folded her arms around my waist and snuggling in impossibly closer. "Yeah, maybe a little bit."

"So, dinner and a movie tomorrow night?"

"Are you going to bring me flowers?"

I blew out a loud breath. "If you promise to be here in the morning, I'll bring you whatever you want."

"Good. Flowers will be another newsie."

I laughed at the memory of her silly list.

Craning her head back to hold my gaze, she said, "You're different."

"So are you," I replied, punctuating it with a kiss.

"You know, that was a very mature conversation we just had."

"Right?" I said proudly. "See? We can do this."

"No. I think it gave me hives." She made a show of scratching her arms.

"Oh, shut up." I dropped a hand to her ass and nipped at her bottom lip.

"You know what I bet would cure my hives?"

"Being tied spread-eagle to my bed?"

"No," she answered. Then she leaned in and whispered, "Well, yes, but maybe later." Stepping out of my grasp, she grandly waved a hand toward my room. "A childish act of rebellion."

"Ash," I warned.

She took off running to my room. "I'm switching all the labels in your bathroom closet."

"Don't you dare!"

I started after her, but I was entirely too slow. She was already in the bathroom before I even got to the bedroom.

I jiggled the handle, but she had locked the door. "Ash, I swear to

God," I growled, but I wasn't angry in the least.

God, I missed her.

"Ash!" I tried the door again, surprisingly finding it unlocked. When I swung it open, I found her wearing nothing more than a teasing smirk.

"Orrrr . . . we could have shower sex."

"Or we could have shower sex," I confirmed, slamming the door behind me.

It was a much better plan.

CHAPTER
Twenty-Four

Ash

BE NICE TO ELIZA.
> *Be nice to Eliza.*
> *Be.*
> *Nice.*
> *To.*
> *Eliza.*

"Hey, I was waiting for you," she said, pulling me into a hug as soon as we walked into the crowded gym. I went stiff—until Flint slid his hand down my back and squeezed my ass.

"Hi!" I chirped, swatting his hand away.

She released me and slapped Flint on the chest. "You're late."

He tipped his head to me. "Her fault. And before you ask . . . don't." He tossed her a wink.

"Ewww," she cried then turned to look at me. "No offense."

I laughed. "None taken."

"Well, you better get back there. Till's been stomping around for some reason. I'd way rather you handle that than me."

"Fantastic," he deadpanned. "Hang on. I need to introduce Ash to someone first."

Eliza looked at me. "I saved you a seat." She pointed to the front row with reserved signs taped to the backs of the chairs. "Just come find me when you're done."

My body relaxed as I watched her walk away.

Flint leaned down and whispered into my ear, "She likes you."

"Oh goodie," I snarked, causing him to chuckle.

Lifting a crutch, he pointed to a door marked *Gym Staff Only.* "Come on."

I followed him as he skillfully navigated through the crowd. I wasn't sure how he did it. I was only using two legs and bumped into more people than he did.

He led me into a large, open office that branched off into three other offices. Two of them could be seen through the glass windows that overlooked the gym, and once I'd seen the names listed on the door, I understood why.

The one on the left sported the On The Ropes logo above the words *Former Heavyweight Champion of the World, Slate "The Silent Storm" Andrews.*

The door on the right had the words *The Silencer* cut out of a sound wave with the title *Former Heavyweight Champion of the World, Till Page.*

But it was the door at the back that really caught my attention: *Head of On The Ropes Sports Management, Flint Page.*

I looked up at him, and his prideful smile matched mine.

"That's really fucking cool."

"Nah, it's no big deal." His smile spread.

I pressed up onto my toes to kiss his cheek. "Liar."

He laughed and pulled a key from his pocket. After unlocking the door, he flipped the light on, not surprisingly revealing a clean and clutter-free desk with three shelves packed with books behind it. A laptop sat on one side, and with the exception of a picture frame and a piece of brick, the rest of the desk was empty.

"Have a seat. I'll be right back." He kissed the top of my head then left.

I chose to sit in his chair behind the desk. Tracing my fingers over the wooden desk, I wondered if he had ever sat in that same spot and thought about me. Just the idea warmed me.

I discovered that the picture frame held a photo of Flint in the box-

185

ing ring. He was mid punch, and judging from his opponent's face at the point of impact, it was a knockout. I smiled to myself as I saw him standing without the aid of his crutches for the very first time. Sure, Flint could take a step or two on his own, but that picture was different. He was strong and fierce. And it left me wondering if that version of Flint would have been so hell-bent on being with a girl like me.

Thankfully, before I got lost in my imagination, Flint interrupted me.

"It's from the building."

"Huh?" I looked up to find him leaning against the doorjamb.

"The brick. It's from the building you vandalized the first night we got together."

I picked it up and spun it around. It was no bigger than an apple, but I could still clearly make out a yellow stripe of paint on one side.

I heard his four-beat gait approach, but I couldn't tear my eyes away from the brick.

"I have no idea if that's a mark you made or someone else, but the day after they tore it down, I had Quarry hop the fence and steal it for me."

"I . . . I was still here when they tore it down," I stuttered, glancing up just as he sat down on the corner of his desk.

He took the brick from my hand and set it down. Then he snagged my arm and tugged me against his side. I went willingly, resting my head on his shoulder as he folded his arms around my waist.

"Yeah, but even then, I was trying to hold on to you."

I melted into his arms.

All. The. Feels.

"Stop talking," I mumbled against his neck.

His hands teased under the back of my shirt. "What? That wasn't even dirty."

Just as I was about to ask for something dirty, a loud and strangely familiar voice boomed into the room.

"I swear to God I hope that boy gave you hell for that stunt you pulled."

My head popped up, and a half laugh, half gasp escaped my throat. "Max!" I cried, scrambling from Flint's embrace.

In a pair of jeans that had probably never seen the dirt and a black

On The Ropes collared shirt, Max glared at me from the doorway. He was pissed . . . and I couldn't have cared less. I rushed over and threw my arms around his neck.

"Oh my God! What are you doing here?" I asked when he released me.

"Me? I work here. What the hell are you doing?"

I spun around to Flint, who was watching us with an amused grin. "He works here?"

He shrugged and crossed his thick arms over his chest.

I looked back at Max. "You have a job?"

"Yep. Your boyfriend there got me the gig not long after you left. Donna too."

"Donna! Where is she?" My eyes jumped to the door.

"Oh, she's not here, baby girl. She shacked up with Slate's old boxing trainer. She lives in L.A. now."

"No. Fucking. Way," I breathed.

"Yep. Jimmy's a good guy, dotes on her like she's the Queen of Sheba. She's still cranky as hell, so brace yourself for when she finds out you're back. Let's just say she is *not* happy with you."

I laughed. "Was she ever happy with me?"

"Nope." He shook his head with a smile. "Listen, I've got to get back out there. I'm pulling security at the back door. We'll catch up at dinner after the fight."

"Okay." I gave him another hug. "I'm so happy to see you."

"You shouldn't be. You and I are going to have a serious chat tonight about that running-off bullshit."

I watched him leave then turned to find that Flint had shifted to his chair.

"You," was all I said as I approached him.

He flipped his computer open, not bothering to look at me. "Me?"

"Wheels, I'm not sure what to say."

He smiled at the screen.

"You got Max and Donna jobs?"

"It's no big deal. They helped me search for you when you left. We became friends."

I teasingly gasped, spinning his chair until he was facing me. "Judgey McGee became friends with two middle-aged, homeless people?"

He shrugged. "They're good people despite their situation. Some chick with a knack for running away told me that."

"She sounds awesome."

He quirked an eyebrow. "She sounds like I'm gonna make her ass red tonight."

I climbed to straddle his lap, briefly taking his mouth. "She sounds like she would love that." I smiled and his mirrored mine.

"Get out of here. I have work to do."

"Does your work involve me riding you in this chair?"

He barked out a laugh. "In twenty-four hours, I've turned you into a fiend."

I latched on to his neck, trailing openmouthed kisses up to his ear. "No, you keep doing sweet stuff that makes me all tingly. I show my appreciation in the same way I apologize."

"Fuck," he cursed as I circled my hips over his hardening dick.

I was reaching down to his button when I heard Till's angry voice behind me.

"You're late! Oh . . . Shit. Sorry."

Embarrassed, I buried my face in Flint's neck, but he let out a loud laugh that had me joining him.

"No, it's okay. I was about to come find you." He guided me off his lap. "Ash is on her way to find Eliza." He pecked me on the lips and nudged me from behind the desk.

"Right. Yes. Find Eliza," I mumbled, smoothing my hair down.

Till lifted his chin toward Flint as I walked to the door. "You keeping that one in check?"

"I was trying," I said sarcastically.

He bit his lip to stifle a laugh. "I can see." He winked and shoved his hands in his pockets as I passed.

I made my way to the row of seats Eliza had pointed out earlier, finding then blissfully empty.

Ducking under the chain blocking them off, I heard, "Sorry, miss. Those are reserved for families of the fighters."

I spun to find a big guy with dark hair and an olive complexion leaning over the railing. As soon as we made eye contact, his head snapped back and his eyes grew wide.

"Holy. Shit."

"I'm here with—"

"Flint," he finished for me. "Hi. I'm Leo James, Slate and Till's head of security." He extended a hand.

"Hi. I'm—"

"Ash Mabie." He once again filled in the blank. "I've spent a lot of time looking for you."

I wasn't exactly sure how to react. Was he mad?

I went with attitude. "Funny, I've heard that a lot."

"I'm not going to lie. I'm a big fan of yours."

It was my turn to snap my head back in shock. "Huh?"

"I hated it for Flint, but I was seriously impressed with how long you were able to elude us. You have no idea how many times we missed you by mere minutes. You're good. Really fucking good."

I tipped my head at the strange compliment. "Thanks?"

"I heard they found you, but I didn't expect to see you here tonight."

I blew out a breath. "Well, you aren't the only one. Flint, however, can be quite persuasive."

"He's a good kid. Dealt a shit hand, but what all of those boys have done with their lives . . ." He paused and shook his head. "Anyway, it was great meeting you. Officially. Enjoy the fight."

I groaned when I caught sight of Eliza approaching as he walked away. Leo paused to hug her before disappearing into the crowd.

"I see you're making friends already," Eliza noted as we both sat down. "Can I please just tell you how much I both love and hate fight nights? You would think after all these years that the nerves would be gone. Nope. I want to puke right now."

I turned my head and mentally grumbled at her attempted conversation before reminding myself to be nice. "You're nervous? About the fight?"

"Yeah. I have no idea why. I could watch Till and Flint box all day long, but Quarry makes me anxious. It doesn't matter that he's six foot three and two hundred pounds. He's still twelve in my book."

"He's six foot three?" I shrieked.

Eliza giggled. "I'm gathering that you haven't seen Q yet."

I shook my head.

"Yeah. He's all grown up. Bigger than Till, smaller than Flint. Same foul mouth though. He graduates from high school in a few months."

"No fucking way."

Quarry was one person I was stoked about seeing again. I'd missed that kid almost as much as I had Flint. Okay, not quite that much. But I thought about him a lot while I was gone.

"Listen, did Flint mention to you anything about Quarry's condition?"

"Condition?"

"Yeah. He's lost a good bit of his hearing over the years. He wears hearing aids when he's out of the ring, and those seem to help, but we use a lot of sign language."

"He's deaf?" I gasped, and my face must have paled, because she reached out and squeezed my hand.

"No! He's . . . just . . . heading in that direction," she amended. "He can still hear some, and with his hearing aids, it's significantly better. I'm only telling you this because tonight, at dinner, you'll probably be the only one who doesn't know sign. Sometimes, when the guys get going, they'll forget to talk."

I stared blankly ahead as the weight of having been on the run for the last three years sank in. "I can't believe I missed all this," I told her without looking in her direction. "First, it was Flint's first steps. Now, Q's deaf."

"Oh, Flint's first steps were no big deal."

"Why does everyone keep saying that?" I yelled entirely too loudly. "He told me the exact same thing. I'm sorry, but walking is a *huge* deal!"

She was sitting only a few inches away, but I'm relatively sure half the gym heard me.

"Shhh," she urged, looking over her shoulder to see how many people had witnessed my sudden outburst. "I didn't mean it like that, Ash. It's just . . . His first steps *weren't* a big deal. It was the day he put away the wheelchair for good that was so huge for him. That was the day he regained a part of his life. I went with him and Till when he donated his wheelchairs. I begged him to keep one—just in case, ya know? But he was adamant that he wanted them all gone. With the exception of this afternoon, I've never in my life seen Flint happier than that day when he walked back to the car wheelchair-free."

With the exception of this afternoon.

I looked down at my lap as my cheeks began to flush.

Yeah, I was pretty happy this afternoon too.

"Besides, you should never listen to anything Flint says is no big deal. He graduated college in two years." She threw up a pair of air quotes then said, "'No big deal.' He landed one of the biggest professional boxers on the scene his first week on the job." More air quotes. "'No big deal.' The kid used a lump sum of money Till had given him as a graduation present to buy a house at twenty-two." She looked at me.

"No big deal?" I guessed.

"Not to Flint." She shrugged. "There has been exactly one 'big deal' as long as I've known him." She leaned in close and reiterated. "*One.* Any guesses?"

Oh, I had a guess. I just wasn't brave enough to utter it. I shook my head instead.

"You," she whispered with a smile before her face shifted to serious. "Ash, you seem like a great girl, and I can't wait to get to know you, but I'll be very honest here. We're all worried about how this is going to go down with you two. The reason we poured every resource we had into finding you is because if Flint thought you were a big deal, then it was infinitely bigger than that. It was the enormous, life-changing, forever kind of deal."

My eyes glistened as I became fascinated with my shoes to hide the emotion her words were causing.

"I don't know what to say," I told the ground.

"Say that you're serious about him."

I could have said that. It would have been the truth. But for some reason, I had more important things to air out.

I lifted my head to stare into her kind eyes. "I hate you," I told her.

"I know," she replied, seemingly unfazed. "You made that pretty clear this afternoon."

"Eliza, by all accounts, you're only one step away from sainthood as far as the Page brothers are concerned. But knowing how he felt about you . . . I can't. I'm sorry."

Her eyes filled with tears, but they were strange. She didn't look like a woman who had just been injured by words. She looked . . . happy.

"And I'm completely okay with that as long as you love *him.*"

Forget the one step. Sainthood has been achieved.

"I . . ." I opened my mouth just to close it again.

"Ash, when this conversation ends, I'm going back to pretending I don't know how you feel about me. All I'm asking is that you truly consider how you feel about Flint before you shred him again over his misinterpreted feelings about me. I think of him as a son and nothing more."

"It was never about the way you felt for him!" I snapped.

She bit right back, "Then let it go! Don't punish the man for the thoughts of a boy." Pausing, she flipped her long, brown hair and looked around to make sure no one was watching our quiet altercation. "When you took off, Flint was a mess. He over-rationalized how he felt about you. He couldn't possibly have fallen in love with a sixteen-year-old girl he'd only known for a month. That shit didn't happen in his guarded and square existence. But it did, Ash. Now, tell me that you share these feelings . . . even in the past. And you can go back to hating me all you want."

I was taken aback by her honesty. I also respected the hell out of her for it.

And for that alone, I answered, "I've always been in love with Flint. It's present tense for me."

"Good," she drawled on a breath.

I dropped my head and watched her from the corner of my eye as I said, "Which is exactly why I'm not sure I can stay."

"I'm gonna do a quick time-out on you hating me." She threw her arms around me in an awkward side hug. "I know Flint and it's present tense for him too." She squeezed me tight for several seconds then released me and reclined in her chair. "Time in," she whispered.

Crossing her legs, she retrieved a sketchpad and pencil from her purse. She didn't attempt to engage me in any further conversation as we waited for the fights to start. Instead, she silently drew an elaborate pair of eyes. I watched in awe as Flint's long, black lashes came to life through the lines on her page. When she finished, she didn't even lift her head to acknowledge me. She just tore the paper out and passed it over to me.

I eagerly took it. Those were Flint's eyes, and they belonged to me—even if it was her hand that had drawn them.

Her kind, sweet, and saintly hand, which I couldn't even hate anymore.

Damn it!

CHAPTER
Twenty-Five

Ash

"WELL WELL WELL! LOOK WHAT the gimp dragged in." Quarry spoke and signed when we walked into the locker room after the fight—a fight he had easily won with a knockout in the third round.

"Oh my God, you're huge!" I squealed as he lifted me off my feet in a bear hug. "Look at you, all grown up." I stepped away and teasingly raked my eyes up and down his body as he proudly flexed and struck different poses. "Damn, Q. if I had known you were gonna look like this, I might have let you feel my boobs all those times you tried."

He busted out laughing. *"Who says I didn't? You're a pretty deep sleeper."* Smirking, he dodged the punch I halfheartedly threw at his shoulder.

"You little perv."

"Dude, where the hell have you been?" He fluidly signed every word as he spoke.

I hated every single second of it.

While we'd waited for Q to shower and change, Flint had filled me in on Quarry's hearing loss. He'd told me that it had started really going downhill around his sixteenth birthday. Thankfully, because of Till, they were all already fluent in sign language, and Quarry was already attending a private school for the deaf, so it hadn't been a drastic change for him. To hear Flint tell it, though, it was "no big deal." I had a sneaking suspicion that Quarry probably didn't feel the same way.

"Well, I've spent the last three years in various mental health facilities trying to get over the horrifying images I saw of you getting out of the shower the night I left."

"*Shut the hell up.*" He laughed.

"I'm serious, Quarry. I hear penile implants are all the rage these days. You should look into it."

"You got jokes, huh?" he said without signing, but only because his hands were busy scooping me up off the ground and tossing me over his shoulder.

I was howling with laughter as he spun in a circle.

"No," Flint suddenly barked when one of Quarry's hands disappeared. "Don't you fucking dare," he growled.

Q's shoulders began shaking with laughter beneath me before he placed me back on my feet. He looked at Flint, but his words were directed at me out of the corner of his mouth. "Apparently, I'm not allowed to slap your ass anymore."

"Anymore?" I asked, also staring at Flint, who didn't appear to be even remotely amused.

"Okay, so you're a *really* deep sleeper."

I punched him in the shoulder, hurting my hand because he'd flexed just before it had landed. "Son of a bitch." I shook it out as Quarry laughed.

His laughing stopped as the door creaked open behind me. I was more focused on my poor knuckles than anything else though. It wasn't until I saw the way the sound had transformed Quarry's bright-hazel eyes into a deep, sexy smolder that I decided to spin to see who had joined us.

An obviously excited girl came barreling into the room.

"Ash, move," Flint urged, but my eyes were glued to her as she all but flew toward us. Her jet-black hair was cut into an adorable pixie cut, with a large chunk of pink covering her sweeping bang. Her jeans had holes that had no doubt been there when she'd bought them in the knees, and she was rocking skull-patterned Converse I was jealous of.

"Ash, move," Flint repeated roughly.

Thankfully, I followed his order and stepped out of the way, narrowly avoiding being plowed over. The girl never even slowed as she launched herself into Quarry's waiting arms. Wrapping her legs around his waist, she didn't waste a second before crushing her mouth over his in something that couldn't even be called a kiss. It was rabid and came accompanied by moans from both parties. Quarry's hands slid from her waist to her butt, squeezing as he carried her over to the table in the corner and sat down without ever breaking the hasty make-out session.

"Uh . . ." I turned to Flint. "Should we leave?"

"I'm not sure yet. Give it another minute to see if she goes for his pants. That's usually my cue."

No sooner had he finished speaking than Quarry let out a loud groan and Flint's eyes flashed over my head.

"Yep. We should go."

I didn't dare turn around as we rushed from the room.

"What the hell!" I laughed when we got outside.

"Don't feel bad. That's pretty much how we all met Mia."

"And what? We just stand out here until they finish?"

"Oh God no. I'm not listening to that shit. They'll meet us at the restaurant." He popped his elbow out, and I all-too-quickly accepted.

Till rounded the corner. "Yo. Where's Q?"

"Too slow. Mia got there first," Flint replied.

Till curled his lip. "He got his hearing aids in?"

"Yeah. He was just talking to Ash."

Till walked past us and banged his fist on the door. "You got two minutes. Then I'm coming in. If I catch you with your dick out, I'm ripping it off."

Flint erupted into laughter. "Good luck with that."

"Yeah, thanks," Till responded then pounded on the door again. "One minute."

"Come on." Flint led me out the back door to his SUV. "You have fun tonight?"

"I really did."

His lips twisted in a smirk. "Even the part where you had to sit with Eliza for three hours?"

"Well, it wasn't as fun as this next part is going to be, but yeah, it was good." I pushed to my toes to take his mouth.

He raked his teeth over my bottom lip. "What's the next part?"

Flint

"Fuck," I cursed as Ash took my cock to the back of her throat.

The moment we'd pulled into the restaurant's parking lot, I'd found out exactly what the next part was.

My hands were tangled in her hair as she hovered over the center console, milking the come from my cock. She swallowed like a fucking champ and continued to work me until I couldn't take anymore.

"Ash. Stop." I tugged at her shoulders, but she continued swirling her tongue around the head, showing no signs of stopping. "Ash," I groaned. Using her hair, I dragged her up, occupying her obviously frantic mouth with my own. I could still taste the saltiness of my release lingering on her tongue, but I couldn't have given two shits. It was in *her* mouth.

She scrambled over the console to mount me. "I want to feel you inside me."

"Baby, not here," I managed to say before she threaded her fingers into my hair to deepen the kiss.

"Please. I need to feel you," she pleaded, rocking against me.

Shit. "I don't have a condom."

She let out an impatient groan. "Just pull out." Then she moved her oral attack to my neck.

"Um. No. As much as I'd love to feel you bare, that is not a chance I'm willing to take."

She sighed in frustration. "God, why are you so responsible?"

"Because the day I get you pregnant, you will have my ring on your finger. Also, knocking you up now would really impede all the plans I have for fucking you over the next few years."

She laughed against my neck and shifted off my lap. "Only you would use words like *impede* during sexy talk."

I might not have been willing to fuck her in the car, but I wasn't done with her yet, either. I followed her with my upper body into her seat. Palming her breasts, I said, "You want to come, Ash?"

Her eyes heated as she nodded.

I looked around the empty back parking lot of the restaurant, knowing that my entire family was probably in the front, waiting for us.

Fuck it.

"Take your pants off and open your legs," I ordered, pressing two fingers into her mouth.

She swirled her tongue around them in a familiar way, sending blood rushing back to my softening cock. I popped my fingers from her mouth while she fumbled with tearing her jeans and panties down her legs.

"This needs to be quick, so I want you to talk to me. Tell me what you like."

Her eyes grew wide. "I like when you touch me?" She phrased it as a question.

I smirked. "I got that much. But how?" I glided my damp fingers over her pussy, spreading her before pushing two fingers inside. "Like this?"

Her head fell back against the headrest.

"Or like this?" I asked before dropping my thumb to her clit.

She all but clawed her way up the seat.

Like that.

"Oh God," she panted as I hurriedly circled the sensitive bud.

She undulated as my fingers continued to pump inside her. I wished it were my cock, but as I watched her lose herself, it was almost better. Her hips rolled into my every thrust until she finally stilled. Her nails bit into my forearm as her whole body tensed. Then a strangled cry escaped from her throat and her cunt pulsed around my fingers.

My thumb continued to circle her clit until the orgasm faded into hypersensitivity.

"Flint, please," she breathed, pushing my hand away—a command I unfortunately had to follow.

"Get dressed. We're eating dinner. Then I'm taking you home for dessert." I lifted my hand to my mouth, licking her arousal off each finger.

She watched me intently as she tugged her pants up. "Are you sure? You just had that for breakfast."

I laughed, dropping my hands to button my own jeans. "Oh, I'm positive. Now, let's get this over with."

CHAPTER
Twenty-Six

Ash

"OH, I SEE HOW IT is. I get yelled at for getting some in the locker room, but when Flint comes limping in looking like he just had an orgy, everyone smiles," Quarry said and signed when the hostess led us to the group already seated in the back.

A gorgeous Hispanic girl slapped him upside the back of his head, while Mia giggled, snuggling under his arm.

"Dumbass," Flint mumbled. "Everyone, this is Ash. Ash, this is . . ." He leaned forward to look all the way down the table. "Jesus, why are all of you here?"

Everyone laughed; then all eyes landed on me.

Great. No pressure.

"All right," he huffed, pointing at the end of the table. "That's Leo James and his wife, Sarah." He swung his arm to the Hispanic girl sitting at the other end next to Quarry. "That's their daughter, Liv. Then you know Max, of course." He pointed to a guy covered in tattoos with his arm draped around the back of a blonde's chair. "That's Caleb Jones, and his wife, Emma, who is Sarah's sister." He waved his finger back to the end of the table. "The ugly guy is Aiden Johnson, and the ogre next to him is Alex Pearson. They run security for Leo, who runs security for Till and Slate." He sucked in a dramatic breath before continuing. "You already know Till and Eliza and Slate and Erica." Lifting his hands to sign, he finished with, *"Oh, and the pink flamingo next to Quarry is Mia March."*

They all laughed as Mia lifted her hands and signed what I could only assume were choice words.

"She loves me," he told me, signing something back.

She flipped him off as Quarry barked out a laugh. Then he tipped her back for a kiss that made the entire table groan in disgust.

"Hi!" I waved with both hands before sitting in the chair Flint had pulled out for me.

All eyes followed me as I sat down.

"Quit gawking and go back to talking," he demanded, and apparently, I wasn't the only one who naturally followed his orders, because within seconds, everyone started chattering again.

"Who the hell are all these people?" I asked quietly as Flint settled beside me.

"Your search party," he answered matter-of-factly, waving a waitress down to order our drinks.

Not. Awkward. At. All.

The girl across from me interrupted my inner embarrassment. "Hi, Ash. I'm Liv. Q's told me a lot about you."

Quarry suddenly became unstuck from Mia's mouth and tossed his arm around the back of Liv's chair.

"The good or the bad stuff?" My eyes flashed to his arm and then back to her.

"Good. He told us you were a pickpocket."

My gaze shifted to Quarry. "That's the good stuff?"

He shrugged, ignoring me to go back to signing with Mia.

"I have been known to lift a wallet a time or two."

Flint choked on a sip of water. "A time or two? You have my wallet right now. Beautiful, don't think I missed you swiping that while I was doing the intros."

"No way," Liv breathed. "Like right now?"

"Yeah, but what he doesn't know is I got his keys too." I placed them both on the table as Flint patted his pockets down, cursing.

"Badass," she breathed.

Mia reached over Quarry to catch Liv's attention, pulling her into their silent conversation.

I looked up at Flint, who was watching them talk while Q sat like a king guarding his harem. "What's the dynamic there?"

"Liv and Q have been best friends since they were kids. She lives in Chicago, so she's only around sporadically. He started dating Mia about two years ago. They've been joined at the pelvis ever since. Mia is all kinds of scrappy. You should have seen the brawl that almost ensued the first time she met Liv. They got over it at some point though. Now, Mia and Liv are best friends and Q's the third wheel."

"Is Mia deaf too?"

"Yeah. She lost her hearing as a kid. Brain tumor."

"Oh, damn," I whispered.

He snuck his hand under the table to rest it on my thigh. "She's fine now. Well, fine enough to jump Quarry on every flat surface in Till's house."

A laugh bubbled from my throat.

"I give her hell, but she's a cool chick. She keeps Quarry's ass in line, so we all love her." He began perusing the menu.

"Hey, Flint," Slate yelled from the end of the table. "What ever happened with that potential fight for Griff in Atlantic City?"

"Oh, let me tell you this bullshit. Four figures. *Four.* Hang on." He turned to kiss me. "I'll be right back." He snagged his crutches and headed down to Slate and Till.

Just as he got close, Eliza excused herself, and Flint filled her chair.

They had a heated discussion both verbally and through sign. I guessed the bad stuff was spoken in sign, since Till looked over his shoulder every time one of them lifted their hands. I couldn't help but laugh at how animated Flint was with his hands. For such a stoic man, sign seemed to really bring out the drama in him.

Suddenly, Eliza slid into Flint's vacant chair beside me. "So, whatcha wearing on your date tomorrow night?" she asked with a huge grin.

She was really taking this pretending thing to a whole new level.

"Um . . ." I raked a hand through my hair. I had exactly three outfits: jeans and a tie-dyed T-shirt, jeans and a black V-neck T-shirt, and jeans and a Grumpy Cat T-shirt. It wasn't a hard question to answer. "Jeans and a T-shirt."

"You want to come raid my closet? What size dress do you wear?

I mean, you're taller than I am, but we're about the same size, right?" She scooted over, measuring herself against me.

I might not have *hated* Eliza anymore after our conversation at the gym. However, going on my first date with Flint while wearing her clothes was never going to happen. *Never.*

Not even an eternity after never.

Never.

"Thanks, but I think I have something." I smiled tightly.

"Okay. If you change your mind, let me know." She must have read my brush-off, because she didn't delay in heading back to her seat.

But she had planted a seed that quickly grew into panic. *What the fucking hell am I going to wear on my date with Flint?* I had twenty-one dollars to my name. Shopping wasn't exactly an option.

Shit. Shit. Shit.

"Why do you look like your head's about to explode?" Flint asked, finishing the game of musical chairs.

"I need to get a job."

His eyebrows popped up, and he scrubbed a hand over the stubble on his jaw. "You going to stay here long enough to work?"

"Well . . . I'm not sure. But I . . . I . . ." I hadn't exactly made my mind up yet, but I also hadn't thought about leaving again. "I'm considering it."

His hand settled back on my thigh before drifting up between my legs. "You're staying."

"I'm considering it," I repeated, spreading my legs to allow him more room to play.

And play he did.

I had just come in the car and I was incredibly sore from the last twenty-four hours, but my body craved him. I bit my lip, trying not to show any reaction while his hand traveled up and down the seam of my jeans.

I figured that, if he could secretly grope me at a table in front of his family, I could do the same.

He caught my wrist just as it brushed over his dick. "Jesus," he whispered, sliding his hand back to my knee and placing mine on top of it.

The waitress appeared beside him. "Are you guys ready to order?"

I hadn't even looked at a menu yet, but Flint eagerly answered. "Yes. Two steaks, medium-well, baked potatoes, and salad with ranch." He paused and looked over at me with a smirk. "In a to-go box, please."

Twenty minutes later, when the food arrived, Flint announced that I was tired. It wasn't exactly a lie. I was ready for bed.

Probably not to sleep though.

We got several knowing looks as we said our goodbyes, but no one argued. Not even Quarry—who offered Flint a high five that got left hanging. After promises of future get-togethers, Flint and I headed home with two steaks in tow.

Sated and naked in Flint's bed, I tipped my head up from his chest and asked, "Hey, you think you can get me a job at the gym like you did Max and Donna?"

"No," he answered curtly.

I looked away, embarrassed that I'd even asked. "Okay."

"Don't act like that. I originally got Max and Donna a job doing housekeeping on the weekends when the afterschool program was off. There is no way I'm getting you a job cleaning the men's locker room."

I sat up. "Oh, I could clean the hell out of that locker room. I'm good at cleaning."

He pointedly glanced over at all of my stuff, which was in a messy pile in the corner of his otherwise pristine room. "I can tell."

"Oh, shut up! I'm messy, but I'm really good at cleaning. Please, Flint. I need to make some money."

"No, you don't. I'll give you money." He pulled me down to rest on his chest.

I sat right back up. "I'm not taking your money," I said, appalled by the very idea.

He laughed. "Says the woman who steals my wallet every chance she gets."

"That's not fair. I always give it back. I've never stolen anything from you for real," I snapped as my heart began to race.

The impulse to run overwhelmed me as his words from the past hit me like a hurricane, stripping me bare before blowing away any hopes I'd been clinging to since Flint had walked back into my life.

I am not a criminal.

Who was I kidding?

That's all I've ever been in his eyes.

"Ash?" he said as I started to slowly scoot toward the edge of the bed. "Where are you going?"

The covers fell away, exposing his nakedness, as he pushed up on his elbows. Crawling out of his bed, I etched the sight into my memory.

He's gorgeous.

Maybe he was right. I was a thief.

Because I had made a million memories with Flint over the last day, and I was taking every single one of them with me when I left.

I pasted on a fake smile. "I'm still hungry. I'm gonna warm up some food. Just go to sleep. I'll be right back." I went to my pile in the corner and tugged some clothes on.

"Ash, what the fuck are you doing?" Flint growled, grabbing his crutches to follow me.

Gathering my hair and pulling it from the back of my shirt, I turned to face him. "I'm just getting something to eat. What are you doing?" I teasingly raked my eyes over his naked body as he approached. Then I let out a laugh, but only to cover the quiver of my chin.

I was dying inside.

Completely withering away at the idea of leaving him again. Yet I had to do it.

"Since when do you need shoes to warm up food in the kitchen?" he snarked, catching my arm.

Suddenly, I became frantic. Lying wasn't working, but I had to get out of there.

I lifted my chin and straightened my back. Very calmly, I demanded, "Let me go, Flint."

We both knew I wasn't just talking about physically.

He flinched but then quickly recovered. His eyes narrowed as he dropped his hand.

Freedom—and a lifetime of agony—was only a hundred-yard dash away.

Unfortunately, my body once again unlocked the magic of teleportation, because in the blink of an eye, I was flat on the ground with Flint on top of me. His crutches were still attached to his forearms as he pinned me to the ground.

"You will not take off on me without an explanation of what the fuck just happened. Not ten minutes ago, you were riding my cock. Now, you're telling me to let you go."

"Please," I whispered, turning my head so I didn't have to see the determination in his eyes.

He'd more than made it clear that he wanted me to stay; I couldn't be reminded of that as I made my escape.

He shook his crutches off one by one then forced my eyes back to his. "Don't you dare shut down on me. What the hell is going on inside your head right now? Start talking."

Flint couldn't walk very well, but he had mastered the pinning-to-the-ground thing. I couldn't have moved if I'd tried.

And I definitely tried.

Finally, I gave up attempting to shimmy out from under his bulky body and said, "I want a job."

"Fine. Get a fucking job. All I said was that I wouldn't get you one cleaning the gym. My woman is not cleaning up after a bunch of nasty-ass men who can't even hit a urinal when they are standing in front of it. No fucking way."

Okay. So that made sense, but it wasn't the root of the problem.

"I don't want your money. I might be a thief, but I'm not a beggar." My traitorous voice quivered at the end.

His tense body slacked in understanding. "You're not a thief, Ash." He tried to kiss my lips, but I turned my head, so it landed on my cheek. "You're not a thief," he repeated into my ear.

I flipped my head to the other side, wishing I'd preemptively pulled a Van Gogh and cut the other ear off.

"You. Are. Not. A. Thief."

But words could never be trusted any more than they could be unsaid—or, in my case, forgotten.

"Get off me."

He was terrible at following orders, because if anything, he got *on* me more. Shifting to cover me completely, he placed a kiss on my exposed neck. "I made a joke about you stealing my wallet. I didn't mean anything by it. If you want the truth, I fucking love when you swipe it. It makes me laugh every time. And that's something I didn't do a whole lot of while you were gone. If a job is important to you, I'll help you find one. Maybe you could do some filing for Till or Slate. Their offices are a wreck.

"But please understand that I want to provide for you. I'm sorry. I know we are just starting over and all that bullshit, but I have worked my ass off, and in the back of my mind, it was always so I could have something to offer you if, and when, I got you back. Ash, I'm half of a man who limps through life on crutches. I'll never be able to scoop you off your feet the way Quarry did today. Even fucking you the way I want is a challenge. I have a lot of limitations in life, but providing for you will never be one of them."

My heart shattered.

I was hurt, but I wouldn't allow him to feel that way.

Turning to face him, I cupped his jaw with both hands. After pressing a reassuring kiss to his mouth, I said, "You are *not* half of a man, and anyone who has ever met you knows that. Especially me." I kissed him again.

His lips twitched against mine. "Ash, you are *not* a thief, and anyone who has ever met you knows that. Especially me."

A megawatt smile formed on his lips.

Son of a bitch!

"Oh my God, you did that on purpose!" I yelled, causing him to laugh and drop his head to my shoulder. "You just made me feel sorry for you to prove a point."

He continued laughing.

"What kind of asshole manipulates a woman's feelings just to use them against her?" My voice broke on a sob.

His head immediately popped up, and his laughter fell silent. "That's not what . . ." he started but stopped mid sentence when he caught sight of my victorious grin. "Oh, you are so going to pay for that." He began tickling me as I squirmed underneath him.

For several minutes, we rolled around on the floor, laughing and acting like the kids we really were. Finally, when we were both out of breath, we climbed into bed. Flint ordered me to undress then promptly juggled me into our position. It was late, and we were exhausted.

I wished I could stay in that bed with him forever.

I wished I could let go of the past and trust his words.

His smartass joke was only a Band-Aid over the gaping wound that was killing our relationship before we had even gotten started.

Or maybe my doubts were killing us.

As I snuggled into his arms, I breathed in deeply, trying to burn that moment into my memory forever.

I would need it more than anything else when I started over again.

CHAPTER
Twenty-Seven

Flint

I WOKE UP EARLY THE next morning with my hands kneading Ash's breasts. She was sound asleep, but my cock twitched between us. I would have given anything to take her right then, but I knew I should wait. She had gone from being virtually untouched for nineteen years to having come at least a dozen times in under two days. That night was our first official date, and I had every plan of ending it with my cock buried to the hilt inside her. So, despite the ache between my legs, I let her rest.

The clock flashed six A.M. but there was no possible way I could have fallen back to sleep. I shifted, trying to scoot out of bed, but unlike Awake Ash, Sleeping Ash *was* a cuddler. She followed me as I tried to inch my way out from under her. Then I chuckled when she all but crawled on top of me.

The sun was just starting to light the room, but coffee would have to wait. I'd been starved of her for entirely too long. Wrapping my arms around her, I spent an hour soaking her in as she slept peacefully on top of me. The last two days played on a loop while the previous years faded into nothing more than a distant memory.

We still had so much stuff to work through—the misunderstanding the night before being the prime example—but I was committed.

I'd talked a big game about making her fall in love with me again and getting to know the real Ash Mabie.

But the truth was that I didn't need to know any more about her.

I love her.

Every crazy, quirky bit of her, I undeniably loved.

As I kissed the top of her head, my eyes drifted to my old book she had used as a journal over the years, sitting on her nightstand.

It was probably a gross invasion of privacy, but I had spent the day prior reading every word she'd written inside that Dave Eggers book. It had taken me a little while to figure out what the highlights meant, but I finally came to the conclusion that they were her streams of consciousness written in code. The random pink-highlighted letters all combined into sentences about how she'd been happy. She'd rambled about people she'd met, books she'd read from the library, and the longest of all was when Judy had baked a cake for Ash's birthday.

The blue seemed to be when she had been sad. She'd written about missing her dad even though she knew she had done the right thing by turning him in. She'd mentioned how hard it had been being on the run, and once, she'd debated stealing food versus being hungry. It was all I could do not to set the book on fire after that.

However, I tried to focus on the green letters. Those were her dreams. There wasn't an F, L, I, N, or T in that book that wasn't highlighted in green. She hadn't been lying. I had been walking in every single dream she'd had. But what bothered me was that I was usually walking out on her.

Her subconscious couldn't have been more wrong. I was never letting her go.

Some time later, I drifted back to sleep with her still snuggled on top of me.

It wasn't until I woke up that I realized that, while I might not ever let her go, holding on to her wouldn't be easy, either.

"Ash?" I groaned, stretching my stiff muscles across the empty bed.

Prying my eyes open, I looked at the clock.

How the hell did I sleep to eleven?

"Ash," I called again, but the house remained notably silent. I pushed to my feet and tugged a pair of shorts and a t-shirt on. Then I headed out to find her.

Wandering around the house, I called her name, but room after room, I came up empty.

"Ash!" I yelled up the stairs that led to the unused spare bedrooms.

I'd bought that house determined to one day be able to navigate those stairs. They were a physical reminder that, while I was up on two legs, I was a long way from full mobility. They both taunted me and drove me on a daily basis.

I started the daunting task of climbing them, but at the last minute, I talked myself out of it, deciding to check the weeds instead.

I checked every possible room in my house, but she was nowhere to be found. My mind began to race with possibilities, stretching the gamut of "She'll be back any minute" to "She's gone and I'll never see her again."

Heading back to my room, I grabbed my cell phone, panic building with every step.

Surely, she wouldn't try to run again?

We'd made some great strides the night before, and we were supposed to have a date that night.

When I rounded the corner of the room, relief settled in my chest—her clothes were neatly folded in the corner. They were a mess the night before, so at some point that morning, she had to have folded and organized them. The relief was short-lived, though, because the messenger bag she used to carry everything was notably missing.

She wouldn't have left her clothes though.

Would she?

There was only one thing I knew for a fact Ash would never leave behind—and unfortunately, it wasn't me.

My pulse spiked as I slowly turned toward her nightstand, praying with all of my heart that I was wrong.

"Oh God," I breathed, stumbling back several steps, almost falling to the ground before getting my crutches back under myself.

The empty spot where her book had once lain gutted me.

She's gone.

"You need to calm the fuck down," Till barked as I threw the malfunctioning coffee maker against the floor.

It had been two hours since I'd realized that Ash had taken off, and just like all the years before, I was waffling between despair and anger. For the first hour and a half, I drove around looking for her. But with every passing minute, hope of finding her faded further out of my reach.

Out of sheer desperation, I'd called Till, who had, in turn, called Leo.

The search for Ash Mabie was on all over again.

"No, what I fucking need is a goddamn cup of coffee and a woman who doesn't run away every chance she gets."

"Well, I happen to agree with you, but right this very second, you have a broken coffee maker and a woman who may or may not be missing. So let's calm the hell down and try to figure this out."

Eliza stopped pacing around my couch long enough to ask, "Do you want me to make a coffee run?"

"No, I don't want you to make a goddamn coffee run," I snapped at her.

Till quickly corrected me. "Hey! Watch your mouth. She was trying to help."

I took a deep breath, closing my eyes and dropping my chin to my chest.

This was not happening.

Not again.

Not when I'd just gotten her back.

"Chill out. We're going to find her. Just like we did last time," Till assured.

I pinched the bridge of my nose. "When? In three years, like last time? Just to keep her for forty-eight hours before she runs again? I *can't* spend my life trapped inside that vicious cycle!" I yelled without lifting my head.

The problem was that I couldn't step out of the cycle, either. Not as long as she was part of it.

Till squeezed my shoulder. "What are you saying? You want me to call Leo off?"

"No! I just want someone to fucking find her and make her love me the way I love her. I want her to *want* to stay with me." I scrubbed a hand through my hair, completely defeated.

Suddenly, Leo's voice joined the conversation. "Well, now, you just sound like a pussy."

My head snapped up to find him and Slate standing behind Till.

Leo took a step forward. "Get yourself together and stop acting like a bitch. Your woman will be here in ten minutes. She was with Liv at a thrift store across town."

My eyes flashed between him and Slate as I attempted to get my emotional breakdown under control.

Only I couldn't do that at all.

The sudden rush of relief left me shaky. Leo was right; I had never looked like a bitch more in my life. But I was completely okay with that.

She's on her way home.

I blew out a loud breath and walked over to the couch, flopping down to hide the effects the adrenaline was having on my already weak legs.

"Awww, she was shopping," Eliza cooed, joining me on the couch.

I cleared the lump from my throat before announcing, "I'm gonna kill her."

Till chuckled. "It's probably easier to buy her a cell phone."

"How the hell did she end up with Liv?" I asked Leo.

"She called Q this morning and got her number. I'll be honest. It was just luck that I found her so quickly. I was looking for my keys to come over here when Sarah told me Liv had taken the car to go shopping. Called Liv to tell her to get her ass back home and she told me she was with Ash." He shrugged. "I'm still billing you though. And just so you know, Sundays are time and a half." He laughed.

I didn't. I was fuming.

I was pissed at myself for having overreacted and assumed the worst, but also at Ash for not at least leaving a note to let me know where she had gone.

But mainly at myself.

"All right. Thanks for coming over, but if she's on her way back, I need all of you to get the fuck out."

Ash

"Where the fuck have you been?" Flint growled from the couch the second I walked though the door.

I set my bags down on the ground and ran my fingers through my freshly trimmed hair. "I'm starting to sense a pattern forming here. Is that the way you're planning to greet me every time you see me? Because I have to be honest. It's not working for me."

"It is when I've spent half the day thinking you took off again."

"What?" I asked, surprised. "Why would you think that? I just went to run some errands."

"You couldn't leave a note?" he asked rudely.

I swayed my head from side to side, pretending to consider it. "I guess I could. I just didn't think about it." I shrugged. "Hey, guess what?"

He didn't ask the obligatory, "What?" He just blinked at me in disbelief.

Finally, I asked, "What?"

"I spent the entire morning worried about you. I destroyed my coffee maker and was about twelve seconds away from a nervous breakdown. And you want me to 'guess what'?" He threw up some very angry air quotes.

"Well I'm sorry to hear that, but it's a really good 'guess what.'" I waggled my eyebrows then repeated, "Guess what?"

He dropped his head back to stare up at the ceiling, mumbling what sounded like a prayer for patience.

Apparently, Flint Page was not a fan of guessing games, so I just went straight to the point. "I got a job! You are looking at the newest shampoo girl at To Dye For. I saw the *help wanted* sign, went in and talked to the owner this morning. Bam! Ten minutes later, I was employed and getting a new *free* haircut. Then—oh, this is my favorite part—Liv and I went to the thrift shop and I found the most adorable little black dress for our date tonight. It's really simple, but it makes my boobs look amazing."

Flint blew out an exasperated sigh then leveled me with a glare. "Ash, just get naked."

I took my shirt off before I asked, "Seriously?"

He pushed to his feet. "I've had the worst day imaginable, and you for some reason have zero grasp of that. You seem to apologize best naked, so I'm cashing in the angry fuck." He grabbed his dick, which was suddenly bulging from the front of his athletic shorts.

My tongue snaked out to lick my lips. "I do like those kind of apologies," I whispered, reaching back to unclasp my bra.

"Go get in bed. I'll be there in a minute."

I continued to stare as his hand disappeared into the front of his shorts. Then I walked over, stopping directly in front of him. "Can I help with that?" I guided my fingers down over the ripples of his abs and under his waistband.

When my fingertips brushed the head of his cock, a firm hand landed against my ass. I dropped my forehead against his chest. Sparks sent blood rushing to my clit, and a strangled moan flew from my mouth.

He removed my hand from his shorts but taunted me by pulling his hard-on out and continuing to stroke it between us. "I said. Go. Get. In. Bed."

"Okay. Okay." I relented, sauntering away.

"You better be naked when I get there, too."

"Bossy, bossy, bossy," I chanted, but I started shimmying out of my jeans before I'd even turned the corner down the hall.

After toeing my shoes off, I hopped into the bedroom, tugging my jeans down my legs. My panties quickly followed as I climbed onto the bed.

Not even a full minute later, Flint entered the room, dragging one of his kitchen stools behind him. He walked straight to the nightstand and retrieved a strip of condoms.

I tossed him my best sultry smile, but he hadn't been kidding about the whole angry thing.

He.

Looked.

Pissed.

"Flip over and put your ass in the air," he demanded, stopping at the foot of he bed. Upon taking his crutches off, he tossed them to the other side of the bed. After dropping the condoms on the bed next to me, he pushed his shorts off and settled on the stool. "And back up."

I didn't argue.

Holy shit. Angry Flint is hot.

Grabbing both of my thighs, he dragged me to the edge of the bed. I was propped up on my elbows with my ass at his eye level, completely exposed in every possible way. But I was with him. Nothing else mattered.

He inched up his stool until it was flush against the mattress. I peeked over my shoulder just as he dragged a finger over my opening and down to my clit. My breath hitched when he looked up into my eyes; his were burning with a mix of anger and desire.

I was turned on by the anger but terrified by the desire. It wasn't the way he usually looked when he was turned on. It was different— and fierce.

"I thought you'd left," he said, holding my eyes and pushing a single finger inside.

As he slowly removed it, I groaned from the loss. "I just went shopping." A hand landed on my ass and his finger darted back inside, mixing the most amazing combination of pain and pleasure.

"I fucking thought you'd left," he growled, deliciously curling his fingers before they were suddenly gone again.

My knees went weak, and I followed him down with my hips, chasing his hand for more. His hand wasn't what I got at all.

"Ass up," he demanded, leaning forward and raking his teeth over the ass cheek.

Chills spread over my body, but I lifted my ass as high as possible. His tongue laved over my core before darting inside.

I rocked back against his face, but just like with his fingers, his mouth disappeared.

"Flint, please. Stop teasing me," I huffed

"I was scared to death, Ash. Looked like a bitch in front of my entire fucking family. All because you didn't leave a goddamn note." He pressed back inside me.

"I'm sorry," I breathed.

"I will never go through that again. Never. Do you hear me?" He twisted his hand back and forth, pushing deeper every time.

My release built. "Oh God. Keep going," I begged.

He stilled his hand as he once more bit my ass. "*Never again.*"

"Okay! I'm sorry!" I cried. "I get it."

"No, you really fucking don't," he gritted out, but his fingers began an unrelenting rhythm. "I need you to come now, Ash. I'm about to fuck you, and I can't swear that you'll get off. So this part is for you—the fucking is for me."

"Stop talking," I whispered, rolling my hips against his hand.

"Hurry up."

I can do that.

Flint added his other hand into the mix, tapping and circling my clit while he pumped his fingers in and out of me. It wasn't long before I was stepping off the edge of climax, calling his name on the descent.

I collapsed face first onto the bed, lost in the post-orgasm fog.

I vaguely heard the crinkle of the condom behind me. The next thing I knew, Flint had lifted me off the bed, settling me on his lap. He was still sitting on the stool, but he had shifted backwards so his legs had room between the stool and the mattress. His chest was to my back, and one of his arms was wrapped tight around my waist.

"Close your legs and put your feet on the bed," he ordered, lifting me to hover over his waiting cock. He guided the tip inside me as I followed his directions. No sooner had my knees touched than he roughly slammed inside me.

"Oh God," I cried as he filled me deeper than ever before.

He folded his other arm over my chest so his forearm rested between my breasts and his hand gripped my shoulder. Then he once again lifted me before roughly forcing me back down.

"You do not run from me." He bit the base of my neck.

"Fuck." I angled my head to give him more room, moaning with his every nip. "I wasn't running."

He slammed into me again. "You will not do that to me again."

Up.

Then down again.

I dropped my head back against his shoulder, turning to capture his mouth. Flint's tongue was rough and demanding, and his stubble rubbed against my face.

He released my mouth in order to shift me for another deep thrust.

I was on top, but there was no mistake that Flint was absolutely fucking me—using his upper body to do the work his legs were incapable of.

"You have completely fucked with my head. I'm a goddamn mess, waiting for the day when you choose to leave again."

Up.

Down.

"Ahhh," I cried as he leaned forward, changing the angle. He wasn't as deep anymore, but it was even better.

"Rock," he demanded, kissing my neck.

I threw a hand up, gripping the back of his hair and used the bed as leverage to move against him. My legs were closed tight, and my clit was squeezed with each movement.

"I need to know if you're planning to stay."

"Flint," I breathed.

"Just fucking tell me!" he yelled, starting a frantic rhythm inside me. His fingers were painfully biting into my hips and my shoulder with every thrust, but his cock was driving me toward the brink of release. "Answer the fucking question. Are you here to stay?"

"Yes!" I cried.

Planting himself to the hilt, he cursed while his cock jumped and twitched as he came.

Out of breath, he panted, "Say it again."

"Yes. I'm staying."

His chest heaved from exertion, but it was his heart pounding against my back that exposed his anxiety. "Swear to me. I need to hear you say it."

What I said probably wasn't what he'd expected to hear, but it was more honest than any oath I could have ever made to him.

I wasn't ready for the rejection I was so frightened I would receive, but I was sick of running from the only thing I'd ever truly wanted to keep.

I'd decided the night before that I was starting over with my life. I was doing it without fear. And *hopefully,* I was doing it with *him.*

"I love you, Flint. I'll stay for as long as you want me."

His shoulders immediately relaxed, and his hands loosened their grip. "Forever."

My eyes began to swim even as a smile crept across my face. Reaching up to my shoulder, I placed my hand on top of his and intertwined our fingers. Then I crossed my arm and did the same with his hand at my hip.

"Then I'm staying forever."

He exhaled a relieved breath. "I don't know how to trust you."

"I think that's something we're both gonna have to learn, but I'm willing to try if you are."

"Even if things get bad, Ash, just talk to me instead of taking off. Don't assume anything. I'm not always going to say the right thing. I'll probably fuck up—"

"Flint." I looked back, interrupting him.

His gorgeous, blue eyes were nervously searching mine.

"Stop talking." I smiled.

He rested his chin on my shoulder but kept talking. "This whole thing between us is absurd. People don't fall in love in a month. And they definitely don't stay in love for three years with no contact. But Jesus Christ, Ash, I love you so fucking much."

I swallowed hard, trying to lock away the tears that were threatening to escape.

He loves me.

Me.

"Stop talking," I choked out.

"I *do* want to get to know each other again. But I need you to know that it won't change anything. I love you. I always have, Ash. *Always.*"

The tears finally spilled from my eyes, but my smile stretched wider.

Always.

"Stop talking," I repeated through my tears.

He sighed contently. "Did I hurt you?" he asked as he softened inside me.

I knew he was talking about sex, but starting over meant full disclosure. "Yes. When I was sixteen, you broke my heart and said some shitty things that made me doubt who I was as a person. For years, I tried to figure out how to be someone you could be proud of, but ultimately, I just learned to hate part of myself." I sucked in a deep breath. "Flint, this is who I am. I may be crazy and quirky, but I'm a good person. And that's something *I'm* proud of. I can't worry about what you think anymore."

"What I think? I think you're an amazing person who deserves more than I will ever be able to give you. But, dammit, I'm going to try anyway. That shit I spouted before you left was about me and my issues. Never you. If you'll just stay with me, I'll spend a lifetime proving that to you. Ash, I'm so fucking sorry."

He reluctantly released me as I stood up. I didn't go far though. Spinning to face him, I climbed back onto his lap, locking my legs around his waist and my arms around his neck.

"It's okay. I forgive you." I kissed him then whispered, "I may have overreacted. I mean, who runs away for three *years?*" I winked, and a small smile quirked the side of his mouth. "I'm sorry about this morning too. I wanted to look nice for our fresh, new start as a couple. No one's really worried about where I was before. I didn't even think about letting you know where I was going."

He nodded, chastely touching his lips to mine before leaning away to catch my eyes. "Why'd you take my book? That's what freaked me out the most."

I laughed. "First off, it's *my* book, not yours. I stole that fair and square before I reformed my ways." He rolled his eyes. "But I wanted to write. I had a lot to catch up on over the last few days."

"What color?"

I knew exactly what he was talking about. I just didn't know how *he* knew what he was talking about. "Excuse me?"

"Pink or green? If it was blue, I'm gonna be pissed."

I slapped his chest. "You read my book?"

"No, I read *my* book . . . that you graffitied with highlighter."

"It's not your book! It's mine."

He thought I was joking, even as I jumped off his lap.

He pushed to his feet, snapping the condom off and knotting it before settling on the edge of the bed. "Ash, I'm not a total asshole. You can borrow it anytime you want."

I gave him an evil side eye. "Wheels, I just told you that I love you. Do not make me regret it. That book is mine."

"Come here." He grabbed my hand and tugged me to stand between his legs. "Say it again."

"It's mine," I told him.

He gave me an unimpressed glare. I knew what he wanted to hear; I just really liked fucking with him.

"The other thing, smartass."

I wanted to keep going, but as he looked up at me through his thick black lashes, I wanted to hear him say it again too. "I love you."

"And," he prompted.

"And no more running."

His lips split into a smile, and the corners of his eyes softened.

Lifting my arm, he kissed the Flint tattoo on my side. "I love you too."

I closed my eyes as he repeatedly whispered it against my skin.

I was so genuinely happy for the first time in my entire life that I couldn't even pretend to stop the awkward bubble of laugher that escaped.

He looked up at me with a questioning expression that I only answered with a shrug as I continued to laugh.

He loves me.

Shaking his head, he said, "Fine. You can have the book, but only if you don't give me shit about reading it."

"You can take your deal and shove it. That's my book, I don't need you to give it to me." I backed away and crossed my arms over my chest.

He barked out a laugh, retrieving his crutches off the floor. "Get dressed, baby. It's date night."

"It's my book," I repeated because, well, he needed to understand.

"Absolutely," he confirmed, walking to the bathroom. "For as long as I let you borrow it."

I could hear his laughter continue as he shut the door.

I wasn't mad. I couldn't have cared less that he was delusional enough to think it was still his.

I was *staying*.
Forever.
With Flint.

CHAPTER
Twenty-Eight

Flint

IT WAS TRULY INCREDIBLE THE way one weekend changed the trajectory of my entire life.

Ash and I had skipped our date in exchange for takeout food and the weed garden. It was far better than whatever cheesy and clichéd date I could have taken her on. It was us. And with her promise to stay, there was officially an us again.

Ash spent the entire night tucked into my side, never letting me stray out of her reach—even while we were eating.

It was incredible. For the first time in my entire life, I wasn't nervously waiting for the sky to crash down on me. The world could have slipped into another Dark Age and I would have been fine. I had a home, a job, money in the bank, and a woman who didn't need any of it.

She just wanted me.

My life had officially begun.

And it was gloriously uneventful.

Ash and I quickly fell into an easy routine. I drove her to work at the salon in the mornings then picked her up at lunch only to drop her off at the college, where she had enrolled in a high school refresher course. She didn't need it. She was insanely smart. However, she was nervous about failing the high school equivalency exam she needed to take in order to start college courses.

I was proud of her for going back to school. She wasn't sure what she wanted to major in, but she was so excited about attending actual classes that it didn't matter. The only problem was she needed an ID before she could enroll and Ash had nothing. We spent weeks tracking down her birth certificate and then her social security card before she finally went to the DMV to get a driver's license—something else she was excited about. Her newsie list was dwindling as she crossed things off left and right.

"Oh my God," Ash gasped as I walked into the DMV. "You came. In a suit!" She left Quarry and Mia sitting in the folding chairs and rushed over to me.

"I had a big meeting with a potential client at noon, but I came straight here afterward. My woman's getting her driver's license today. This is a big deal." I leaned down to take her lips.

Her eyes flashed surprise as she dodged my mouth. "Oh shit. Let's go." Grabbing my arm, she pulled me toward the door.

"Where are we going? Did I miss your test already?" I asked, doing my best to keep up with her as she dragged me toward the door.

"No. But you need to see a doctor. I think you had a stroke."

I threw the brakes on, stopping just before we exited the building.

"Don't stop! I can't have you dying on me! Who will nag me about leaving my shoes in the middle of the floor if you croak?" She bit her lip, but the smile escaped around it.

"I'm missing the joke, funny girl. I'm gonna need you to explain."

"You said something was a big deal. Clearly, you have some neurological issues going on."

"It *is* a big deal."

"No. It's just a driver's license. I've been driving for years." She shrugged before adding, "By the way, you look hot in a suit."

I shook my head at her randomness. "You're insane," I told her, wrapping her in my arms and kissing the top of her head.

"I think you're insane. You relearning to walk again after spending years in a wheelchair was nothing. But me getting a little plastic card that allows me to legally do something I've been doing for years is a big deal?" She folded her arms around my hips, hugging me tight, before sliding her hand down into the back of my slacks.

"Would you stop?" I laughed, swatting away her hands.

"What?" she whined innocently. "It's the suit. I can't help myself."

"Right. What was it last night when you jumped me in kitchen?" I quirked a questioning eyebrow.

"Uhh . . . I'm sorry, but sweatpants leave nothing to the imagination. If you don't want to be sexually assaulted by your girlfriend, then you should really put on something else."

"Insane," I whispered, kissing her again. "Besides, the driver's license isn't a big deal because you can drive. It's a big deal because it will have our address on it as your legal residence. There's no getting rid of me now."

"I'm pretty sure I could just change it when I move out."

"You planning to move out?" I joked. It was an idea that, a few weeks ago, would have spiked my pulse. But Ash wasn't going anywhere. Of that I was sure.

She was mine in every possible way.

"Well, I don't know. Are you going to stop wearing the sweatpants?" She slid her hand back down into my pants.

"No. I love those sweats."

She squeezed my ass and winked. "Then I'm definitely not moving."

Smiling, I leaned forward to take her mouth, and it wasn't going to be sweet. It was going to be completely indecent, regardless that we were in a very public place. Judging by the way her eyes flashed with desire, she was okay with that.

Unfortunately, Quarry and Mia noticed our moment too. Catcalls echoed through the DMV, earning us quite a few glares from the employees.

"Ash Carson?" the older woman called from behind the desk.

"*Mabie,*" Ash corrected on a mumble.

"We'll, get it changed," I assured her the same way I had when she'd melted down the day her birth certificate had come in the mail.

Ash hadn't spoken to Ray again since the night she'd turned him in to the police. Nor had she shown any desire to visit him in jail. She just hated the fact that Mabie wasn't listed as her legal last name. I had full intentions of helping her change it from Carson, but it was never going to be Mabie.

Ash Page had a nice ring though.

While I wasn't jumping into the whole marriage thing yet, I was positive it was where we were headed. I was planning to give it some time. But every day that passed only cemented the fact that I wanted to spend the rest of my life with her.

I wasn't a rash person.

But it was *Ash*. I lost my fucking mind when it came to her.

We had only been back together for eight weeks, but it had only taken four for me to fall in love with her when we'd first met. Eight weeks felt like an eternity.

"Wish me luck," she said, pushing up to her tiptoes and pecking me on the cheek.

"You got this, baby."

"Then I'm getting that." She waggled her eyebrows suggestively, backing away. "Oh, wait." She turned to Quarry, snapping her fingers. "Keys."

Quarry dropped the keys to his sports car in her hands. "Be gentle with her."

"Right. The same way you were gentle with Flint's SUV when you took it out mudding last week?" She smirked, knowing she'd just thrown him under the bus.

My eyes jumped to his.

Quarry didn't seem fazed in the least though. "*Oh, don't even start. It was a puddle. You don't even have four-wheel drive. Those hand pedals sucked too. Pushing a lever really takes the sexy out of peeling out.*" He draped an arm around Mia's shoulders when he finished signing.

She giggled, squeezing against his side.

"Ash Carson?" the woman droned again.

"Oops. Gotta go." She patted me on the ass then jogged away.

I looked over at Quarry as I sat down in the chair next to Mia. "*You are never allowed to borrow my car again. I don't care if yours is in the shop.*"

"*Meh. I'll survive,*" he signed back before scooping Mia out of her chair and settling her on his lap.

I began checking my e-mails on my phone. "Please don't molest her in here."

"Huh?" she said and Quarry's hands translated for her.

Mia slapped my arm to get my attention. *You're one to talk,* she signed, not bothering with saying it aloud since Ash was gone. *I threw up in my mouth a little.*

Whatever. You look like you're twelve. Q looks like he's older than I am. Everyone in the room is assuming he's a pedophile right now, I replied.

Q interjected, *Hey! I wasn't the one getting a sixteen-year-old girl naked in the back of my child molester van.*

Yes, you did! That's why I had to sell it. I don't even want to know what you two did in that thing before Till bought you a car.

Q laughed. *Oh, come on. That's not why you sold it.*

The floor was sticky, you dick. I punched him on the shoulder.

"Damn it," he cursed, rubbing his arm.

Mia stared into space dreamily and signed, *God, I miss that van.*

I gave her a disgusted look then went back to scanning my phone.

Quarry asked, *"Hey, why didn't you tell us about Ash's birthday?"*

"It's not for another month. I'll let you know when I plan something," I answered absently.

"Dude, her birthday was last week."

My head snapped up. "Her birthday is April eighteenth."

Mia's hands lifted as her jaw fell open. *You idiot! You missed her birthday.*

I looked back at Quarry and repeated, "Her birthday is April eighteenth."

He shook his head, pulling Ash's birth certificate from the folder she'd left on her seat. "March eighteenth."

What the fuck?

I distinctly remembered her telling me that it was in April the first night we were lying in the weeds. "What astrological sign is March eighteenth? Aries?"

They both shrugged, so I picked up my phone and did a quick Internet search.

"Pisces," I whispered at the screen of my phone. "Why the hell would she have lied to me?"

"This is going to cost you big time. You should buy her a car and pretend this was all part of your plan. Make her think you forgot her

birthday on purpose," Quarry suggested.

Mia excitedly nodded her agreement.

It wasn't a bad idea, exactly, but I was more focused on why she would have lied to begin with than the repercussions of flubbing the date.

For the next ten minutes, I stared a hole in the DMV's door, waiting for her to come back inside.

Finally, she bounced around the corner, laughing with the once disgruntled DMV employee. "You just let me know when. You can borrow his car anytime," Ash told the woman, flashing her eyes to Quarry.

"Hey!" He quickly shifted Mia back to her seat and rushed to retrieve his keys. "You pass?"

"Psh, did I pass?" She gave him a disgusted look. "Tonya didn't even make me take the test. We just took turns pulling the parking brake and sliding into the parallel parking spot."

Q snatched the keys from her hand. "Shut up. You did not."

I pushed to my feet and joined them. "You pass?"

"You're in a suit!" she squeaked.

"How many more times are you going to say that?"

"You're in a suit."

Shifting my weight to one arm, I wrapped the other around her waist. "Are you stuck on repeat?"

"I'm not sure. Get naked and let's see."

"Jesus, woman. Just answer the question."

She grabbed my tie and tugged my head down, whispering in my ear, "I think we should celebrate my brand-spanking-new driver's license by having sex in your back seat."

I smiled down at her when she added, "This. Suit." I let out a loud laugh.

Pointedly nodding toward my zipper, she let me know just how serious she was.

"All right. Keep your pants on," I said, backing out of her grasp.

The woman at the camera station called her name. "I'll be right back." She sauntered away, swaying her ass and ensuring that, as soon as I got to the bottom of the whole birthday lie, I'd be using the suit to my full advantage.

Ash

"You seriously took the rest of the day off?" I asked when Flint surprised me by climbing out of the car instead of just dropping me off at home.

He unlocked the front door and swung it open. "Yep. I told you. Big deal."

"You called in after you saw how much I loved the suit, huh?" I made a show of checking him out before walking inside.

"I mean, that didn't hurt my decision. But I'm more interested in why you're lying to me," he replied with a hard edge to his voice.

I spun to look at him. "What?"

He closed the distance between us, stopping only inches in front of me. "Your birthday is March eighteenth," he stated definitively. "But I can't for the life of me figure out why the hell you would lie to me about that."

"Uh, 'cause maybe I'm not *lying*," I snapped, taken aback by his accusation.

"Bullshit. I saw your birth certificate when you were taking your driving test. You *are* lying and I want to know why. *Now.*"

I loved bossy Flint. I actually even loved angry Flint. But asshole Flint made me want to resort to violence. Fortunately for him, he was still wearing that suit.

"So let me get this straight. You see something that's different than what I've told you and your immediate conclusion is that I'm lying to you? You don't ask me about it. You just jump straight to liar. Thanks for the vote of confidence."

"You *did* lie to me! You point-blank told me that your birthday was in April."

"My birthday *is* in April!" I yelled, quickly losing my temper.

"Stop fucking saying that. Your birthday was last week. What the hell are you trying to hide from me?"

I blinked at him. "Are you kidding me here? Now I'm hiding shit from you?" I said, a little bit hurt. Okay, a lot hurt.

"I don't know! That's exactly what I'm trying to figure out!"

"There is nothing to figure out!" Taking a step away, I closed my eyes and attempted a calming breath. "Listen, you're acting like an asshole right now. Let me know when you want to talk. I'm happy to explain, but I'm not sitting here, listening to you toss out accusations." I turned and stomped to our bedroom, slamming the door behind me.

So maybe I was acting like an asshole too. I was hurt though. Flint was the one person who knew my buttons. Yet, like a little kid on an elevator, he was pushing every single one of them.

I collapsed onto our bed, toeing my shoes off then kicking them over the edge. I groaned to myself when I heard his steps against the hall's hardwood floor. I needed a few minutes to collect myself and get rid of the bitter taste he had left in my mouth. The door opened, but he didn't come inside.

Propping himself against the doorjamb, he said, "You're right."

"I know I am," I snarked back.

"For what it's worth, I wasn't assuming it was some nefarious plot or anything. I thought maybe you had lied to keep some distance between us when you first got back. I don't know. That doesn't even really make sense." He ran his fingers through his hair then used his hand to comb it back into place. "It's just . . . I missed your birthday, and now, I feel like a dick."

"Are you ready to listen now instead of jumping to conclusions?" I asked, sitting up and crossing my legs underneath me.

He looked down sheepishly. "Yeah."

"You didn't miss my birthday, Flint. My mother killed herself on March eighteenth, so when I was a kid, I picked a new day to celebrate."

His head shot up. "Shit," he breathed, becoming unstuck and walking to the bed to join me.

"As far as I'm concerned, my birthday *is* April eighteenth. I wasn't lying to you, but the fact that you automatically assumed I was . . ." I trailed off.

He cupped my jaw to force my eyes to his. "I'm so sorry. I didn't know."

"But that's exactly the problem. There's a lot of stuff you don't know, Flint. You can't always assume I'm lying or hiding shit from you every time a new truth comes out."

The bed dipped under his weight as he settled on the edge. "I want to know everything about you, Ash. I *should* have known something as big as March eighteenth." He leaned forward, kissing me all too briefly.

"Look, we've been back together for two months. The get-to-know-you portion of this relationship is not going to happen overnight."

He arched an eyebrow. "Sage advice from a woman who's only been in one relationship." He smiled, kissing me again.

"Nah. I read a lot of romance novels."

His head snapped back. "Do you really?" he asked skeptically. "Seriously, or are you fucking with me?"

"No. I really do. The dirtier the better." I shrugged.

His eyes flashed wide as he fell back against the bed, laughing. "How the hell did I not know that?"

"You never asked!" I defended.

Grabbing my arm, he tugged me down, juggling me into our position. Sighing, he kissed the top of my head. "What else should I know about you?"

"Well, my favorite color is neon green, but only for accessories. You'll never catch me in a neon-green shirt or dress. I prefer black with splashes of color. My favorite flavor anything is apple, but I hate actual apples. I love olives of all colors and prefer vanilla over chocolate." I paused to tap on the corner of my mouth. "I feel like I'm missing something."

"Maybe the important stuff." He squeezed me tight.

"I can't tell you the important stuff, Flint. That kinda comes out randomly. Hell, the stuff you think is important might not even be the important stuff to me. But the good news is I'm here for forever, so long as you stop making assumptions, time is something we have." I pushed up on an elbow and pressed a kiss to his jaw.

Turning his head, he captured my mouth. "I love you."

"I know you do."

"And I'm sorry. You can have whatever birthday you want."

I kissed him more deeply then moved to straddle his waist. "What if I want my birthday to be today?"

"Sorry. No can do." He suddenly sat up, shifting me to the side as he scooted toward the edge.

"Where are you going?"

"Shopping. I just found out my girl has a fetish for suits."

I chased him off the bed, catching him just before he was able to retrieve his crutches. "Well, then why don't you let her enjoy this one? *Then* go shopping." I dropped to my knees in front of him only to be lifted right back to my feet.

"Because torturing her with a day at the mall then fucking her to sleep sounds like more fun." He winked.

I would have argued, but it did sound like fun.

I could live with that.

CHAPTER
Twenty-Nine

Flint

Three weeks later . . .

"HAPPY BIRTHDAY," I SAID, PULLING a little, black, velvet box from my pocket and placing it on the table after we'd finished lunch.

I'd wanted to take her somewhere nice, but in true Ash fashion, she'd picked a greasy burger joint with paper menus. It was her birthday though. If she wanted burgers and milkshakes, then damn it, I would make sure my girl got them.

"Oh my God," she breathed, staring at the box as if I'd just unleashed a venomous snake. "I can't open that."

I nudged it a little closer. "Yeah, you can."

Tears filled her eyes. "Flint."

"Just open it."

She shook her head and bit her lips.

"Ash, open it."

"No!" she yelled. Then she pleaded, watching me intently, "Are you sure? Like, really, really sure?"

I grinned, pushing the box even closer. "I'm positive, Ash. Absolutely positive."

She looked back down, sucking in a deep breath before extending a shaky hand to pick it up. "I love you," she whispered.

"I love you too," I replied, waiting for her reaction as she slowly pried it open.

Staring down, with tears in her eyes, she exclaimed, "You asshole!"

I burst out laughing. "Ash, baby, we've been together for three months. Did you really think I was going to propose at a burger joint on your twentieth birthday?"

"No!" she snapped. Then she looked to the side and mumbled, "Maybe."

I continued laughing but took her hand and lifted it to my lips.

"I'm glad you think this is funny," she bit out, pulling the silver dog bone from the box. "What is this?"

"One step at a time, Speedy. I figured maybe we could get a dog until you're old enough to legally drink at your own wedding."

"Just so you know, there was no guarantee that I was going to say yes."

"You cried."

"So?"

I winked and pulled the box from her hand. "You were gonna say yes."

She rolled her eyes then laughed. "I was totally going to say yes."

"That's really fucking good to know for future reference." I reached back into my pocket, and her eyes grew wide again. "Oh God, stop! It's not a ring." I revealed a small, pink collar and twisted the silver dog bone onto the loop.

Her shoulders fell, and I laughed all over again.

"I should not have started with that damn box. I had no idea that you would assume it was a ring."

I'd known with one hundred percent certainty she would think it was a ring. Ash had found the engagement ring I'd bought her while she'd been snooping around my office at On The Ropes. I knew because she'd put it back in the box upside down and then spent the rest of the day tearing up every time she so much as looked in my direction. I got the best sex of my life that night. She rained I love yous over my entire body, focusing the majority of her attention on my cock.

I got hard from just thinking about it.

"I thought we could go pick out a puppy. I've never had a dog, and I figured maybe you'd want one. But . . . I mean, if you don't—"

"No! I do. I really do," she interrupted, snatching the collar from my fingers.

"Are you sure, because you didn't seem too excited?"

Leaning over the table, she planted a kiss on my lips. As she tucked the empty box into her purse, she said, "Let's go get a dog."

I drove Ash to a pet store, where I had full intentions of buying her a small and fluffy lap dog—something yippy she could fawn all over. However, she refused to even go inside, stating that there were plenty of dogs at the animal shelter waiting for a new home. So, after a quick search on my phone, we were on our way to the adoption center at the local pound. Ash painfully paced up and down the rows of caged animals, apologizing to each and every one for not being able to take them home, before finally settling on the ground in front of a Chihuahua puppy. She sat there for several minutes, poking her fingers through the chain link and letting him chew on the tips.

"You want that one, baby?" I asked when she started to push to her feet.

She pointed to the dog next door. "No, I want that one."

"No," I said firmly even though I knew exactly how worthless it truly was.

"Yep."

"No," I repeated.

"Yes, that's our dog. Isn't he handsome?" she cooed.

"Damn it, Ash. I said a puppy."

She cocked her head to the side and folded her arms over her chest. "It's my birthday. You don't get to argue with me on my birthday."

I let out a huff, knowing she had a point. With a groan, I turned to the woman who worked there and said, "We'll take him."

Ash clapped, bouncing on her toes as they began preparing the adoption paperwork on a sixty -pound, three-legged basset hound named Julio.

"I cannot believe you picked that dog," I mumbled an hour later while we waited for our brand-new bundle of slobber to be brought out.

"Don't you dare talk about Julio. He's perfect." She hugged me.

"We're going to have to buy him a new collar. I don't think this one is gonna fit." I pulled the pink collar from my pocket, accidentally on purpose dropping a black, velvet box to the ground. "Shit," I cursed.

Her back went stiff.

"Damn it. You weren't supposed to see that yet."

"Flint," she whispered, bending over to pick it up.

"Well, I guess it's too late now." I kissed her forehead. "Happy birthday, Ash."

Her eyes sparkled with tears as she slowly opened the box. "You asshole!" she declared for the second time that day, lifting a Volkswagen key from the box.

I burst out laughing all over again. "What? You thought that one was a ring too?"

"I hate you," she mumbled then joined me in laughter. "You got me a car?"

"I'm getting busy at the gym, and it's becoming harder to match up our schedules so I can run you around all the time. Plus, you can't drive mine because of the hand pedals. This just made sense."

She threw her arms around my neck. "I've never had my own car!"

"It's pretty sweet too," I told her proudly. "Go see if Julio is ready and let's go home and check it out. Q and Mia should have dropped it off by now."

Pushing to her toes, she placed a lingering kiss on my lips. "Thank you. For Julio, for my car, for you."

"For me?"

"Yeah, especially for you." She kissed me again before skipping away to the front desk.

I should have been the one thanking her.

"What the fucking hell is that?" Quarry asked when we arrived back at the house.

Ash struggled to lift the dog out of the back of the car. "His name is Julio, and shut your face . . . and your hands," she snapped.

He's adorable! Mia signed, settling on the driveway, where Julio promptly covered her in sloppy kisses.

I never in a million years would have chosen that dog, but he definitely made it easy to see why Ash had.

I looked over at Quarry, who was watching Mia's tongue bath in disgust. I wolf-whistled to grab his attention. "Where's her car?"

His eyes slid to Ash. "Shhhh."

"She already knows, jerkoff. Now where is it?"

He tipped his chin toward the garage.

Using the panel on the outside wall, I typed in the code to open the door.

Ash's head popped up as the garage door lifted. Nestled inside our garage was a black convertible Volkswagen Beetle with a custom license plate that read: *WHEELZ.*

Much to my dismay, there was already some asshole who'd claimed wheels. My eye had twitched when the lady at registration suggested substituting with the Z. I'd succumbed to the pressure though.

"Shut up." She stood up, tossing Julio's leash to Mia, and then jogged over. "Shut up," she repeated, snatching the door open to reveal the custom neon-green floor mats that had cost a mint.

I didn't have a ton of money, but she needed a car, and I'd wanted her first one to be something she loved. Ash deserved to have something that was all her own. Not a hand-me-down or something she'd picked up on sale. She deserved something that was created custom for the crazy woman who would be driving it. Well, actually, she deserved more, but it would take time for me to give her that. Thankfully, according to Ash, time was the one thing we had plenty of.

"Flint, this is too much," she said, gripping the steering wheel and running her hands over the dash.

I rounded the hood to the passenger side. "Christ, this thing is tiny," I complained, attempting to fold my body inside.

"I don't mean to sound ungrateful, but can you . . . I mean, can we . . . afford this?"

I smiled at her concern. "I put a chunk down. Then we'll make the payments. It might cut into my suit budget, but we'll survive," I joked, but for quite possibly the first time since I'd known her, Ash didn't laugh at all.

"I don't know what to say. I mean, you told me you bought me a car, but . . . I just didn't expect . . ."

"Expect what?" I asked, popping the glove compartment open and retrieving a small, black, velvet box.

She swallowed hard when she saw it. "I'm not even going to get excited this time."

"You should probably get excited, Ash," I said, offering her the box.

"Stop," she whispered, warily taking it from my hands.

Staring deep into her eyes, I urged, "Open it."

Nervously chewing on her bottom lip, she popped open the top.

Then I ducked as she hurled it at me.

"Son of a bitch!" she screamed.

I roared with laughter. "What is your problem?" I said, snatching the long balloon she'd found inside the box from her hands and blowing it up.

"You told me to get excited. Now, you're just being mean."

I tied off the end of the balloon and handed it to her. "You should be excited. There's a clown in the backyard waiting to make that into whatever animal you can possibly think of."

Her glare softened as a smile grew on her mouth. "A clown? Seriously!"

"I remember I kinda hijacked you from the one at Blakely's party. Figured I should start making that up to you."

She quickly scrambled from the car, pausing only long enough to say, "Stop fucking with me, but I love you." Not bothering to wait for me as I climbed back up on my crutches, she sprinted out the back door.

I chuckled when I heard her scream as all of the guests hiding in the backyard shouted, "Surprise!"

I didn't follow her out the door though.

I needed a minute.

Sucking in a breath, I filled my lungs with every bit of the future I never thought I would have. Then, closing my eyes, I became lost in the present I never wanted to leave. Five years earlier, I wouldn't have been able to imagine a day when the constant fight finally became worth it.

Maybe she was the reason for the struggle all along.

I remembered it all.

I *heard* the gun.

I *felt* the bullet.

I saw her fall.

In less than a second, my life as I had known it was over.

But unquestionably, I would do it all over again.

For her.

"Don't you dare hide in here. The clown just handed me a little, black box."

My eyes popped open, and she was smiling in the doorway with the bright afternoon sun lighting her from behind.

"Yeah, about that," I said, starting in her direction. "You should probably stay out of the bounce house."

"Flint!" she squealed as I crushed my mouth over hers.

For Ash.

CHAPTER
Thirty

Ash

"DID YOU HAVE FUN TODAY?" Flint asked as we lay in the weeds, staring up at the night sky.

Rolling off his shoulder, I propped myself on an elbow, facing him. "Fun would be the understatement of the century. I can't even begin to tell you how amazing today was." I paused. "Even your stupid boxes."

That day was easily one of the best of my entire life. Flint had gone above and beyond throwing me a birthday party in the backyard. Most twenty-year-old women would have scoffed at how juvenile it all was, but not me. From the clown to the bounce house, right down to all the people who came and covered a table with gifts, it was perfect.

With the exception of the occasional cake my father had bought when I was a kid, I'd never had a birthday party.

I'd also never had a car.

Or a dog.

Or a man I wanted to spend the rest of my life with.

Yet, suddenly, I had them all.

Flint's chest shook with humor as he pulled me back down. "You know, for a girl who laughs as much as you do, you sure didn't act like those boxes were very funny."

"Oh, shut up."

He scooted out from under me and shifted to his side. "Also, for a woman who spent her formidable years pickpocketing and hustling for your father, you sure weren't very careful when you put that engagement ring back in the box after finding it in my desk." He arched a knowing eyebrow.

Shit! "You knew?" I squeaked.

He winked. "I know everything, Ash."

I slapped him on his chest. "I panicked, okay? I heard you coming back from lunch, so I just threw it in there."

"Sounds like an excuse to me," he teased, reaching out to grope my ass—a grope I quickly returned.

Smirking, he held my gaze until I worked up the courage to say, "Sooooo . . . about that ring?"

"I'm glad you asked." He pulled yet another little, black box out of his pocket.

I'd seen the bulge in his pocket earlier, but I'd seen so many of them over the course of the day that it didn't even excite me anymore. Actually, that's a lie. Each one had excited me, but I'd given up hope that any of them actually contained a ring.

Until he produced that one.

"Ash, I love—"

Snatching the box from his hand, I yelled, "Give me that!"

"Hey!" he objected, but I jumped out of his reach before he could take it back.

My heart raced as I slowly opened the box, revealing . . .

"A piece of paper? You have got to be shitting me." I threw the box at him, but while he did bat it away, he didn't laugh.

I glanced between Flint's serious stare and the tightly folded notebook paper for several beats, trying to figure out what the hell was going on. It wasn't a ring. But what I couldn't figure out was why he looked nervous.

Flint sat all the way up and grabbed his crutches as I unfolded the paper.

<u>Newsies</u>

~~Get shot in the back.~~
~~Become a horrible human being.~~
~~Pineapple banana juice.~~
~~Graffiti a building.~~
~~Fall in love with Ash Mabie.~~
~~Make Ash Mabie fall in love with me.~~
~~Treat her like an asshole.~~
~~Regret it more than anything in my entire life.~~
~~Learn to walk again. (Not in a strawberry field.)~~
~~Buy a house with hopes that she will come home.~~
~~Tear up the grass to make a patch of weeds.~~
~~Chase her to the ends of the Earth.~~
~~Make Ash Mabie fall in love with me. Again.~~
~~Get a dog.~~
~~Propose to Ash Mabie.~~
Make Ash Mabie Ash Page.
Spend the rest of my life making sure she never stops laughing.

My heart stilled and the breath was stolen from my chest. A large lump formed in my throat, but my lips split into an impossibly wide smile.

"Propose to Ash Mabie" was crossed off.

Oh my God.

"Don't say a single word until you hear me out," he growled when I finally tore my eyes from the paper in my hands.

Flint was kneeling in front of me, using one of his crutches to balance. I awkwardly laughed, forcing tears I hadn't known I had produced to spill from my eyes.

"Ash . . ." He cleared his throat then started again. "Ash, you're twenty years old, and we've only been back together for a few months. It would be ridiculous to rush into something as big as marriage when we barely even know each other."

I opened my mouth to object, but he got there first.

"Not a word."

"Fine," I huffed.

"As I was saying, it would be ridiculous to rush into something when we are still getting to know each other. But the other night, after you fell asleep in my arms, I realized I knew enough. I know you're crazy and messy and you take great pleasure in screwing with me."

I nodded at his assessment.

"I also know you're one of the kindest and most generous people on this planet. I mean, let's be serious here. I took you to get a puppy today and you picked the ugliest, most pitiful animal in there." He swayed his head from side to side. "Which explains a lot about why you're with me, but it also speaks wonders about who you are as a person.

"Ash, I know the way you make me feel and I know I will never in a million years be able to find anyone who could even come close to filling your neon-green Converse."

I giggled.

"And more than that, I don't want to. So yeah, this is probably ridiculous and rash and reckless, but I also know it's exactly right." He lifted a square solitaire engagement ring I immediately recognized. "Ash, I love you. Marry me."

I'd always tried to be careful when it came to Flint's mobility. He could walk with his crutches, but I knew that his balance was still sometimes an issue.

He had just proposed though. Careful was not in my vocabulary.

After racing forward, I launched myself into his arms, knocking him down as I fell on top of him. Julio barked from the other corner of the yard, and Flint immediately started cussing.

"Damn it. I dropped your ring."

"I don't care," I replied, sealing my mouth over his.

He turned and patted the ground above his head. "Ash, stop. I can't find it."

"I don't care," I repeated, forcing his mouth back to mine.

He rolled me over. "You better care. That's your engagement ring, and it wasn't cheap."

I groaned as he pulled his cell phone out to use as a flashlight. "You know, I can still say no."

"Got it!" he exclaimed, looping an arm around my waist to drag me back on top of him. With a huge smile, he pecked my lips. "What do you say? You want to spend forever with me?" He lifted the ring between us.

"I'll check my schedule," I smarted, taking the ring from his hands and sliding it on my finger.

"Your schedule?"

"Yep," I answered, admiring the diamond.

"Ash, stop messing around and say yes," he growled, causing my smile to once again spread.

"I'm sorry, Flint, but now that we are getting married, you really should start getting used to me messing around with you."

"Well, Ash, you need to either say yes or get used to me *not* messing around with you." He tipped his hips against mine.

"Oh my God. You're already threatening to withhold sex." I laughed as he began tickling me. "Sex is not a weapon!"

"Say yes," he demanded as I shifted to flip so I was on top. His eyes warmed as he swept my hair off my shoulder. "Marry me, Ash."

Bending down, I rested my hands on his chest. Despite his playful exterior, his heart was racing. Brushing my lips across his, I proved once and for all that I was not clairvoyant. Not even my dreams had been bold enough to conjure that moment.

"Yes," I whispered.

Flint's breath hissed from his lips as his hand gripped the back of my neck and he took my mouth in a languid kiss. It didn't turn frantic or desperate like it usually did with us.

We didn't need the rush anymore.

There was plenty of time in forever.

CHAPTER

Thirty-One

Flint

Three years later...

"FLINT! WE NEED TO GO. Eliza just called and she needs a ride to that press conference thingy. Till has to be there early to set up the gym," Ash yelled up the stairs.

"Thingy." I laughed to myself. "I know. We have to go early too," I replied, closing my computer. After snagging my suit coat off the back of my chair, I grabbed my cane to head out of my home office.

"What?" she yelled again. "I thought Till and Slate were the only ones who had to be there early?"

"As his agent, it's kinda my job to be there." I gingerly made my way down the stairs to find her standing in the kitchen with a half apron tied around her waist. "Don't you look like Betty Crocker?" I smirked.

"Hey, I take my job as head rainbow-cupcake maker very seriously." She blew the hair out of her eyes.

Using my thumb, I rubbed the flour off the tip of her chin. "I can tell." Once I'd hung the hook of my cane on the counter, I put my hands under her arms and lifted her to sit on the counter.

"Don't knock over my food coloring!" she squealed.

I glanced over her shoulder, noticing that it was too late for the red.

"I'm not," I lied, taking her mouth. "So, did you think any more about our talk this morning?"

"It was two hours ago . . . and I've been baking. So no." She pecked my lips.

"Come on. We can work in a quickie now." I moved my hand between her legs, rubbing against the seam of her jeans.

She swatted it away. "One, we have to go. Two, even if I agreed, birth control doesn't just stop on demand. And three, I'm not conceiving a baby on the counter next to Quarry's celebratory cupcakes."

"Does that mean it's a yes?" I asked, raking my teeth over the sensitive flesh of her neck.

She moaned sensually but pushed me away. "No. It means I'm still thinking. Now, can you let the dogs out while I finish packing up these bad boys?"

I groaned, accepting my temporary defeat. "Does Q know you made *rainbow* cupcakes? The media is going to be there, Ash. I'm relatively sure he was assuming you'd make something a little more masculine for his professional boxing announcement."

Her mouth fell open in amused outrage. "Of course he doesn't know! That's the entire point of making rainbow cupcakes!"

I shook my head in humor. Some things never changed.

Heading to the back door, I clapped my hands and called, "Julio. Rico. Let's go!"

Julio came barreling around the corner with our one-eyed pug, Rico, hot on his limping heels.

After closing the door, I started toward our bedroom to nervously change my tie for the tenth time, but a knock at the door rerouted me.

"That's Liv! Can you open that for her? She probably has her hands full," Ash called, but before I even got to the foyer, Liv had already let herself in.

"Too slow," she said, walking in carrying half a watermelon shaped like a basket. Various fruits were carved into flowers, complete with a pineapple bumblebee on the top.

"Wow. That is . . ." I began laughing, unable to complete the thought. "Rainbow cupcakes *and* a watermelon fruit basket. I see you and Ash have been conspiring."

She giggled. "Wait until you see what Eliza had made."

"Holy shit. You got her in on it too?"

She nodded proudly. "Let's just say, right now, a table-top ice sculpture of Quarry riding a unicorn is out for delivery."

My eyes went wide as I gasped, "No way."

"Yep," Ash confirmed, walking over to take the fruit from Liv.

"You do understand that I'm trying to market him as a professional heavyweight boxer, right?"

They burst out laughing, throwing each other high fives.

"You two are horrible. This is his career we're talking about," I said sternly as they continued giggling. With a resigned sigh, I gave up on the worthless attempt at a lecture. "Okay, let's get out of here. I need to see this sculpture."

Ash

"Where the fuck is he?" Till boomed as we all huddled in Flint's office at the gym.

Eliza paced the floor while Flint ran damage control, assuring the numerous media outlets that Quarry was on his way.

If he really was though, none of us knew. Quarry was officially two hours late to his own press conference announcing his much-awaited transition to professional boxing.

Over the previous three years, Q had dominated every single facet of the amateur boxing world. He'd been widely followed because of his connection to Till and Slate, and Q did not disappoint. He was a virtually untouchable beast who was equally as charismatic inside the ring as he was out of it. Gracing the pages of sports magazines everywhere, he was the new golden boy in professional boxing—even though he had yet to even step in the ring. When Flint had scheduled an exclusive press conference months earlier, the boxing community had gone nuts with hopes and speculation that Quarry would, in fact, finally make the crossover. Hopes we all shared.

Slate had held Quarry back for as long as possible, determined that his rise was not going to be the slow, uphill climb Till's had been. And as much as it had ticked Q off, thanks to Slate and Flint, he already had six-figure contracts in the works.

But that was all assuming we found him.

"I'm going to kill him. He's bitched for two years for this, and now, his dumb ass doesn't show. That's it. I'm dropping him. He wants to act like a little fucking prima donna, he can find a new trainer." Till ran a rough hand through his hair then kicked an empty chair over.

I quickly grabbed the brick and the frame off Flint's desk, tucking them into his drawer before they ended up broken on the ground.

Liv walked back into the room with her father, Leo, behind her. She nervously knotted her fingers as she said, "Okay, he's not at his apartment. And no one answered at Mia's parents' either. Her car was parked out front though, so I'm pretty sure they're together." She shrugged. "I honestly have no idea."

"I tried tracking his phone—" Leo said, and Till quickly interrupted.

"Why didn't you do that two fucking hours ago?" Till's eyes narrowed in a murderous glare I'd thought only Flint possessed.

Leo stepped toward him, crossing his thick arms over his chest. "It's dead, jackass. Calm the fuck down. It's a goddamn press conference. You can always reschedule."

But it wasn't just the press conference. No one had heard from Quarry since he and Mia had gone out to dinner the night before. Till was worried, and judging by the hole Eliza was pacing in the floor, so was she.

"Right," Till bit out, storming past him.

Just as he got to the door, Johnson came flying around the corner and announced, "We found him. We need to go *now*."

"Don't you fucking touch her!" I yelled through the burn in my lungs. Stepping protectively in front of Mia's lifeless body, I blocked her from view.

"I'm not going to ask you step away again."

I watched his hands form the words, but my brain was no longer able to process rational thought.

No one is taking her from me.

I sucked in a hard breath then snarled. "Back. The fuck. Up."

"You need to leave."

My chest heaved as I frantically tried to find a way out of my nightmare, but my mind was riddled with memories of her tiny body seizing in the passenger seat of my car as I rushed her to the hospital. "Fuck you. You're not touching her. Ever."

"Quarry, please. She's my daughter."

"She's my life!" I roared.

Her mother stepped forward, tears streaming from her deep-jade eyes—Mia's eyes. *"And you think she would have wanted this?"* Her words never made it to my deaf ears, but I heard her voice break all the same.

I couldn't bring myself to consider what Mia would have wanted at all.

I needed her.

I lifted my shaking hands to sign when my voice lodged in my throat. *This is not your decision to make. You don't get to play God.*

Her mother shook her head in regret. *"We didn't make it. She did—six months ago when she found out there was no treatment for the newest tumor they discovered."*

My legs buckled as the excruciating pain hit my gut.

She knew. Oh my God, she knew all along.

"You're lying," I declared. "She would have told me."

She shrugged. *"Come on, Quarry. You of all people know how stubborn Mia was. She didn't want you to worry."*

I stumbled back a step.

She hadn't wanted me to worry?

I was dying right alongside her. I'd have given anything to have more than just a few hours to adjust to the fact that I was never going to see her again.

No.

I wasn't letting her go.

I could fix this. We'd find some new doctors. Get a second opinion. She'd wake up and be fine.

I'd fight for her, because she would have fought for me.

"I don't care. I'm unmaking her decision. I should get a say in this, and I say she lives." I swallowed hard, packing my desperation down. "You will not fucking touch her," I seethed, swinging my gaze between her parents.

"*I'm done.*" Her short, overweight father stepped forward. "*I will not stand here listening to you throw a temper tantrum at the side of my daughter's deathbed. If there was hope, trust me, we would be clinging to it. But that is the shell of our Mia. She has no brain activity. People don't just come back from that. We all loved her. But she didn't want to live like this.*" He choked on the admission.

"Love. I *love* her. She's not gone, and I will not let you take her from me!"

He stepped even closer. "*Either you get the hell out right now or I will have security escort you out.*"

I ground my teeth, and my entire body flexed, preparing for war. "Then make your call, because there isn't a force in the world that could drag me away from her." I menacingly bumped my chest to his, forcing him to stumble.

Suddenly, a pair of hands slammed into my chest and Liv slid in front of me. I read her lips as she yelled, "Stop!"

My head snapped up as Till, Flint, and Slate filed into the room. My shoulders slacked at the sight of reinforcements.

"Get them out of here," I barked at Till while nodding to Mia's parents.

"*You need to come with me,*" he replied with his hands and voice and then grabbed my arm.

I snatched it away. "Fuck you."

When motion at Mia's bedside caught my attention, I turned to look over my shoulder.

Liv's silent wails as she clung to Mia's hand drained my soul.

What the fuck is going on?

My mind swirled as devastation sank in.

She can't be gone.

Not Mia.

Epilogue

Ash

MIA MARCH WAS TAKEN OFF life support less than twenty-four hours after her parents had produced a notarized do-not-resuscitate order dated six months earlier. We all attended her funeral, although Quarry's presence was limited to physical. His mind seemed to be lost in her deceit while he watched his heart being lowered into the ground. The whole Page family rallied around him, but we all struggled to make any kind of headway as he retreated into his own self-inflicted solitary confinement. News of Quarry's sudden loss hit sports pages everywhere, and Flint was flooded with phone calls as Quarry's popularity skyrocketed.

He hated every single second of it.

We were all rocked by Mia's death. Suddenly, forever didn't seem as long anymore.

After months of debating, Flint and I decided to start a family. I was just finishing up college when Flint and I welcomed Cole Page into the family. He was born with red hair that eventually turned strawberry blond. He had Flint's bright-blue eyes and my wide smile.

Having a baby was not as difficult as everyone had warned it would be. Cole was a blast. It was the second one who flipped our world upside down. I thought Flint was going to have a stroke when they informed us that I was already pregnant again at my first postpartum appointment.

I cried.

Flint just held Cole and blinked a lot.

But in the end, when Chase was born looking exactly like his brother, we all laughed.

Bottles, diapers, and sippy cups became our life. Time marched on, only at a slightly quicker pace.

When the boys were two and three, we buried Julio in the corner next to the weeds in the backyard. I was a mess, but that day, I made the decision to go back to school and become a veterinarian. Flint was making excellent money, so upon graduation, I was able to volunteer at the local animal shelter. They were grateful for my *free* expertise, but Flint was slightly less than excited by the constant stream of injured animals parading in and out of our house. He sat me down one night and gave me a firm lecture about not being able to save them all. I rolled my eyes and kept trying.

Over the years, Flint and I laughed a lot. We also argued a good bit too, but we always made up. I continued to dream, and Flint continued doing everything he could to fulfill them.

The day Flint finally put his cane away for good was a big deal—even to Flint. I cooked dinner that night and then the boys and I danced around the living room singing "Eye of the Tiger" at the top of our lungs while Flint laughed in the corner.

That night, as we fell asleep tangled in each other's arms, Flint whispered in my ear just before I dozed off. "You stayed."

"Huh?" I mumbled sleepily against his chest.

"You stayed and I'm walking." He tipped my chin up to take my lips in a reverent kiss. "Maybe those weren't dreams. Maybe they were our future all along."

My eyes popped open as I bolted upright. "Oh my God," I breathed as my heart began to race. "Do you know what this means?" I swallowed hard.

His eyes flashed with alarm. "Jesus, Ash, what the hell are you talking about?"

"I really am clairvoyant!" I exclaimed.

His shoulders fell as he glared, unimpressed with my joke.

"No, wait! We're *both* clairvoyant. Hurry, get up! We need to start training the boys to harness their powers for good and not evil."

Grabbing my waist, he flipped me to the other side of the bed and covered me with his body. "Funny girl, huh?" He began tickling me only to silence my howls of laughter with his mouth. Pinning my wrists above my head, he glided a hand between my legs, instantly finding my clit with his thumb.

I threw my head back against the bed. "Oh God."

"What's wrong, smartass? You didn't see that in your future?"

I rolled my hips off the bed, grinding against his hand. "Oh, I did. All of these years have been a meticulously crafted plan just to get to this exact moment. You better not disappoint me now."

He laughed as I began pushing the sweatpants off his hips.

Seconds later, he was inside me.

And he didn't disappoint.

Ever.

FIGHTING SHADOWS
THE END

Fighting Solitude

Winter 2015

Quarry Page is just climbing through the ropes.

About the Author

About the Author

Born and raised in Savannah, Georgia, Aly Martinez is a stay-at-home mom to four crazy kids under the age of five, including a set of twins. Currently living in South Carolina, she passes what little free time she has reading anything and everything she can get her hands on, preferably with a glass of wine at her side.

After some encouragement from her friends, Aly decided to add "Author" to her ever-growing list of job titles. So grab a glass of Chardonnay, or a bottle if you're hanging out with Aly, and join her aboard the crazy train she calls life.

Facebook: https://www.facebook.com/AuthorAlyMartinez
Twitter: https://twitter.com/AlyMartinezAuth
Goodreads: https://www.goodreads.com/AlyMartinez